● ● ● ● ● ●

"But remember, Brick House is your company too," he continued. "Everything I have is yours. I believe that if you and I work together and let Devin and Stephanie run Texas Builders, we will all win. I can't tell you how much I'd love to walk into my office and see your face every day. Hell, we could ride to work together."

The more Korah thought about it, the more she liked the idea too.

"You'll know when Stephanie's ready," Brick said. "When that day comes, you gotta let her fly. And then you can come and take your rightful place as the queen of our Brick House empire."

Her smile returned. "Damn, baby. You just made my heart flutter."

"And I made myself hard," he said, without the slightest bit of shame.

"I don't know how you managed that," Korah said with a giggle, "but it sounds like a personal problem."

"It doesn't have to be," Brick said. He leaned over the table with an all-too familiar look in his eyes. "What say me and you get out of here and find a quiet spot to park for a little while, before we hit the road?"

She shook her head. "No way. I'm too full."

"Oh." His smile deepened. "At least you turned me down for a good reason, instead of because you're a prude."

She laughed. "I'm not a prude, darling. You know I would never deny you."

He watched her intently as she spoke. "Oh, well if that's the case, how about a quickie hand job?"

She chuckled and shook her head but said, "Okay."

"*Nice*," Brick said, rubbing his hands together. "Now I'm thinking I should've asked for a blow–"

"Whoa," Korah said, looking around. "Sir, this is a family restaurant."

"You're right. I'm sorry."

"I didn't say I wouldn't do it."

Brick's hand shot up in a flash. "Check, please!"

● ● ● ● ● ●

BRICK HOUSE 3

KEITH THOMAS WALKER

KEITHWALKERBOOKS, INC
This is a UMS production

BRICK HOUSE 3

KEITHWALKERBOOKS

Publishing Company
KeithWalkerBooks, Inc.
P.O. Box 331585
Fort Worth, TX 76163

For information write
KeithWalkerBooks, Inc.
P.O. Box 331585
Fort Worth, TX 76163

ISBN-13 DIGIT: 978-0-9967505-4-7
ISBN-10 DIGIT: 0-9967505-4-1
Library of Congress Control Number: 2016916742
Manufactured in the United States of America

Second Edition

Visit us at www.keithwalkerbooks.com

This book is for Kim Tanner

MORE BOOKS BY KEITH THOMAS WALKER

Fixin' Tyrone
How to Kill Your Husband
A Good Dude
Riding the Corporate Ladder
The Finley Sisters' Oath of Romance
Blow by Blow
Jewell and the Dapper Dan
Harlot
Plan C (And More KWB Shorts)
Dripping Chocolate
The Realest Ever
Jackson Memorial
Sleeping With the Strangler
Life After
Blood for Isaiah
Brick House
Brick House 2
One on One
Brick House 3

NOVELLAS

Might be Bi Part One
Harder
Primal Part One
The Realest Christmas Ever
Hotline Fling

POETRY COLLECTION

Poor Righteous Poet

FINLEY HIGH SERIES

Prom Night at Finley High
Fast Girls at Finley High
Bullies at Finley High

Visit keithwalkerbooks.com for information about these and upcoming titles from KeithWalkerBooks

ACKNOWLEDGMENTS

Of course I would like to thank God, first and foremost, for giving me the creativity and drive to pursue my dreams and the understanding that I am nothing without Him. I would like to thank my wife for being my first and most important critic, and I would like to thank my mother for always pushing me to be the best I can be. I would like to thank Janae Hampton for being the best advisor, supporter and little sister a brother could ever have.

I would also like to thank (in no particular order) Beulah Neveu, Deloris Harper, Denise Fizer, Michele Halsey Hallahan, Priscilla C. Johnson, Tia Kelly, Melissa Carter, Cathy Atchison, Lanita Irvin, Ramona Weathersbee, Jason Owens, Chanta Rand, Ramona Brown, Sharon Blount, BRAB Book Club, and Uncle Steven Thomas, one love. I'd like to thank everyone who purchased and enjoyed one of my books. Everything I do has always been to please you. I know there are folks who mean the world to me that I'm failing to mention. I apologize ahead of time. Rest assured I'm grateful for everything you've done for me!

CHAPTER ONE
FULL SERVICE

He said
Baby, I love you
She said
I know you do
He said
Let's get together
For an eternity or two
He said
I'll make you happy
Keep you satisfied
I'll worship the oasis
Between your creamy thighs
She said
Boy, you're so sweet
Handsome and fine
But eternity is a very
Very long time
We'll discuss this later
But in the meantime
Continue to worship the oasis
Between my creamy thighs

On Thursday, May 19th, Stephanie Stewart stepped out of her walk-in closet with dramatic flair. Her four-inch heels sank into the plush carpet in her master bedroom. Her only other article of clothing, a full-length graduation gown, flowed majestically as she performed a slow strut from her closet to her king-size bed and then back again. The shimmering, purple fabric caught a slight breeze as she turned, briefly exposing her bare legs from the knees down. Her skin was smooth, silky brown.

Her audience, a tall, handsome brother named Theo, grinned appreciatively as he sat on the corner of the bed and watched her. He leaned forward and reached for her when she stepped closer to him, but Stephanie stopped a few inches away from his groping paws and struck a pose.

"What do you think?" Her smile was as bright as her lustrous, purple gown, which was only half as bright as her future.

Theo continued to lean forward with his forearms resting on his knees. "You look good," he said. "You know you do."

"I love this gown!" Stephanie exclaimed. She returned to her closet and admired herself in the full-length mirror. "Oh, I forgot the cap," she noticed. She found it on a closet shelf. Her heart swelled as she lifted the cap and placed it atop her head. The fit was almost perfect, but she planned to secure it with a few bobby pins when she wore it during the ceremony tomorrow.

With the cap and gown on, everything looked official. Stephanie's smile was so wide, her seldom seen dimples had appeared. She left the closet again and returned to Theo. He looked her up and down as she approached him.

"Damn, you making that outfit look good," he commented. "Come here."

Stephanie continued to grin as she stepped between his legs. Theo placed a hand on each of her hips. She pushed him away and took a step back.

"No, don't get it wrinkled," she warned. "I won't have time to take it to the cleaners."

"I'm not gon' get it wrinkled," Theo replied, but he didn't reach for her again. "Are you gonna wear those heels?" he asked, looking down at her feet.

"Yeah." She nodded. "You like 'em?"

He shrugged. "They're fine. Are you gonna wear a dress under your gown tomorrow or go commando?"

Stephanie thought his grin was devilish. She loved Theo's eyes; they were a couple of shades lighter than brown, but not quite hazel. He was tall, with fair skin that he'd chosen to decorate with an assortment of bold tattoos. None of the markings were gang-affiliated, and according to Theo, the few that featured a female's name were in reference to relatives; his mother, grandmother and daughter.

Stephanie wasn't a huge fan of tattoos, but she had to admit that she found them appealing when they first met nine months ago. Theo had approached her at a gas station and asked if she'd like him to pump for her. The request was uncommon, considering full-service stations went out of style before Stephanie was born, and Theo did not work for 7-11. She thought his chivalry was endearing. She didn't even judge him when she noticed he had stepped away from a late model Suburban that was badly in need of a paint job and new tires.

"What's your name?" he'd asked as he slid the pump nozzle into her Navigator.

"Stephanie," she'd replied as she watched him. "Thanks. I can't remember the last time someone asked to pump my gas."

"No problem," Theo had said as he studied her features. "How old are you?"

The question caused Stephanie's eyes to narrow. "Why?"

He smiled, revealing one of the main things Stephanie noticed when she met a man. He had nice teeth. She also appreciated Theo's height and build. He wore a tee-shirt that showed off his strong arms and flat stomach. His chest wasn't necessarily brawny, but Stephanie didn't need a muscle man in her life at the time. In fact, she didn't believe she needed a man at all.

"I was just noticing your ride," he had commented. "Not many women successful enough to roll around like this at your age."

"You don't know how old I am," Stephanie had replied, flirting now.

Theo moistened his lips before responding. It was a slight gesture, but Stephanie's eyes were glued to his mouth as she watched him. Theo was clean-shaven, his lips pink and full.

"I don't mind pumping your gas either way," he commented. "But if I'm filling up your *man's* car, I don't want to embarrass myself by asking for your number."

Stephanie half-rolled her eyes. She thought his pickup line was subpar, but she had to give him props for his approach. She gave him props for his height and looks as well. And then there were those tattoos. As the digital readout on the gas pump inched closer to the $40 it usually took to fill-up her SUV, her attention moved to his arms. Neither had a full sleeve of tattoos, but he had an interesting mural on display. She decided she wouldn't mind studying it in more detail.

"I'm twenty-one," she had told him.

"You got a man?" Theo had asked.

She shook her head. "No. Not right now."

"Can I get your number then?"

Stephanie gave it some thought, but she didn't have a lot to go on at the time. Nothing she'd observed thus far put the stranger in her *husband material* category. But who the hell was looking for a husband?

"Alright," she decided. "What's your name?"

"Theo."

She didn't think she'd reacted to that, but she must have, because he told her, "I was named after my granddad."

"I think it's a nice name," she said. "Short for Theodore?"

He nodded. Behind them the pump shut off, indicating her gas tank was full. After he returned the nozzle, Theo produced his cellphone and handed it to her, so she could input her number. When she was done, he inquired again about her ride.

"So is this your truck?"

Stephanie was able to hide her suspicion as she nodded.

"Nice," he'd said, admiring the Navigator. "You must be balling. What you do for a living?"

"I'm still in school," Stephanie replied as she returned to the driver's side. By then she was wondering if he was *one of those*.

Nine months later, she was still on the fence in regards to whether Theo was a male gold-digger or not. If she had to say yay or nay, she'd probably respond in the affirmative. But Theo wasn't like any of the leeches she'd met thus far. Since they'd been dating, he only asked to drive her car twice, and he didn't seem upset when she turned him down. He sometimes complained about his living situation (he shared an apartment with a friend who was not always timely with their portion of the rent), but Theo never asked Stephanie if he could move in with her.

As their relationship progressed, and he learned more about her, Theo was increasingly impressed with her status and ambition. He now knew Stephanie was the heir to her family business, Texas Builders. It was one of the largest construction and contracting companies in the state. Theo knew she owned her home and car outright, and earning her college degree in construction management was highly recommended but never a formal requirement from her mother, who was the current CEO of Texas Builders.

Theo knew Stephanie became a millionaire when her first trust fund matured on her 18th birthday. He also knew she'd have access to another trust fund tomorrow (when she officially graduated from TCU), and funds from a third account awaited her on her 25th birthday.

Stephanie often wondered if money was the reason Theo allowed her to assert dominance over him and their relationship – which she openly referred to as a *friendship*. He sometimes complained that she was too bossy, but the grievance was never strong enough to push him out the door or out of her life.

Even when Theo said things like, "One day you gon' meet a man who won't put up with all that mouth," and Stephanie would counter with, "Maybe so, but it won't be you," he would simply grin and nod, as if he was privy to a secret that might change her life. She doubted if he had an ace up his sleeve, but in the meantime she enjoyed his company. Theo was good-looking and loyal. And he was a skilled and devoted lover.

He liked to tell her, "I don't make love to you. I pay homage."

Stephanie believed her oasis was more valuable than diamonds, so his devotion was befitting.

● ● ● ● ● ●

"What are you doing after the ceremony?" Theo asked.

Stephanie removed her cap and placed it on the dresser. She checked her hair in the mirror mounted on the solid, oak furnishing and smoothed it down with her hands. She wanted to go with curls for graduation, but she decided to keep her mane straight, so the cap would fit snugly. She smiled at her reflection. In the past six months she'd lost nearly twenty-five pounds. The weight loss was most noticeable in her waist and face.

She liked her looks when her cheeks were fuller, but there was no denying she looked better now that her features were slimmer. She thought she was starting to look more like her mother, and that was a good thing. Korah was a beautiful woman. Interestingly, Stephanie thought her mother was becoming more attractive as she approached her 50th birthday. She and Korah both hard dark, rich skin. Stephanie wished she had her mother's height, but she never felt uncomfortable with the woman who stared back at her in the mirror. Even when she was short and chubby, Stephanie knew she had it going on.

A breath of air skated up the back of her legs.

Stephanie reached back, and her hand came in contact with Theo's. She didn't realize he had risen from the bed. He appeared in the mirror's reflection, looking over her shoulder. He had lifted the gown up to her thighs. She playfully pushed his hand away again.

"Why you tripping?" He watched her eyes in the mirror.

"I told you I don't wanna get it messed up," she said.

"You think I'ma mess it up, just by touching it?" he asked.

She didn't respond.

"Why you ain't got no drawers on, if you don't want me to look?" he wondered.

Stephanie didn't want to admit it, but she liked Theo's hood accent. He had a bright, red tattoo on his neck of two plump lips, and she liked that too. She liked to lick him there, though she sometimes wondered how many other women enjoyed the same thing.

He raised her gown again. She didn't stop him this time. She smirked at him in the mirror, but he didn't notice. His gaze had dropped down to her waistline. When he had the gown high enough to expose her ass, his eyes brightened. His smile was genuine. He let the gown fall and met her eyes in the mirror.

"Why don't you take this off, so it won't get messed up?"

"Don't you have a job to go to?" Stephanie inquired.

He shook his head. "I'm off today. They cut my hours again."

She turned to face him. Theo worked as a waiter at Cattleman's Steakhouse downtown. When she first met him, she found that hard to believe. But she and a few girlfriends showed up unannounced one evening, and there he was; waiting tables. That night he wore a long-sleeved button-down that covered all of his tattoos, except the lips on his neck.

She had asked to be seated at one of his tables and was surprised by how proper Theo spoke as he took their orders and made sure everything was to their satisfaction. Even with Stephanie at the table, he was very flirtatious. She could see how he managed to generate $200 in tips on a Saturday night. A lot of women are attracted to thugs who can change their vernacular when the setting called for it.

"Why'd they cut your hours?" she asked him.

He shrugged. "They hired a couple of new people. I think everybody's hours got cut, to make room for them."

Stephanie wasn't sure if she believed his explanation and was grateful that it didn't matter. She wouldn't like it if her *man* was a slacker, but she could care less what her *friends* did.

He knelt suddenly. Stephanie's heart froze, thinking he'd dropped to one knee. Was this the moment he'd been waiting for? He'd put up with her shit for nine, long months, and now that she was graduating, it was time to capitalize. Stephanie already had her own home and personal fortune. Theo had been looking forward to the day when she'd take his last name and share her world with him.

But when she looked down, she saw that he was on both knees, rather than one. And he didn't have a ring in hand or a hopeful smile she'd have to shatter into a dozen pieces. Theo smiled as he lifted her gown and ducked his head under it. She started to protest, but the feel of his warm breath between her legs effectively silenced her.

Theo's large hands rose up the back of her legs, sending tingles through her thighs and spine, until he had a firm grip on her ass. He urged her forward, until his mouth came in contact with her sex. Stephanie shuddered as she gripped his crew cut through the gown.

"I thought you said—"

She cut him off by lifting one leg over his shoulder and drawing his face deeper into her core. His nosed pressed her clit, igniting a pleasant trickle of fire that flowed down both legs and up to her stomach.

Theo muttered something that sounded like, *"You don't know what you want,"* against her labia.

Why are you still talking? Stephanie wondered. She grinded harder against his mouth, imploring him to finish what he started.

Their position wasn't optimal for what she hoped to accomplish, so she wasn't upset when he began to lean backwards, until he lie flat on his back. She followed him down, refusing to allow his lips to become unlatched. When she had his face successfully straddled, she began to worry about her gown again. She decided a few wrinkles were better than a wet stain that smelled of her essence, so she lifted the garment up to her chest.

The added benefit of this move was it provided her an opportunity to look down at Theo's face, well the top half of it at least. Plus she figured he'd be able to breathe a little better. That was sure to prolong his offering.

He watched her as his lips and tongue titillated her most sensitive region; sucking and caressing until the fire in her belly became a whirlwind in her chest. He savored and slurped as if she was the juiciest peach ever. His tongue did magic tricks. He gripped her ass tighter; inviting her to put more weight on him.

Stephanie fought to hold onto the gown, but as her ecstasy gained momentum, she needed to stabilize herself. She dropped the garment over his face and leaned forward, planting both palms on the carpet. With this position, she could ride him fully. She grinded on his mouth as if it was his manhood. Theo licked and sucked her clit dutifully, allowing her to manage the momentum of her pleasure.

Stephanie checked the clock on her nightstand and saw that it was a little after one. She didn't know if the nearest drycleaner would launder her gown while she waited, but she did know that money talks. She had yet to encounter a business that wouldn't bend a few rules for cold, hard cash.

She also decided that not being able to see Theo's face didn't detract from the ecstasy he provided. On the contrary, looking into his eyes would only remind her that he was a real person with *feelings*, and he might want her to reciprocate the pleasure he was giving her. Stephanie was generally okay with that, but as her graduation day neared, she felt special. She didn't feel like sucking dick today. Today she felt like cumming on Theo's face and then sending him on his way.

So that's what she did.

CHAPTER TWO
KORAH AND BRICK

A man who finds a good wife
Has found life
He's found light in a wasteland
Of darkness and strife
He's found warmth in a world
That's grown frigid to love
A soft touch
A kind smile
Always lifting him up
Because she shines when he shines
Her tears spill when he cries
He has no kingdom or throne
Without her by his side
Her devotion is unquestioned
Her character refined
Their union is blessed
Their lovemaking divine

Three hundred miles away from Stephanie's love nest, in the fair city of Lubbock, Brick Avery pulled his F-150 King Ranch into the parking lot of an enormous worksite. He navigated his truck smoothly between heavy-duty vehicles, personal cars and trucks and an endless stream of construction workers.

The majority of men on the site wore tee-shirts or golf shirts with their company logo boldly emblazoned on the front or back. This was the same logo on both sides of Brick's truck. His passenger worked for a different company, but she was not envious of the project Brick House had landed. She did not bid on this contract, but even if she had, she would rather lose it to Brick than any other contractor in the lone star state.

He pulled to a stop near the entrance of what would one day be a Dillard's store and exited the vehicle. Korah waited and watched as he moved around the truck to open the door for her. Brick wore a white button-down that was tucked into a pair of faded jeans. The jeans fit him nicely, drawing attention to his perfect waistline and tight butt.

He wore a pair of Justin work boots that were designed to look like western wear, yet still offer the steel-toed safety needed for construction sites. His bronze skin was radiant beneath the hot, Texas sun. He and Korah had been married for over two years, but her heart still beat sweetly when he opened her door and offered a hand to help her out of the truck.

"Thank you," she said, looking into his eyes.

Brick took in a deep breath as he raised both arms overhead and stretched his travel-weary muscles. The drive from Dallas to Lubbock took four and a half hours, but Korah didn't mind. She was excited to see her husband's new property, and Brick was always eager to show off his accomplishments.

She stepped out of the F-150 wearing tan slacks with a purple blouse. Brick reached into the bed of the truck for her spare work boots. Korah steadied herself with a hand on his shoulder as she stepped out of her pumps and into the boots. When she was done, Brick surprised her by kneeling so he could tie the laces for her. When he finished, he rose to his full height and noticed her smile and the appreciation in her eyes.

"What's up?" he asked.

"Nothing," Korah said. "Just, thanks." She knew he didn't consider his behavior *gallant* or worthy of pointing out at every turn. This was just one of many perks that came with being married to a cowboy.

"Don't forget your hard hat," he told her. "Will you grab mine too?"

Korah turned and opened the truck's back door to retrieve the hardhats from the seat. Her eyes widened when she felt an unexpected slap on the rump the moment she bent over. She gave her beau a playful look when she turned back to him.

"You shouldn't put that thing in my face, if you don't want me to touch it," he commented.

"You don't see me complaining," Korah replied as she handed him his hardhat.

Brick grinned and put it on. Like his boots, the hat was fashioned to look like a Stetson, while offering all of the safety of a typical hardhat. Korah thought he looked supremely handsome when he was all suited up and ready to inspect the site.

"You won't believe some of the designs we got going on here," he boasted as they stepped away from the truck. "I'm talking state of the art."

"I'm sure I will believe it," Korah said. "You already showed me the blueprints, remember?"

"Babe, don't spoil the surprise," he complained.

She shook her head, smiling. Brick was as happy as a teenager with a new car. She knew that building things was one of her husband's greatest joys in life. Next to that was showing off the things he'd built.

"I'm sorry, dear," she replied. "Please show me your *grand creation.*"

"That's the plan," he said, as if he didn't notice her sarcasm. "Maybe one day your little company will get a contract this big."

That comment earned him a good-natured elbow to the ribs. Brick shook it off with a country boy chuckle.

● ● ● ● ● ●

For the next hour, Brick gave his wife a tour of his latest project. She had to admit it was very impressive. The sleepy town of Lubbock was currently behind the times when it came to shopping experiences. The malls in Dallas, Overbrook Meadows and even Arlington put their shopping centers to shame. That would all change in 2018, when Brick House was expected to complete the Hendrick Mall.

The massive construction would be home to more than 100 stores and restaurants as well as a full-scale ice skating rink and a futuristic movie theater. Brick had successfully bid on a number of noteworthy projects in recent years, but the sheer magnitude and splendor of the mall was on another level of extravagance. And he was right; the blueprints Korah had examined last year did little to prepare her for her husband's grandiose construction.

As they toured the property, she was equally pleased with his employees, who worked together with the efficiency of a well-oiled machine. The respect they showed Brick never failed to impress her.

Midway through their visit, Brick noticed an unattended jackhammer next to one of the fountains.

He looked Korah's way and said, "Hey, babe, check it out. Your favorite toy. You wanna play with it?"

She smiled and blushed, despite her dark skin tone. "You know I want to."

"Go ahead," he offered.

Looking around, she said, "Really? With all of these people here?"

He chuckled at their private joke. "Nah, you're right. No point in starting something we can't finish."

Afterwards he took her to a home-style restaurant for lunch. Korah sat quietly while he bragged about the eatery's architecture before she told him, "Brick, I know you built this restaurant."

"Really?" he said with a grin. "How'd you know?"

"It used to be on your website," she reminded him.

"This restaurant hasn't been on my website for over a year," he commented. "How come you remember?"

"I didn't at first," Korah replied as she took a sip of her tea. "I thought it looked familiar. But then you started going on and on about how nice it is, and that's when I knew for sure."

He laughed. Korah loved his smile, his lips, his teeth, even the crow's feet that appeared in the corners of his eyes when he squinted.

"Okay, well if you *didn't* know I built it, what would you think of this place?" he asked.

"I think it's beautiful," she said honestly. "Anything you put your hands on turns to gold."

He nodded appreciatively. "We only had two trucks when we started work on this restaurant," Brick reminisced. He looked around with nostalgia glinting in his eyes. "I was at this site every day. I stayed in a hotel up the street."

"Now look at you," Korah said. "You've come a long way."

"Yeah." He nodded and looked her in the eyes. "We both have."

They ordered chicken fried steak with baked potatoes and black-eyed peas on the side. The food was amazing. Korah tried not to eat to the point of lethargy, but it was hard not to.

"Glad *I'm* not driving back to Dallas," Brick said when he pushed his plate away. He leaned back and patted his belly. "I think I'll take me a nap, while you fight that traffic."

"Lucky you," Korah said. "If I had known we were going to eat this good, I would've volunteered to drive down here, instead of the return trip."

"I'm sure you would've. No take-backs."

Korah rolled her eyes, but she wasn't upset with him. She loved when they could spend a whole day together. Usually their careers pulled them in different directions, and she couldn't even count on Brick to make it home for dinner.

"You excited about tomorrow?" he asked.

The smile that lit Korah's face said it all.

"Me too," Brick said. "I can't wait to finally put our team together."

Her eyes narrowed. "I hope you're not still talking about consolidating our companies."

He shook his head. "No. I know better than that. Texas Builders is doing great. You'd be a fool to merge with anyone."

Korah agreed wholeheartedly. "Then what do you mean by putting our team together?"

"I mean *our* team," Brick said. He reached across the table and took her hand. "Me and you. I've always hoped we could work together. I want you to take over my offices, so I can get more involved with the constructions. It'll be perfect."

This was news to Korah. "How long have you been planning this?" she wondered.

"From the moment I met you. Over the past few years, the things you've done with your company are phenomenal, Korah. I can't fully express how impressed I am with you. You're incredible."

His praise meant the world to her. Her chest flushed with heat. "Thank you. But why would I give all of that up – to work for you?"

"Not *for* me, baby. *With* me. Do you have any idea how far we could take Brick House if you were there? I'm talking skyscrapers, all across the country."

"You already have someone running your offices," she pointed out. "And he's pretty good at it."

"I don't think Isaac would mind if you brought your expertise to the table."

"What does Stephanie's graduation have to do with this?" Korah wondered.

"You said you were going to hand over the reins when she graduated," Brick reminded her. "If she's CEO, what do you plan to do there, file papers?"

"Actually I haven't given much thought to it," Korah admitted. "But I never said she'd take control of the company immediately. There's still a grooming process. She's not ready."

"You've been grooming her for the past four years," Brick stated. "And it's not like you won't be around to help her. Plus she's got Yolanda and Priscilla. She'll have all the support she needs."

"You've put a lot of thought into this," she noticed.

"Seems like I've been thinking about it more than you," he said, still cradling her hand. "How long do you plan to stay on after she graduates?"

"I don't know," Korah said. "But I know she's not ready. She's only twenty-two."

"She's more ready than you were when you took over," Brick noted.

"That was different. It was an emergency situation, and I had to take a crash course; learn on the go. I made a lot of bad decisions in those early days. I bumped my head plenty of times."

"You learned from all of those bruises," her husband said. "You grew stronger. I'm not rushing you. We've got our whole lives to make this work. Just give me some idea how long you think it'll take to get Stephanie where you want her to be. I'll keep my best office warm for you."

Korah appreciated the gesture, but "Even when Stephanie does take over the company, what makes you think I want to go right back to work for you?" she asked with a smirk.

"*With* me."

"Either way, honey... Maybe I plan to spend my retirement, I don't know, bird-watching or something."

He laughed at that. "Come on now. You're too young to retire. And construction is in your *blood*. You'd go crazy if you had to sit at home and watch everything get built without you."

"That's why I planned to stay at Texas Builders, maybe in an advisory role."

"Really? That's your plan?"

She shrugged. "I'm sorry, but I don't have anything concrete yet. I'm glad my baby is graduating, but as far as turning over the company to her, I'm just not there yet."

"That's fine," Brick said. "Like I said, no pressure. If you wanna hold her back–"

"I'm not holding her back."

"If you wanna hold off because she needs more training, that's understandable. But if you wanna hold off because you enjoy the job too much to give it up, then I would much rather you come and do the same work at Brick House."

"Brick…" She placed her other hand over his. "Texas Builders is my family business. It's my legacy. I have to be extremely careful about the moves I make."

"Yes, you do," he agreed. "And you know I would never do anything to cause Texas Builders to falter. I would sell my company to save yours, if it ever came to that."

She looked into his eyes and knew he was telling the truth. His declaration warmed her, all the way down to the core.

"But remember, Brick House is your company too," he continued. "Everything I have is yours. I believe that if you and I work together and let Devin and Stephanie run Texas Builders, we will all win. I can't tell you how much I'd love to walk into my office and see your face every day. Hell, we could ride to work together."

The more Korah thought about it, the more she liked the idea too.

"You'll know when Stephanie's ready," Brick said. "When that day comes, you gotta let her fly. And then you can come and take your rightful place as the queen of our Brick House empire."

Her smile returned. "Damn, baby. You just made my heart flutter."

"And I made myself hard," he said, without the slightest bit of shame.

"I don't know how you managed that," Korah said with a giggle, "but it sounds like a personal problem."

"It doesn't have to be," Brick said. He leaned over the table with an all-too familiar look in his eyes. "What say me and you get out of here and find a quiet spot to park for a little while, before we hit the road?"

She shook her head. "No way. I'm too full."

"Oh." His smile deepened. "At least you turned me down for a good reason, instead of because you're a prude."

She laughed. "I'm not a prude, darling. You know I would never deny you."

He watched her intently as she spoke. "Oh, well if that's the case, how about a quickie hand job?"

She chuckled and shook her head but said, "Okay."

"*Nice*," Brick said, rubbing his hands together. "Now I'm thinking I should've asked for a blow—"

"Whoa," Korah said, looking around. "Sir, this is a family restaurant."

"You're right. I'm sorry."

"I didn't say I wouldn't do it."

Brick's hand shot up in a flash. "Check, please!"

CHAPTER THREE
GRADUATION

On Friday afternoon Korah, Brick, Devin, Yolanda and a host of other friends and relatives arrived at the Schieffer Arena on TCU's campus to celebrate Stephanie's graduation. Due to the size of the graduating class, the master of ceremonies implored everyone to hold their applause until the last student had stepped across the stage. That request was mostly ignored.

Decorum was certainly thrown to the wayside when the MC called Stephanie's name. They weren't in competition with any other family, but Korah believed the thunderous racket that erupted as her daughter accepted her degree was the loudest by far.

And though it had always been a given that Stephanie would graduate college and follow in the footsteps of her father, mother and brother, Korah couldn't help but get emotional as she watched her little girl take the next step towards professionalism and maturity.

When Stephanie looked out into the crowd and yelled, "Mama, I did it!" with her degree held high, Korah lost the last of her resolve. Joyful tears filled and leaked from her eyes. Brick draped an arm around her.

"Look at your girl," he said, leaning close to her ear. "You did it, baby!"

She didn't believe she deserved much credit for Stephanie's accomplishments, but she accepted his compliment. Korah was born in a home with no college graduates. When her first husband passed away and left the company in her hands, she found herself on the verge of defeat many times.

But despite it all, she didn't fold. Korah got her degree, while struggling to keep Texas Builders and her family afloat. She made sure her son Devin went to college as well, so he could carry on the legacy. Now that Stephanie had done the same, Korah felt she could finally take a step back and relax, knowing Texas Builders would always be in good hands.

● ● ● ● ● ●

The university hosted a reception for the graduates and their families immediately following the commencement ceremony, but for Stephanie and her group, the real fun was scheduled for later that day.

At seven p.m. everyone met up again in the Garden Ballroom of the downtown Hilton for Stephanie's graduation party. Korah pulled out all the stops for the celebration. The buffet-style dinner featured rotisserie chicken, barbecue ribs and leg of lamb shish kebabs. There was also an open bar and a DJ spinning tunes for guests with varied tastes in music.

The dress code was semi-formal. Korah thought everyone looked great as the guests began to fill the room and mingle. Malcolm, her assistant from work, was one of the first to arrive. He helped Korah with last minute arrangements and remained tethered to her hip until she told him, "You're not at work today, Malcolm. Everything's taken care of. Go on, enjoy yourself."

"I know, Mrs. Avery. I just wanna make sure everything's perfect for Stephanie."

Malcolm was tall and thin, with fair skin. His suit fit him perfectly. He'd been with the company for a little over two years, and Korah still considered him a godsend. It was hard to find any fault with him, but if she had to pick something, it would be that he was a bit overzealous at times.

She reached to loosen his tie. "You know you don't have to wear a tie tonight."

"I know, Mrs. Avery, but–"

"Go, have a drink," she said, gesturing towards the bar.

"Okay," he said. "What would you like?"

"I'd like for *you* to go have a drink," she said with a chuckle. "I'm paying good money for that bar. I don't want it to go to waste."

"Oh, okay," he conceded. "But you'll let me know if you need anything?"

"If I need anything, I have plenty of servers here to get it for me." She turned him towards the bar and started him in that direction. "Go on, now. Have fun."

He sighed quietly. A slight smile curved his lips. "Okay, Mrs. Avery, but if–"

"Nope, nope, nope," Korah said, shooing him away. "Have a nice evening, Malcolm." She shook her head, grinning, as he reluctantly walked away.

Other guests from Texas Builders included Priscilla, their longtime bookkeeper, accompanied by Hiram; her husband of more than forty years. Korah was surprised that he chose to attend, given his reserved nature and his insistence that Priscilla hurry and retire from the company, so she could spend more time with him. Korah greeted them when they entered the ballroom.

"Good evening! Glad you could make it."

"You know I wouldn't miss it for the world," Priscilla said.

"I love your dress," Korah told her.

"Thank you. Where's the woman of the hour?"

"Not here yet. You know how these youngsters always wanna make an entrance." Korah looked to Hiram and said, "Thanks for coming. It's great to see you again."

"Happy to be here," he said with a nod. "'Cilla says you have an open bar."

"*Hiram*," Priscilla said with a frown. "Is that the first thing you ask for?"

"You know how long it's been since I had a good martini," he told her. He reached into his jacket pocket and produced an envelope. "Here, for Stephanie."

Korah took the envelope, rather than direct him to the table she designated for graduation gifts. "Thank you, Hiram. I'm sure she'll appreciate it."

"I hope your bartender's up to snuff," he said as he turned and headed that way. He moved with a slight hobble, but other than that, he looked good for a man in his late sixties.

"Sorry about that," Priscilla said when he was out of earshot. "I would've left him at home, but he's been craving a martini ever since I told him about the party."

"No, he's fine," Korah replied. "Not half as grouchy as I expected."

Priscilla reached and took hold of both her hands. They stood facing each other, smiling broadly.

"I still remember the first day I met Stephanie," Priscilla said. "A fireball with pigtails."

Korah's heart warmed. Priscilla had been working at Texas Builders since Korah's late husband founded the company. She was family now, as much as Devin and Stephanie.

"It's been awesome watching her mature into the woman she is today," Priscilla continued.

"I don't know about *mature*," Korah joked, "but she's certainly grown up."

"Have you set a timeline for when you'll let her take over as CEO?"

"No," Korah said. "You know I have reservations..."

"Why, because she's so bossy?"

"Bossy, cutthroat, spoiled, borderline *rude*. I worry about how she'll respond when she runs into some of those chauvinists. There are plenty of investors who don't want to respect a woman in my position."

"You seem to have handled those chauvinists pretty well," Priscilla noted.

"That's because I learned how to finesse them. Stephanie's not one to humble herself."

"She'll learn," Priscilla predicted, "just like you did."

"I know, but..."

Priscilla's smile widened. "Sounds like someone might be afraid to let go."

Korah got a laugh out of that. "Look who's talking. How many years has it been since you semi-retired?"

"Touché. But you're much too young to retire. Have you given any thought to what you'll do whenever you decide Stephanie's ready?"

"I already got a job offer," Korah told her.

Priscilla's eyes brightened. "Really? Where?"

"Brick House," Korah said with a chuckle. "My husband wants me to work alongside him."

"I think that would be wonderful!" Priscilla exclaimed. "But it doesn't sound like you're sold on the idea."

"Texas Builders means everything to me," Korah acknowledged. "It won't be easy to let go and shift gears. Do you think the CEO of McDonalds could give it all up and go work for Burger King?"

"Probably not – unless he fell in love and married the CEO of Burger King. Then, anything's possible."

Korah smiled but said, "I think I'd miss everyone at Texas Builders too much."

"You could always take me to Brick House with you," Priscilla offered.

"Oh no. If I leave, you have to stay there to look after my baby."

"Understood."

The women laughed and embraced like sisters.

● ● ● ● ● ●

By eight o'clock most of the guests had arrived, but the honoree was still nowhere to be seen. Korah was reluctant to start dinner without Stephanie, but some of the natives were getting restless.

The ballroom was filled with family, friends and a horde of construction workers from Texas Builders and Brick House. Korah had never seen most of these men outside of the workplace. She was delighted by how nice they looked in slacks and collar shirts, rather than jeans and hardhats. Isaac, Brick's right hand man at his company, was there as well as their lead foreman Hector and a slew of other employees from the Dallas office. Everyone thought Korah was the perfect hostess, and they were ready to get the festivities started.

"Mama."

She turned to see her son Devin approaching with his lovely wife. Before Malcolm came along, Yolanda was Korah's assistant for years. She didn't approve when Devin informed her that the two of them were dating, but so far Korah's worries were unfounded. After three years, Devin and Yolanda were still going strong. They'd given Korah her first grandchild. And Yolanda's belly was currently swollen with the second.

"Hey, baby." Korah gave her son a hug and then turned to dote on her daughter-in-law. "Yolanda, you look beautiful!"

"Thanks, Mama. But I don't feel like it, not with this dress on."

Over the years, Yolanda transitioned from calling her boss *Ms. Stewart*, then *Mrs. Avery*, and finally *Mama*; which pleased Korah immensely.

"Oh, you look wonderful," Korah said. She placed a hand on her visible baby bump. "I wish I'd carried my babies as well as you do."

"Um, where is your daughter?" Devin asked, interrupting them.

"She'll be here soon," Korah told him.

"This party started an hour ago," Devin complained. "I'm hungry. My wife is hungry–"

"Mama, I'm just fine. Don't listen to him," Yolanda said.

"I'm not the only one staring at that buffet like a starving refugee," Devin told her. "I know you got those servers over there guarding it."

Devin was tall and handsome, with broad shoulders and large hands. His muscular physique was evident, even with a blazer on. He looked so much like his father, for a moment Korah felt like she was in a time warp.

"Stephanie texted me twenty minutes ago and said she was on her way," she told them. "She should be here any minute."

"Hey, baby."

Korah felt an arm snake around her waist. A moment later, she noticed the familiar scent of her husband's cologne. Brick pulled her to him and kissed her cheek, just as she turned to face him. After two years of marriage, Korah was surprised that her body still wanted to melt in his arms.

"Where's Stephanie?" he asked.

Brick wore a black suit with a white shirt and no tie. His coat was perfectly squared on his shoulders. With one button fastened, the jacket followed the contours of his back and sides perfectly. He was clean-shaven and as dapper as ever. Even though she saw him on a daily basis, Korah was taken aback by how fine her man looked.

"Like I was telling this one," she said, "Stephanie will be here any minute. I know you're not that hungry."

"No, not me," Brick said. "But Isaac's asking me to sneak him a plate of ribs. And I heard a few of your workers talking about bum-rushing the buffet tables. They don't think the servers can stop 'em, if they all go at once."

"I'm with them," Devin said. "Where they at?"

Korah shook her head, laughing. "Y'all need to quit."

"*Heeeey!*"

Everyone's attention was drawn to the entrance of the ballroom. Korah was grateful to see her daughter, accompanied by her latest boy toy, walking down the aisle. They were followed by a throng of ladies from Stephanie's sorority and a few dates they had brought with them.

"I'm here, everybody! *Now we can get this party started!*" Stephanie announced.

Since the graduation ceremony, she had changed into a party dress that was short and form-fitting. It was perfect for showing off the weight she'd recently lost. Korah was proud to say her daughter's fitness plan had paid off, and Stephanie could no longer be referred to as *chubby*. She was still thick in the hips and thighs, but there weren't a lot of black men who considered that a fault.

Upon seeing her, the ballroom erupted in cheers. Korah knew everyone was happy to see her, but some of them were even happier that they could finally start dinner.

CHAPTER FOUR
OBJECT OF DESIRE

*I spy
With my pretty brown eyes
A dark, chocolate prince
With godlike features
As tall as the sun
Strong shoulders and defined chest
My heart rate increases
As my eyes roll up and down his frame
A destructive fire
Blazes deep within me
My carnal desires peak
When he looks my way
And smiles
My heart shudders
I know he feels it across the room
I gather my courage
And make my way to him*

After everyone settled down enough for a prayer, the guests were finally allowed to attack the buffet. The DJ continued to spin soft tunes while they ate to their heart's content. Towards the end of the meal, Korah and a few others stood to toast the most special lady in the building.

"My baby," Korah said, already struggling to hold back her tears. "I remember when you were just a little thing; following your father around when he remodeled our first home. I used to get scared to death when I saw you running around with those screwdrivers. But Devin Sr. would tell me, 'She's gotta learn. But more importantly, she *wants* to learn.' It didn't take long before I saw that he was right.

"Y'all should've seen Stephanie when she was four," Korah said. "Couldn't even say *crescent wrench*, but she'd be sitting next to her dad's toolbox while he worked under the sink. When he'd ask for something, she'd dig in the box and come out with the right tool. I always knew she'd follow in his footsteps. Today she took another big step forward, but everyone knows Stephanie decided her future before she took her first class at TCU. She has always wanted to be just like her dad."

Thinking about her first husband and her daughter's achievements caused Korah's eyes to mist over. She felt Brick reach to squeeze her hand comfortingly. She looked down at him and smiled appreciatively.

"Stephanie, I know you'll continue to excel and make all of your dreams come true," she continued, "because you are a *Stewart*, and you never take no for an answer. Growing up, that line of thinking got you in a lot of trouble..." The audience agreed with lighthearted laughter. "But in the business world, it's gonna help you get things done. And I know you're gonna go about it the right way. Your future's so bright... I'm going to enjoy watching you take Texas Builders to the top. I love you, baby. I'm so proud of you!"

After the applause died down, Devin stood with his glass raised.

"I see that Mama remembers everything with *rose-colored glasses*. But for me, Stephanie is and will always be the same bratty sister who used to drink up all the Kool-Aid, tell on me when I did something bad and run to her daddy whenever she pissed me off enough to chase her around the house."

His comment brought laughter from every table.

"And then she had the nerve to get *bossy* as she grew older," Devin said. "Her teenage years..." He shook his head. "She didn't have enough authority to tell the mailman where to drop off packages, but she had an opinion about *everything*. And you best believe she let you hear it – whether you wanted to or not."

"Hey, I didn't know this was a roast!" Stephanie called from her seat. But she was smiling, as was everyone else in the ballroom.

"I may not get another chance to tell everybody about the *real* you," Devin joked.

"Better watch it," Stephanie warned. "You know I got stories too!"

"Naw, I'm just kidding," Devin said chuckling. "Everyone knows how awesome you are. I've been watching your steps since the very first one – *literally* – and you've never failed to amaze me at every turn. I think the most impressive thing about you, like Mama said, is the fact that when you set your sights on something, you don't stop grinding until you see it through to fruition.

"I used to make fun of how competitive you are; how aggressive you can be. But in this business, we need some of that. You're gonna have a lot of people who look at you as *A*, a woman and *B*, a black woman. Some of them won't give you the respect you deserve. But I know you'll earn their respect at the end of the day, because you refuse to take a loss, and your work is irreproachable. For that reason, I'm so happy to be on *your* side!

"But you might wanna be a little worried," Devin said to Brick, "because when Stephanie takes over, she'll try to take every contract you even *think* about bidding on."

"And I'ma get 'em too!" Stephanie shouted.

Even Brick had to laugh at that.

"I love you, lil' sis," Devin said. "And I'm forever proud of you. I look forward to working by your side. Under your leadership, I know we'll take Texas Builders to the top in the state, and then, maybe the whole country!"

"No maybe about it," Stephanie added. "We're gonna do it. I love you too, big bro!"

The crowd responded with *awws* and more applause.

● ● ● ● ● ●

After dinner the party became more lively when Stephanie and her crew hit the dance floor, and the DJ played music with their tastes in mind. The older crowd still had a ball congregating with familiar and unfamiliar faces and learning the new dance moves. And of course the open bar kept everyone in good spirits.

By eleven o'clock the first of more than 100 guests decided to call it a night. But as far as Stephanie was concerned, the party was just getting started. She and her sorority sisters were tipsy and without inhibition as they danced with themselves and their dates. Devin approached his mother with a sly look in his eyes.

"Hey, baby." She embraced him fully. "How long are you and Yolanda staying?"

"You know we got a room upstairs," he reminded her. "Her mom's watching the baby all night."

"That's good; for you two to get some time to yourself," Korah said.

"You and Brick got a room too, right?"

Korah nodded. "Stephanie did too, and a bunch of her friends from school. Not too many people wanna drive home after this party."

"What's up with your future CEO?" Devin asked, nodding towards the dance floor.

At the moment, Stephanie and her crew were having what appeared to be a twerk-off, while their dates (and a lot of other guys in the ballroom) looked on wolfishly.

"She's just having fun," Korah said, blowing him off.

"Of course. Not rachet at all," he commented sarcastically.

"Ratchet? Oh, I suppose you don't see your wife out there." Devin searched the crowd until he spotted her.

"She's not dancing like Stephanie and them."

"Hmmm. I see a little booty-popping going on," Korah noticed. "And Yolanda's *pregnant*. For shame!" She laughed at the look Devin gave her.

After a moment, he laughed too. "Naw, but for real, are you sure you're ready to let Miss New Booty take over the company?"

"*Miss New Booty*?"

"Ever since she got that weight off, she's been acting a little different. I know you noticed."

"You mean more confident, sure of herself?"

"Yeah, like we needed more of that."

"What are you saying?" Korah wondered. "Are you worried about where she'll take the company?"

"Are you saying you're not at all concerned? She's young, demanding, spoiled. I think her favorite comeback when she doesn't get her way is, '*The hell with this. I don't need you.*'"

Korah couldn't deny that was the case.

"That worked out okay in college," Devin acknowledged. "And with her boyfriends; I'm glad she takes a hard line with them. Saved me the trouble of having to whoop up on 'em. But I don't see that attitude working in a boardroom, when she's negotiating contracts..."

Korah wished that wasn't a concern, but everyone familiar with the situation knew that it was. When it came to getting her way, Stephanie had a pit bull's tenacity. But oftentimes their line of work required poise and patience.

"I think she can turn it on and off, depending on the situation," she said.

Devin looked doubtful. "Really?"

"Stephanie has a lot of friends," her mom noted. "And she's had her fair share of boyfriends. I don't think all of those people would like her, if she was constantly bossing them around."

Devin nodded. "I guess so."

"Anyway, I don't think you need to be worried about that tonight," Korah said. "The girl just graduated."

"That only means she'll want to take over as soon as possible," he pointed out. "Have you given her a timeline, for how long you need to train her before you retire?"

"No, and I'm not thinking about that tonight," Korah insisted. "Go on. Have fun. The company's fine, and you need to stop worrying. And, unless I'm not hip enough to know the difference, it looks like your wife is definitely twerking now."

Devin followed her gaze and saw that, sure enough, Yolanda had both hands on her knees. Stephanie and her friends cheered her on as Yolanda proved that despite being pregnant, she could still get down with the best of them.

"She looks good though, don't she?" Devin said, grinning.

"Yes, they all do," Korah agreed. "Not ratchet at all."

● ● ● ● ● ●

By midnight the crowd had thinned even more. Most of the folks over the age of 45 wished Stephanie well before bidding her and her family adieu. The buffet table had been broken down and carted away, but the bartender was still mixing spirits. The DJ was as lively as ever. Stephanie had taken off her heels and had no idea where she left them. She was alert and excited when she approached her mother's assistant Malcolm.

"Hey, where's Mama?" she asked as she scanned the remaining guests.

"I think she and Brick went upstairs," he informed her.

"She left without telling me bye?"

"No, she said she'd be back to check on you," Malcolm replied. "But Brick was tired. He may be gone for the rest of the night."

"That's cool," Stephanie said. Her eyes were as bright as her smile. "Have you seen Baron?"

Malcolm smiled knowingly as he joined her in looking around the room. "There he is right there."

He gestured towards a tall, dark chocolate gentleman wearing a blue suit with a tie.

"Damn, he's fine," Stephanie said as they watched him interact with another employee.

"Yes, Ms. Stewart, I'm well aware of how you feel about Baron," Malcolm said.

Stephanie used to find it awkward when Malcolm referred to her as *Ms. Stewart*, considering he was older than her, and she didn't have an official title in their company. But now she thought it was fitting, and she appreciated how respectful he was. Malcolm was currently her mother's assistant, but Stephanie knew that one day he might work directly under her.

"Is he still single?" she asked, her eyes locked on Baron.

"I'm not sure," Malcolm replied.

"Come on, I know you know something."

"That's not something we've ever discussed," Malcolm said honestly. "It hasn't come up in any team meetings. But you're there most of the time, so you already know that."

"Don't be a smart-ass."

"I'm sorry, Ms. Stewart. Why don't you ask your brother? Devin works with him more than anyone at the office. He would probably know for sure."

"You know I can't ask Devin about him," Stephanie said, "just like I can't ask Mama about him."

"You know, Ms. Stewart," Malcolm said, "if you feel like you have to keep your feelings about Baron *secret*, that may be a sign that you shouldn't pursue it."

"I don't know why Mama doesn't want me to talk to him," Stephanie complained. "Devin and Yolanda worked out. They're married, and everybody's happy."

"That's not the norm, when it comes to workplace romances," Malcolm cautioned. "What usually happens is two people hook up, things get messy, and they can't stand to see each other when the dust settles. You know your mom doesn't want that to happen with you and Baron, especially since you're taking over the company some day. Once you're his boss, that would be all kinds of inappropriate."

"Did Mama say when she was going to let me take over?" Stephanie asked, barely listening to him.

"No," he said with a chuckle. "You mean you haven't asked her?"

"I tried to earlier," Stephanie revealed. "She told me to let the ink dry on my degree, before we get into all that."

Malcolm nodded. "Sounds like good adv—"

"Whoops – gotta go," Stephanie said, walking away from him. "Looks like somebody's trying to bounce without telling me goodbye."

Malcolm sighed and shook his head wistfully as he watched her pursue her most lingering object of desire.

● ● ● ● ● ●

"Leaving so soon?"

Baron turned and saw the heir to the Texas Builders' throne standing before him. Without her heels, the top of Stephanie's head barely reached his chin. He smiled down at her good-naturedly.

"Oh, um, yeah, it's getting late," he said, checking his watch.

Baron was clean-shaven, but Stephanie was accustomed to seeing a little hair on his face; sometimes a light moustache and beard. He had thick eyebrows, smooth skin and large hands that were calloused from hard work with heavy machinery.

Next to Devin, he was the top foreman at their company. That meant Stephanie was fortunate enough to see him at their team meetings on Monday mornings. Her school schedule had kept her away from the bulk of those meetings, but with school over, she looked forward to seeing a lot more of him.

Her infatuation had been active for the past two years and was common knowledge at the company. Stephanie even told her mother that she wanted to get to know Baron better. Of course Korah advised her against it. At the time, Devin and Yolanda's relationship had just become public. Everyone was worried about how the atmosphere in the office would suffer if things didn't work out with them.

But that was a long time ago, and Devin and Yolanda's relationship didn't end catastrophically. In fact, it was great having Yolanda officially in the family. Stephanie was pretty sure her mother would still prefer that she didn't date Baron, but it didn't look like Korah was around to object at the moment. Stephanie didn't see her nosey brother around either.

"You can't leave without dancing with me," she said as she hooked her arm in his. She could smell his cologne now that she was closer. It was alluring, but faint. She wanted to bury her face in his neck to smell more of it.

Baron barely budged as she attempted to lead him to the dance floor.

"Um, I'm not sure if that's a good idea."

His deep, assertive voice never failed to induce a response from Stephanie's body. This time she felt goose bumps sprout on her forearms.

"Why can't you dance with me?" she asked, looking up at him with her best doe eyes.

His eyes left hers and searched the room, no doubt looking for Korah or maybe Devin.

"My mama's not here," Stephanie told him. "Nobody will mind."

"If you had to wait until she left before you approached me, that says a lot," Baron replied.

Jeez. Everyone was starting to sound like the same broken record.

"Come on," Stephanie insisted. "This can be my graduation gift."

"I already gave you a gift," he said. "It's on the table with the others."

Stephanie sighed. Baron couldn't help but notice her breasts as they rose and fell. She didn't have a lot of cleavage exposed, but she didn't need it to draw attention. Baron noticed her figure a lot more in the past few months. As her waist slimmed down, he was aware that her breasts had not.

In a different environment, he may have told her how appealing she was. But his position at Texas Builders wasn't just a job for him. It was a career; the first one he ever had and a rather lucrative one. If all he had to do to keep things going smoothly was avoid the boss' daughter, he could certainly do that.

"What if I don't want that gift?" she said. "What if all I want is a dance?"

"You don't even know what I got you," Baron replied.

Stephanie turned to glance at her gift table. "Is it a box or an envelope?"

He grinned. "It's an envelope."

"Then I think I do know what it is," she said. "And as much as I appreciate it, I would still rather have a dance."

Baron couldn't respond right away. Stephanie's flirting had never been this bold. He knew the alcohol she'd consumed played a part in it, but he wondered if other factors weren't involved. With graduation, she was closer to taking her mother's position as CEO of Texas Builders. Maybe Stephanie believed her power over the company extended to everyone who worked there.

Baron was grateful when her date stepped to them. The boy's eyes were medium brown, but at that moment they were green with envy.

"Hey, babe. You ready to head up to our room?" He put a possessive arm around her waist, despite the fact that Stephanie's arm was still hooked around Baron's.

The graduate was so upset, she could've slapped the shit out of him. She knew this was her own fault for bringing Theo as her *date* and inviting him to spend the night in her suite. But she never figured him for a cock blocker.

Baron graciously withdrew his arm and smiled at the couple.

"You kids have a nice evening," he said before turning and walking out of the ballroom.

Kids? That comment left Stephanie even more frustrated. Did Baron think she was too young for him? Based on snooping she'd done in his personnel file, she knew he was 28. That made him six years her senior. That wasn't enough years for him to refer to her as a *kid*. She was about to run the whole company, for Chrissake.

"Don't ever do that again," she growled as she and Theo turned back to the party.

"Do what?"

"Interrupt me when I'm talking to an employee."

Her eyes were knitted together in anger, but Theo didn't back down.

"It didn't look like you were talking to an employee," he said. "Looked like y'all was macking."

"And if we were?" she said, pushing him away. "You are not my man. You're lucky I even invited you."

Theo remained in that spot while Stephanie stormed off towards the bar. He shook his head. It was starting to look like no matter how long they dated, she would never acknowledge him as her boyfriend. With any other girl, he wouldn't have tolerated it. But Stephanie was special. The problem with that was she knew she was special.

Instead of allowing resentment to set in, Theo relaxed and blew it off. Regardless of how she labeled their *situation*, there was no denying they were in a relationship. He still had time to turn things around, or *fuck some sense into her*, as his brothers would say. They had a fancy room waiting for them upstairs, so tonight Theo would have another opportunity to accomplish his goal.

CHAPTER FIVE
A DECENT PROPOSAL

On Monday morning Korah was greeted by a sexy cowboy when she stepped out of the shower at 7 am. Brick hadn't finished getting dressed yet. He was topless, wearing only a pair of faded jeans. He sat on the corner of the bed watching her. When they locked eyes, he leaned forward, resting his forearms on his thighs. The light from the bathroom revealed his sculpted trapezius muscles and his powerful chest, which had a clear crease down the middle.

Both he and Korah were pushing fifty, but Father Time had yet to soften Brick's muscles or loosen his skin. Korah stopped short and took a moment to admire her man as she dabbed the remaining moisture from her neck and shoulders. Brick stood and approached her with what Korah would've described as *lust* in his eyes – if not for the fact that it was 7 am on a workday. They both had important places to be. Brick's commute was much longer than hers; considering they were currently residing in Overbrook Meadows, and his office was in Dallas.

Korah smiled when he placed his hands on her sides and kissed her lovingly.

"Good morning," she murmured.

Her throat caught when he deepened the kiss and moved from touching to caressing her hips. He took her hand and led her to the bedroom. He relieved her of the towel before he backed her towards the mattress.

"Brick," she said with a giggle. "What are you doing?"

Rather than respond, he laid her back on the bed and stood between her legs. Her stomach tightened when he ran his hands from her ankles to her knees. He stared down at her kitty and then knelt, until all but his face had disappeared from sight.

"Brick..."

He hushed her with soft kisses on her sensitive folds. Korah's heart drummed. She sat up on her elbows and looked around the room anxiously.

"What, what are you doing?"

She gasped when he sucked her clit before responding. His hands gripped her outer thighs now, as if he was preventing her from escape.

"I'm tasting my wife," he said, and his tongue joined his lips in pleasing her. He hummed gruffly before telling her, "You should relax."

"What, what about Flora?" Korah stared at the bedroom door, half expecting their housekeeper to enter with a stack of neatly folded linens in her hands. She could imagine the embarrassed shock that would appear on Flora's face before the older woman quickly backed out of the room.

"Today's *Monday*," Brick reminded her between licks.

Korah knew that, but with the way he had her head spinning, she wasn't even sure which way was up anymore.

Hiring a housekeeper was Brick's idea. Korah wasn't raised with such extravagance, and although her home had six bedrooms, she'd been keeping up with it just fine. That all changed when her husband moved in and with the new edition Devin and Yolanda added to the family. Korah kept her granddaughter as often as possible. And Brick didn't always kick the muck off his boots before coming inside. Korah finally agreed that she could use a little extra help on the weekends, and they found a gem in Flora.

Brick found another gem when Korah submitted to his advances. She lie back on the mattress and allowed him to spread her legs further apart. He lapped her juices rhythmically, until the rise and fall of her stomach became erratic, and the pulse of her clitoris caused visible tremors to roll down her legs.

"Oh. *Baby, don't stop*," she whispered.

Her husband was obedient. In fact, Korah would say he went above and beyond the call of duty. Her ass began to grind on the mattress, as Brick's head bobbed up and down. He sucked all portions of her labia, clearly savoring every lick and nibble, but he saved his best loving for her clitoris. He licked the bulb until it hardened. He sucked it until Korah's eyelids fluttered, and her mind went blank. Her mouth hung open in what would've been an embarrassing expression in any other setting. But it was only the two of them, and even Brick couldn't see her face, so she felt no shame in moaning loudly, one eye half open, the other barely a slit.

Her lips quivered when the jolts of energy traveled from her center and up her spine, creating muffled explosions in her head and chest. Her orgasm rained down hot and sticky. Brick's hands moved between her legs. He tried to hold them apart, but Korah's climax forced them closed with the power of a bear trap. She scooted away from him and rolled to her side, gripping the sheets tightly as tidal waves of pleasure washed over her.

Brick stood and looked down upon the artwork he'd created before he backed away and stepped out of the room.

● ● ● ● ● ●

Korah freshened up and got dressed for work. She stopped short a second time that morning when she opened the bedroom door and detected the scent of toast. Her smile remained, but her expression became suspicious as she walked through her home and entered the kitchen. Brick stood, still topless, at the counter. He had prepared breakfast for her: Orange juice, grapefruit, toast and two strips of bacon. This was Korah's favorite morning meal. He looked up at her and smiled.

"Morning, babe."

As pleased as she was, about everything, Korah couldn't get over how obvious it was that he was buttering her up. She shook her head and chuckled.

"What?" he asked, looking as delectable as a stripper.

"This must be really big," she said.

"What's that?"

She walked to the counter and stood beside him. She placed an arm around him and kissed him on the cheek as she reached for a piece of bacon.

"Aren't you gonna be late?" she asked.

The commute to Dallas took nearly an hour. It was seven-thirty, and she knew he liked to get there at eight.

When they first married, deciding which home they would reside in was no easy task. While Korah's house in Overbrook Meadows was beautiful and very spacious, Brick's Dallas home (affectionately known as the Avery Manor), was larger and just as desirable. After living in both houses for the past two years, alternating on a weekly or monthly basis, Korah eventually gave in. In three months the Avery Manor would be their official residence. Rather than sell her house, Korah opted to rent it. In August her first tenants were arriving from London.

Korah didn't have time to eat breakfast, thanks to her husband's bedroom surprise (which was well worth the time), but she took a seat at the kitchen table and indulged him.

"Okay, Brick. Tell me what you want."

He brought her plate and sat across from her. "Darling, whatever do you mean?"

She laughed and got started on her meal. "You're going through all of this trouble to make me happy, even though it's making you late for work."

"Nothing wrong with a fella doing for his wife every now and then."

"Doing for his wife?" She met his eyes. "Since when do you do for me without wanting something in return?"

He frowned. "Now, I'm offended by that comment."

"In the *bedroom*," she clarified. "It's not like you to get yourself excited and then walk out, like it's no big deal."

He grinned. "Okay. You got me there. I do need to talk to you about something, baby."

"Mmm hmm. It must be a doozy."

He propped his elbows on the table. His smile gradually fell away. "You remember I told you about the problems I've been having with Hector?"

Hector was his lead foreman. Korah knew he'd been a cause of concern, because he was having trouble laying off the bottle. But his problems never caused Brick to miss a deadline.

"Yeah. I thought he was better," Korah said. "I saw him at Stephanie's party. He looked great."

"I thought so too," Brick said. "It's probably my fault for inviting him. I don't know a lot about AA, like what those guys can be around and stuff. I know some recovering alcoholics can go to a ballgame and sit right next to folks who are drinking with no problem. But I guess there's the other kind who can't stand to see people drink, without wanting to be a part of it."

"Oh no," Korah said. "Did he relapse at the party? I didn't see him drinking."

"I didn't either. But he must have. I guess he was too smart to go full blast at the party. He said everything happened afterwards."

"You talked to him?"

"Called me from jail last night, but I didn't talk to him until this morning. He picked up another DUI on Saturday, so I can't let him drive any of our trucks."

"That's..." Korah caught herself. First sex, now sympathy. Brick certainly had a dilemma, but, "What can I do to help with your, um, situation?"

"I need a foreman," Brick stated. "Just to borrow," he added, when Korah started shaking her head.

"Brick, I am not giving you a foreman."

"Baby, you gotta help me out," he pleaded. "We's married. We gotta be there for each other."

She laughed at that. "Me being there for you as a wife has nothing to do with doing a favor that could hurt my business. You have plenty of foremen."

"I need a *lead* foreman. My workers are stretched thin. I can't start that new dealership with what I'm currently working with. I had Hector lined up to run that job, but he's gonna be out of commission for a while."

Korah knew the Mitsubishi dealership in Irving was a big deal to Brick. They broke ground on the project last Friday.

"Fine," she conceded. "But we're gonna have to work out a contract. You would have to pay him as much as he would get paid on one of my sites."

"Of course," Brick said. "Thank you, baby. We really need to get moving on this, because I need him out there tomorrow. Today I'll lead the crew myself, but you know I can't be out there all day like that."

Korah understood that. But she still didn't like the idea of loaning her talent to the competition – even if it was her husband. She sighed.

"Alright. I think we can spare Monte."

Brick surprised her by shaking his head. "No, baby. I need Baron."

Her eyes widened. *"Baron?* No way."

"Korah, I'm sure Monte's a nice guy and all, but I don't know him. Do you think I'm comfortable giving a project this big to just anybody? I worked with Baron before. I respect him, and I know he does great work. That's the guy I need."

"Yeah, I'm sure you do. Do you think I forgot how you offered him a job?"

That sneaky move occurred a few years ago. Brick had won a bid on a new high school and subcontracted Texas Builders to construct the football field. Baron ended up running their portion of the project. He did so well, Brick had the nerve to ask if he wanted to jump ship and join his ranks.

"That was a joke," Brick said chuckling. "And it was years ago."

"The only reason it hasn't happened again is because you haven't been given another opportunity."

"Well, send me Devin," Brick suggested. "You know I would never try anything underhanded with him."

"Brick, you know I'm not gonna send you Devin. He's supervising all of our sites."

"Then send me Baron. I hate to say it, but you're starting to sound a little selfish, darling."

Korah's jaw dropped. She felt like she was on the wrong end of one of Brick's notorious negotiations. She had to take a step back and ask herself if she'd be willing to loan another company one of her employees *if she wasn't married to their CEO.* On a business level, it wasn't totally out of the realm of possibility, but it would come at a hefty price. The problem with that was she wouldn't feel comfortable accepting an outrageous sum from her husband. But if she agreed to this, Brick would have to pay well.

"I'll talk to Devin," she said.

Brick grinned, knowing he'd closed a deal once again. He stood and kissed her before exiting the room. "I gotta hurry and get ready for work."

Korah rolled her eyes. She didn't think her orgasm played a part in her decision, but thinking about his head between her legs gave her a pleasant aftershock. She was glad he hadn't asked for more.

● ● ● ● ● ●

Thanks to her sexy, conniving husband, Korah was ten minutes late to her Monday meeting at Texas Builders. If anyone was upset about it, they didn't dare complain. A lot of the eager faces in her conference room were blood relatives, but Korah considered all of them family. In addition to Stephanie and Yolanda, Priscilla was there along with Malcolm, her right hand man. On the construction side, or as Devin referred to them, *The Hardworking Men*, there was Baron, Monte and her beloved son; the head of construction at the company.

As a group, they discussed their current projects, the bids they were waiting to hear back on and any concerns they needed to keep in mind throughout the week. No one had a significant issue, so the meeting ran smoothly. Their most important project was an expansion of one of Overbrook Meadows' busiest freeways. The work had cut the four-lane highway down to two lanes for the past five months. Commuters would be happy to know that Texas Builders planned to complete their portion of the work by July. Korah was glad the end was finally in sight.

She asked her son to stay back after she concluded the meeting. Once everyone cleared out of the conference room, she took a seat across from Devin and told him about Brick's dilemma. In the past, Devin was known to have a bit of a temper, which could make conversations like this dicey. But he'd been a lot more composed since marrying Yolanda. Korah thought the birth of their daughter loosened him up even more.

When she was done speaking, he smiled at her. "Mama, why you let him do you like that?"

"I knew you were going to say that. But I assure you, he's not getting over on us."

"You're telling me you'd loan out our talent for – how long did you say this job would take?"

"I didn't. But according to Brick, six months."

"You'd loan out our talent for six months, to our competition, no less?"

"We subcontract all the time," Korah pointed out. "We got guys at Industrial Works right now."

"Yeah, and we're making them pay out the ass." He caught himself swearing. "Oh, sorry."

"Who said Brick's not gonna pay?"

"How much?"

"I don't know. Whatever Baron's salary is right now. I'll have Yolanda–"

"*Baron*? You offered him *Baron*?" Devin didn't want to go without their second best foreman any more than Korah did.

"Initially I offered him Monte."

"*Mama*," he moaned, shaking his head.

Korah considered the bedroom activities that led to her agreeing to that. Her face flushed with heat. Rather than suffer quietly, she turned the tables on her son. "He only wants Baron because he worked with him before. And the only reason he worked with him was because *you* got yourself kicked off that school job."

"I didn't get kicked off. I left on my own."

"Um, you better check your memory, baby."

"We had a difference of opinions," Devin said, thinking back to the spat that got so ugly, he and Brick nearly came to blows. "That was a long time ago," he said. "You know we get along great now."

"Yes, and I love that," Korah said. "But the fact remains, you're the reason he even knows Baron exists. So you should bear some responsibility."

He laughed. "Okay, now I *know* you feel guilty about going along with this. What'd he do to convince you, Ma? Wait, never mind!" He shook his head. "I don't even wanna know."

Korah laughed with him. "If we can't spare Baron, tell me," she said seriously.

"Nah, we'll be alright," Devin said. "Unlike your husband, we have plenty of talent at *our* company. Apparently we got enough talent to share with others." He gave her a side eye.

When they left the conference room, Korah was not happy to see that her daughter had the foreman they were just discussing cornered near the doorway. She imagined Baron was trying to exit the building when Stephanie stopped him. The girl appeared to be in full flirt mode. Korah couldn't tell if Baron was interested or entertaining her out of politeness.

"How long has she been barking up that tree?" Korah asked her son.

"On and off, since before me and Yolanda got married."

Korah was not amused. "What does he have to say about it?"

"I don't know. He's probably scared," Devin joked. "Your little girl can be pretty intense."

"Good," Korah said. "I hope he's scared to death."

Maybe getting Baron away from their sites for a while wasn't such a bad idea. Now that Stephanie had graduated, she might be ready to get serious with one of her boyfriends. Korah wasn't impressed with the one she brought to the graduation party, but she'd rather Stephanie devote her attention to that tatted-up fool, if it kept her mind off Baron.

"Go," Korah told Devin. "Hurry up and get your people out of here."

"Gladly," he said with a chuckle. "When does Baron start at the dealership?"

"Tomorrow," Korah said. "Could you let him know?"

"Brick must be a *master* negotiator," Devin said, laughing again.

"Have a nice day, son." Korah turned and headed for her office.

CHAPTER SIX
NO MEANS MAYBE

Korah wasn't always in a great mood on Mondays, but after the glorious morning with Brick and later confirming she could help with her husband's dilemma, she was chipper and upbeat. She felt so good, she invited her office staff to lunch; her treat.

They went to Chuy's on 7th Street for authentic Mexican cuisine. Korah always felt the food there was delectable. The only downside to going at lunchtime was her desire to wash the meal down with a Corona.

"I could probably get away with ordering one," she joked with Yolanda, "now that Stephanie is out of school and ready to take over the company."

Her daughter jumped on the opportunity to get clarification on the subject.

"And, um, when will I get that CEO title?" Stephanie asked.

"I don't know," Korah said noncommittally. "I was thinking two to three years."

"*Two to three years*?" Stephanie's expression made it clear she was not expecting to wait that long.

The group sat at a circular table that was big enough to give them all a fair amount of elbow room. Everyone found Stephanie's impatience amusing, but Korah knew her daughter was dead serious.

"Honey, that's not a long time," she told her. "I know you didn't expect this to happen overnight."

"No," Stephanie agreed. "But I thought we'd get things moving a lot sooner than that."

"We will," Korah promised.

"Starting when?" Stephanie wanted to know.

Korah smiled at her. "We've been working on your transition for months already."

"It doesn't feel like it," Stephanie countered. "Maybe if you tell me what this transition looks like, I'll know what to expect."

Korah nodded. She didn't think that request was unreasonable. She continued to smile as she looked her daughter over. Today Stephanie wore a gray pantsuit with a beige blouse. She had her hair pulled up in a professional bun. Her makeup was faint. Her skin, dark and lovely.

It was clear that she had been watching her mother for years; taking note of how she should dress, stand and even speak in the workplace. Korah had to admit that Stephanie would probably make a better contractor than her one day, given her natural tenacity and unwillingness to settle. But it would take time.

"Stephanie's right," Korah told her crew. "We should discuss this, because it will affect the whole office."

The group paid close attention as they continued their meal.

"It's no secret that Stephanie is going to take over my role in the company," Korah continued. "I offered the CEO position to Devin, because he's older and he's been working longer. But he declined. He prefers to continue as lead foreman and supervise the sites. That's probably the best move for the company, so I have no objections."

Everyone nodded their agreement.

"That brings us to this little girl..."

Stephanie beamed at her mother.

"You all know how hard Stephanie has worked to get through college and learn the business while attending school," Korah said. "In the past four years, Stephanie has operated in whatever capacity we needed her. She was an excellent assistant, before we hired Malcolm. Yolanda believes she could even fill in as bookkeeper. On top of that, Stephanie has a vast knowledge of construction. She can operate anything, from a forklift to a crane. She can read blueprints too, almost as well as Devin."

Stephanie's smile grew larger as her mother listed her qualifications.

"I won't lie and say I'm ready to step down," Korah acknowledged. "Building our company to what it is today has been my life's work. Every day, for the past thirty years, I've poured everything I have into Texas Builders. The thought of backing off completely and handing it over to someone – even if it's my own daughter – it's, well, quite frankly it's scary. I'm not only worried about the future of the company. I'm worried about what I'll do with myself when I don't have to show up at eight am every morning. Priscilla, I'm sure you know what I mean."

Priscilla nodded empathetically. Three years ago, when she suffered a stroke, the company was thrown into turmoil as they scrambled to train Yolanda to take over as the bookkeeper. After she recovered, Priscilla began to show up at the office, initially to offer Yolanda guidance. Her husband was not happy with that at all. He wanted her to retire. But Priscilla defied him and eventually came back to work full time. She said she wouldn't know what to do with herself, if she stayed at home every day.

Stephanie's smile faded when she said, "Oh, Mama. I'm sorry. I guess I never thought about how this would affect you."

"No, don't worry about me," Korah said. She managed to restore her game face. "If my husband has his way, I may never get to retire."

She told them about Brick's offer for her to take over the front offices at Brick House. Prior to then, Priscilla was the only one who knew.

"Mama, that's perfect!" Stephanie exclaimed. "If you do that, then I won't worry about you sitting at home, all bored and depressed."

Korah laughed at that. "Well I'm glad you don't have to worry. But that still leaves the first part of my argument: How long it will take before I feel comfortable enough to hand the company over to you...?"

"I hope it's not really three years," Stephanie complained. "You just said I know how to do every job in the office."

"Every job *except mine*," Korah corrected her. "But you're right." She sighed. "It won't take three years to get you ready. Starting this week," she said, addressing the group again, "we're going to take more steps to groom Stephanie for the position. I expect every one of you to help make this transition as seamless as possible. With Stephanie out of school, she can shadow me fulltime. I'll take her with me to meet with new clients and shareholders.

"Yolanda, I want you to work with her too; show her how to put a decent bid together. Malcolm, I want you to start CC'ing Stephanie on my incoming emails – except the ones from Brick. Those may be personal."

They all smiled at that.

Malcolm said, "Yes, Mrs. Avery."

"For now, Stephanie and Malcolm will accompany me when I check on our sites," Korah continued. "But over time, I'm going to leave it to just the two of you."

Stephanie nodded eagerly.

"Honestly, I think I can start taking days off within the next few months," Korah said. "I'll remain active in a consulting role for at least a year after the transition. I know I said I was worried about what would happen to the company in my absence, but honestly, that's more of a personal issue than a real concern. I know everyone at this table will do their very best to assist Stephanie, and you won't hesitate to call me if she makes a boneheaded move."

No one commented, but Korah knew they all had her back.

"Remember, it's not just Stephanie who'll suffer if the company falters," she said. "It will affect everyone's livelihoods. For you, Yolanda, this is not just a job anymore. It's your family legacy, just as much as it is mine. I know you won't let anything happen that would have a negative effect on your children's future."

"No, ma'am, I won't," Yolanda assured her. "But Stephanie's gonna do just fine. You'll see."

"I know she will," Korah said, looking her daughter in the eyes. "She always makes me proud."

● ● ● ● ● ●

After lunch, Korah asked Malcolm to catch a ride back to the office with Yolanda and Priscilla, so she could have some time alone with her daughter. When they hit the road, Stephanie expected to hear more details about her takeover.

Her mom surprised her by asking, "What were you talking to Baron about this morning?"

Stephanie's eyes widened. She didn't have an immediate response to that. Before she could come up with something, Korah said, "Girl, don't lie to me."

Stephanie swallowed the lie she was about to tell and shook her head. "Nothing, Mama. He was waiting on Devin, and I was just, you know, keeping him company. It was just small talk."

"And at your graduation party," Korah said. Her attention left the road for a second, so she could look Stephanie in the eyes. "What were y'all talking about then?"

Stephanie felt like she had fallen through some sort of time warp. Last time she checked, a 22 year old woman talking to a 28 year old man was perfectly legal. Her mom hadn't gotten into her business like this since she was in high school.

"How do you know we talked at the party?"

"We have a big company," Korah said. "But it's not that big."

Stephanie's eyes narrowed. She wondered who snitched on her. Neither Korah nor Brick were around when she approached Baron. She hoped it wasn't Malcolm, because she considered him a confidante. If she couldn't trust him, she couldn't keep him as her assistant when she became the CEO.

"We were just talking," she said vaguely.

"How did your date feel about that?" Korah asked.

"Theo's just a friend," Stephanie said with a roll of her eyes. "It doesn't matter how he felt about it."

"Oh, is that right?"

Stephanie was torn between wanting to assert herself as an adult and needing to be obedient to her mother. She hoped they could find a happy medium.

"Mama, I don't like Theo like that."

"You've been dating him since last year," Korah recalled.

"Not exclusively."

"So, he's not the one?"

Stephanie shook her head. "No. Not even close."

"Have you and Baron gone out?"

Stephanie continued to shake her head.

"You're not trying to make a move on him?" Korah asked.

"Mama, you know I like Baron. But we've never seen each other outside of work. We never even talked on the phone."

Korah could tell she was being honest. "You do realize that as CEO, it would be improper for you to initiate a relationship with any of the guys who work for us," she stated.

"Yeah, but I won't be CEO for two years," Stephanie retorted. "You said it may take up to three…"

"Is that supposed to be funny?"

"Yes, Mama," Stephanie said, smiling now. "You need to loosen up. You're getting all worked up over nothing."

"Am I, Stephanie?"

"Yes, I think so. I mean, Baron is fine. Everybody knows that. But he's not interested in me."

Korah tried to hide the joy that news brought her. "Why do you say that?"

"Because I tried to talk to him a bunch of times, and he never flirts back. I don't know what more I can do. You saw how good I looked at the party. But when I walked up to him – nothing. He didn't stare at my boobs or *nothing*."

"I won't tell you I'm disappointed that Baron chose not to ogle the boss' daughter," Korah said with a smirk.

"I'm more than just the boss' daughter," Stephanie quipped. "Plus I lost all that weight. I can't believe he's still ignoring me. Do you think he's gay?"

Korah got a laugh out of that. Why was that such a common retort from vain women, when faced with a man who didn't respond to them? "Either that, or he's not stupid enough to touch the boss' daughter," she reiterated. "Either way, I appreciate it."

Stephanie shook her head and let the conversation end there. They were both in good moods, and the situation seemed settled. It wasn't settled, but Korah thought it was, and that would keep her off the subject – at least until something happened to pull her back in.

Stephanie had paid close attention to everything her mother said, and she was grateful that a flat out ban didn't cross her lips. Korah never explicitly ordered her to leave Baron alone. Stephanie would take heed and not try anything foolish once she became the CEO. But until then, she had time to close the deal.

She didn't believe for one second that Baron was gay. He may be shy and leery of her, but he was *all man, all day long*. That much she was certain of.

CHAPTER SEVEN
TWO MASSAGES
ONE HAPPY ENDING

His squeezes
Illustrious
Enticing
So appealing
His strokes
Are commanding
My body's begging
I'm so demanding
Skin like lava
Hot and sticky
Please don't stop
Taste me
Lick me
Take me
Make me
Scream
If I'm too loud
Fill me up
My mouth
My mind
All of my wet places

By nine pm that evening, Korah was home, well fed and freshly bathed. She lie on her stomach in the center of her bed, while her husband straddled her lower body. She was completely nude. Brick wore only a pair of boxers. He used a scented lotion to massage her arms, shoulders and sides. Korah didn't believe her day was stressful enough to warrant this attention. She told him as much. But easing her tension wasn't Brick's only goal. In the two years they'd been married, Korah learned that his massages were as therapeutic for him as they were for her.

Brick loved her skin, the warmth of her body, the softness of her contours. He loved to see her smile, loved to watch her body melt beneath his deft fingers and strong hands. He loved her thighs, hips and ass. He had told her that a massage afforded him the opportunity to fondle her fully, every inch of her, for as long as he wanted. When it came to eroticism, he said nothing turned him on more.

Korah closed her eyes and hummed her approval when she felt him move further down her body, until he hovered over the back of her knees. She felt his manhood brush her calf. He was hot and hard, maybe fully erect. His hands continued to caress and smooth the muscles on either side of her spine as he continued downward. He stopped for a moment to apply more lotion before he got down to the serious business of massaging her ass. Korah felt a rivulet flow between her legs the moment he groped both cheeks.

"Thank you, baby," Brick said. His voice was deep and sultry.

"Is that why I'm getting a massage tonight?" Korah wondered, "because I got Baron for you?"

"Hmm? No," Brick said, his eyes glued to her derriere. "Of course not. I don't need to bribe you, do I?"

"Then what are you thanking me for?" Korah murmured. She felt so relaxed, she didn't know if she would cum first or pass out.

"I was thanking you for growing such a luscious ass," he told her.

Korah chuckled. "I think that's mostly genetics."

"Maybe," Brick said. "But you helped it along with biscuits and cornbread, two slices of bacon for breakfast."

"Are you saying I'm getting fat?"

"As long as it keeps piling up back here, go for it."

Brick's hands moved up and down, side to side, squeezing and kneading. Korah didn't even know butt massages were a thing before she met him. Now she wondered how she ever lived without them.

"What about this morning?" she asked. "That wasn't a bribe either?"

"Oh, yeah that totally was," he admitted, much to his wife's amusement. "But I knew you wouldn't let me down."

"Are you sure you don't need a spare forklift driver, or two?" Korah asked. "I think I like being bribed."

"Nah, I think I'm good," Brick said with a chuckle. "But I'll let you know if something changes. Did you get the contract drawn up for Baron?"

"No, but Yolanda's on it. Should have it ready tomorrow morning."

"Any idea how much it's gonna run me?"

"He makes forty-five a year," Korah informed him. "If you need him for six months, it'll be half that."

"You're not gonna tax me?"

"No," she said, smiling. "But Devin did ask me that."

"Whaa?" Brick feigned disbelief.

"We discussed how much we'd charge if it was some other company," Korah said. "If it was anyone but you, we would definitely tack on a little extra."

"Then by all means, tax me."

"No, baby. It's fine."

"You're asking that man to go and work on a competitor's worksite. I'd say that's worth a little extra pay."

"I can give him a bonus. *Ooh, baby.* That feels good."

"No, let me do it," Brick countered. "It would look better on paper, if it comes from me."

"Okay. I'm sure he'll appreciate it."

"Speaking of bonuses..." Brick moved his knees between her legs and began to spread them apart. He raised her hips, pulling her towards him, until she was in the proper doggy-style position.

Korah's face remained glued to the pillow. Her smile widened when she felt movements behind her and knew he was taking off his boxers.

"Wait," she breathed.

Before he could take a plunge, she turned, swiveling on her knees until she faced him; or came face to face with his manhood, to be more precise.

"Ah, baby, you don't – *ahmmm...*"

He swallowed his words as she attempted to swallow him whole.

"I love my wife," he muttered as he stared down at her.

I love my life, Korah thought as she watched his features dissolve into a pool of pure pleasure.

● ● ● ● ● ●

Twenty miles away, in the Berry Hill neighborhood, Baron Grant found himself between the long, cocoa colored legs of Lisa Franklin; a natural beauty by any man's standards. He sat on the floor in his living room, topless, while Lisa sat behind him on the couch. She rubbed the tight muscles in his neck and shoulders with slender hands that were surprisingly skillful.

Like Korah, Baron didn't request this attention. But unlike Korah, his body was in need of soothing after his long workday. Baron didn't work as hard as he used to, now that he was a lead foreman at Texas Builders. But he was never one who could sit back comfortably and watch men sweat.

Today they had an issue with two temps at the end of the day. The slackers started eyeballing the clock at five o'clock. By five-thirty they were verbally complaining. At six they put their tools down and refused to help straighten up the site, so everyone could go.

Unfortunately for them, leaving trash and tools lying around was not part of Texas Builders' protocol. Baron cursed the temps out, banned them from ever picking up another shift with his company and promised to call the temp agency to leave a bad report.

"The day's done when *I* say it is, not your goddamned watch!" he had told them.

"But, but they said we were only working till five," one of the men complained.

Baron was so upset, with what he considered a full day of loafing from the temps, he could barely control his temper. "Get the hell out my face, before I slap the shit outta you!"

The men had retreated, and Baron instructed one of his workers to take them back to the agency. Now three men short, he worked alongside the remaining crew, until they got their tools put away and all the trash hauled off to the dumpster out back. By the time they were done, the sun was starting to set, and his muscles were sore from stooping and lifting heavy objects.

To make matters worse, Baron had to start a new job tomorrow on a Brick House site. He'd be working with a crew he was unfamiliar with, and he hadn't even seen the blueprints for the dealership yet. He needed to be as fresh and well-rested as possible.

When Lisa called during his drive home, he initially declined her request to come over.

"Please," she said. "I need to talk. I got some shit going on."

When didn't she have some shit going on? Baron wondered. "Nah," he told her. "I'm tired. All I wanna do is go to bed."

"You sound stressed," she noticed. "Let me come over. I can give you a massage."

And that was the magic ticket. As annoying as Lisa could be at times, she was a legitimate masseuse; took a three-month course and had a certificate to prove it. The certificate never helped her find gainful employment in the field. Six months after completing the class, she accepted a job as an administrative assistant and had been working in that capacity ever since.

But her massages were on point.

"Fine," Baron had said. "But I can't stay up too late."

"That's okay," Lisa responded. "I just wanna talk for a minute..."

The minute turned out to be a two-hour bitch fest about her latest heartbreak. According to Lisa, her boyfriend of three months had a lot of suspicious activity with his cellphone. She ignored it for a while. Towards the end she hoped she'd find out he was a drug dealer. That wasn't something she'd be okay with, but it would've been better than the dark suppositions swirling through her mind.

Last night she got hold of his cellphone before the screen timed-out and left her locked out. It turned out Mark was just your average, everyday cheater. Mystery solved. Now Baron was in the dubious position of offering a shoulder to cry on.

He and Lisa had been friends for more than two years. During that time they gave love a try twice. The first time was a drunken sexcapade that left them both feeling embarrassed the next morning.

The second time they were able to maintain a full-fledged relationship for a couple of months. When it ended, they both acknowledged the part they played in the breakup: Lisa complained too much about Baron working long hours, how he didn't take her out enough and about him not allowing her to move into his home; which was clearly big enough for three to four more people. Baron complained about her incessant complaining.

They decided to go their separate ways, but Lisa called him again a few months later. She was having trouble with a new boyfriend, and she wanted a male's perspective. At the time, Baron missed talking to her. He didn't mind lending his ear. A year and a half later, this pattern had repeated itself several times. Lisa didn't always have a hard-luck story when she called, but things had gotten to the point where Baron was surprised when she didn't.

Thankfully she was always appreciative of his advice, and she adequately reimbursed him for his time. Usually she'd bring beer and food from one of his favorite restaurants. If not, the least she could offer was one of her world-class massages.

Baron felt the stress from his day dissipate as she rubbed his dark skin and rambled on and on about the latest in a long line of no good dogs she somehow kept falling in love with.

"How come I'm not good enough?" she wondered. She wasn't crying yet, but Baron could tell by the quality of her voice that she was getting close. "Why do they always do this to me?"

"It's not the same every time," he said.

Baron loved the feel of her legs on either side of his torso. He savored her touch. Even her voice was soothing, despite her inner turmoil. He was starting to feel so relaxed, he feared he'd fall asleep while she was talking.

"It feels like it is," Lisa said. Her hands moved from his shoulders to his neck. She kneaded his muscles with her thumbs and the heel of her palms.

"Last time you said you got in an argument in the movies," Baron recalled. "You said he disrespected you; tried to put his hand up your skirt."

Lisa didn't respond, just kept rubbing.

"The time before that, you said it didn't work because his mom didn't like you. You said she tried to clown you at a cookout."

Lisa's hands moved from his neck to his chest. She leaned forward and groped his pectorals. Her hair brushed the back of his head. Her cheek came to a rest on his, as she hugged him from behind.

"You remember all of that?"

"Course I do. You think I just sit here and let it go in one ear and out the other?"

She smiled; he could tell by the warmth of her breath when she exhaled. Her hands continued to move about his chest. She was no longer massaging him, but her caress still felt good. Things didn't get awkward until she said, "That's why I like talking to you. Nobody listens to me like you do."

Baron's chest rose and fell as he sighed quietly, knowing what her next comment would be.

"Don't you think we could—"

"Uh uhn."

He rose to his feet, forcing her to release him from her grasp. She watched him curiously as he took a seat next to her. Across the room, Baron's terrier, Pearlie, lifted her head and watched both of them.

"What are you—"

"I'm stopping you," he said, "before you try to take it there."

She registered more confusion.

Baron wore a pair of athletic shorts. He found his tee-shirt on the arm of the couch and pulled it over his head, hoping to further distance himself from whatever romantic feelings she had. Lisa wore stretch pants with sneakers and a tight tee that made her boobs look huge. She was tall and thin, with a plump booty that was nearly disproportionate to the rest of her body.

Lisa sometimes complained that her ass attracted more attention than her face or her personality – yet she consistently shopped for clothes that drew attention to her apple bottom. Then again, that phatty was pretty hard to downplay, no matter what she wore.

"Where do you think I'm trying to take it?" she asked. Her eyes were large and wet, but her cheeks were dry. She didn't have on any makeup, and she didn't do anything special to her hair for this visit. She would say that was clear evidence that she considered their relationship platonic, but Baron knew better.

"Whenever you break up with somebody, you start looking my way again," he noticed.

"No, I don't."

"Okay, not every time. But at least half the time."

She shook her head. "Baron, we're just talking. Just because I give you a massage..."

His eyes asked her to keep it real.

"Okay, but I don't see why that's such a bad idea," she admitted.

He shook his head in disappointment.

"What, Baron?" she asked, becoming agitated. "What is it about me that's so unappealing?"

"Nothing, girl. Nobody said it was anything wrong with you."

"Then how come every time I bring it up, you got the same response?"

"Because we tried that. You know it didn't work."

"That's because–"

"What are you doing? Do we really gotta go down this road again? You just broke up with your boyfriend. You don't see anything wrong with you trying to push up on me the very next day?"

Her lips started to tremble a moment before the first tear fell.

Ain't this some shit. Baron wondered how the hell he allowed this to happen again. "So now I'm the one who broke your heart?" he asked her.

"No. I didn't say that."

"Well, you come over here to talk about some fool that did you wrong. But now all of a sudden I'm the one who's hurting you."

"It's because you won't listen," she blurted. "Every time I try to talk to you about this, you shut me down."

Baron clenched his jaws and swallowed down his next response, thinking it would be too hurtful. Despite all of her obvious issues, he still considered Lisa a friend. She was the only female friend he spoke to on a regular basis.

"Okay." He leaned back against the cushions and resigned himself to playing this out. "What do you wanna say?"

"I just think things could be different, if we gave it another try," she offered. "I know I had my problems. I was the reason we didn't work out. But I've changed, Baron. I don't need to know where you are all the time. I'm not gonna ask to move in here. I know you need your space. I just think, if we really tried, we could make it work. We have a lot of fun together. We have a lot in common. We already care about each other. I can tell you things I can't tell anyone else. I just..." She lowered her gaze. "I just wish we could be closer..."

Baron waited a good amount of time before he responded, so she would know he had heard her and considered her ridiculous proposal. When she looked up at him again, he shook his head.

"I'm not going there with you, Lisa. We not good for each other. Right now, you're not good for *anybody*. I think you know that. Plus I don't even want a girlfriend."

She lowered her gaze again. "Is this because of Yvette?"

His countenance grew dark in an instant. His eyebrows bunched together when he said, "What?"

Lisa didn't notice his change in demeanor, so she trudged on foolishly. "I feel like, because of what happened with Yvette, you won't give anybody else a chance." She met his eyes then. His expression froze her heart.

"Why you wanna bring her up?" he growled. "You're the one having relationship problems, not me. Yvette ain't got shit to do with this."

He watched as her features slowly melted into an expression that personified grief. The tears sprang from both eyes now. She brought her hands up and cried into her palms. Baron knew he hadn't done anything wrong, but she made him feel like an asshole. He reached for her. The moment his hand touched her shoulder, she collapsed into him. The move reminded Baron that although her sorrow may be real, there were still a lot of theatrics involved.

But what kind of friend would he be if he didn't comfort her? He checked the clock as her tears wet his tee-shirt. It was 11:32. He needed to go to bed by midnight. He didn't like his chances of getting her out of his home by then.

By 11:45 she had stopped crying, and her breathing sounded normal. Baron felt like a dick for putting her out, but he'd be a fool to let her troubles ruin his day at work tomorrow. He knew that Brick Avery had a favorable opinion of him, and he wanted to keep it that way.

He told her, "Hey, I gotta—"

"I know you gotta go to bed." Lisa's voice was grief-stricken, but it sounded like she had come to her senses. "Can I stay with you?" she asked. She must have felt his body stiffen, because she followed that with, "I'm sorry I said we should get back together. I know I'm just upset, and you're right; we're not good for each other, not like that. I just want you as a friend. I *need* you as a friend. I don't wanna be alone tonight, Baron."

Who could turn down such a desperate plea? He wanted to, but despite the fact that he hadn't attended church in nearly four months, he considered himself a Christian.

"Alright, let's go."

He stood and helped her to her feet. When they reached the bedroom, she kicked off her shoes and bent to remove her socks. He stopped her when she started to push her tights down her hips.

"Naw, keep those on. Your shirt too."

She gave him a look but didn't question him. She crawled into bed and lie on her side. Baron turned off the lights and joined her. He liked to sleep on his side too, so he didn't object when she backed into him, until her back pressed against his chest and her ass was planted in his lap. He draped an arm over her midsection and managed to fall asleep while enjoying the slight fragrance of whatever shampoo or hair tonic she used.

She only woke him twice throughout the night. The first time was when she left the bed to go to the bathroom. The second time was when she returned from the bathroom and kissed the corner of his mouth before settling back in bed. Baron chose to feign sleep and pretend he didn't notice.

When the alarm clock went off at 6:30, Lisa was still snuggling in his embrace. Before he could get out of bed, she reached back and touched and then wrapped her hand around his erection. Baron brushed her hand away and rose to his feet. She rolled over and watched him, her dreamy eyes filling with lust as she examined the noticeable bulge in his shorts.

"Why you running?" she asked.

"You know nothing's happening," he said on the way to the restroom.

"Come on, Baron. It doesn't have to mean anything." She crawled out of bed and followed him.

"You're out of your mind." He grabbed his toothbrush and toothpaste. "Girl, you're on the rebound. If I take that swim, you liable to get sprung all over again."

She chuckled. "Yeah, right. You so full of yourself."

He watched her reflection in the mirror. "So I'm lying?"

She bit her bottom lip. She reached around him and tried to grab his meat again, but he bumped her with his hip.

"Watch out. For real. It ain't happening."

"Then why you so hard, if you don't wanna do nothing?"

"That's morning wood," he said as he stuffed his toothbrush in his mouth. "It would be here even if you wasn't."

She smacked her lips. "Alright, fine."

He winked at her in the mirror, to let her know there were no hard feelings. "You still my nigga, though," he said around his toothbrush.

Even though his comment reaffirmed their friend-zone status, she smiled.

"Thanks, Baron. For last night."

"No problem. I'll always be here for you."

Her smile deepened as she backed out of the bathroom.

CHAPTER EIGHT
BOSS FOR THE DAY

When she got to work on Friday, Stephanie was surprised that she'd beaten her mother to the office. She entered the building and saw that Priscilla wasn't there either. There was only Malcolm and Yolanda.

"Where's Mama?" she asked as she approached Malcolm's desk.

"She's not coming in today," he informed her. "She wants you to call her."

"Is she okay?" Stephanie asked, her eyebrows bunched in worry.

"Yes, she's fine," Malcolm replied. "Her and Priscilla are playing hooky."

Stephanie's confused expression remained as she entered her office and dropped her purse on the desk. She took a seat and called her mother from the office phone.

"Morning, sweetie."

"Morning," Stephanie said. "What's going on with you and Priscilla?"

"We're going to Winstar today," Korah said, referring to a casino in Oklahoma.

"Winstar? On a workday?"

"I checked my schedule. I don't have anything too pressing going on. I thought it would be a good chance for a three-day weekend."

"Really?"

"Um, is that a problem?"

"No, Mama. Of course not. It's just, you didn't say anything about it."

"Maybe I would have, if you called more often. Just because we see each other at work doesn't mean you can't call at home sometimes."

"Mama, I call you all the time," Stephanie said, not wanting to get goaded into that little argument. "Anyway, are y'all going to gamble? How come you didn't ask if I wanted to go?"

"We're gonna do some gambling, but the main reason we're going is to see Dolly Parton. She's in concert this weekend."

"*Dolly Parton?*" This story was getting stranger by the second.

"Priscilla loves her," Korah said with a laugh. "But she's never seen her in concert. She figures this might be one of the last chances she has."

"But you don't like Dolly Parton."

"Hey, I may not listen to her all the time, but I do like her," Korah said. "You know I love *9 to 5*. I like *Jolene, Yellow Roses*. She has a lot of hits. You know she sang *I Will Always Love You* before Whitney – but Whitney did do it better."

"Okay, I'm glad you didn't invite me," Stephanie said. She couldn't imagine herself enjoying the honky-tonk crowd Dolly Parton was sure to court. She didn't think her mother would like it either, but apparently Korah was open to such things.

"That's not the only reason I didn't invite you," her mother said. "Without me there, I thought this would be a good opportunity for you to get a taste of being on your own, even if it is just for a day. Do you think you can hold things down till I get back?"

Stephanie felt a sudden rush of adrenaline. *CEO for the day?* Hell yeah she was ready for that! Her smile was ear-to-ear, but she took a deep breath and managed to sound calm when she said, "Yes, Mama. I can handle that."

"Sorry, I don't have anything exciting for you to do," Korah said. "I already talked to Malcolm. I want you to stick with him. I need you to check on a few of our sites, approve some invoices. And if you have time, I need you to interview a few guys for construction. We've been using temps, but Devin says they're unreliable."

"Okay," Stephanie said. Those tasks didn't sound too vexing. "I've been meaning to ask you; with all of this expansion, why don't we have a Human Resources department?"

"That sounds great. Do you want to spearhead that?"

"Yes." A whirlwind of power thundering in her chest gave Stephanie goose bumps. "I can handle that."

"Great," Korah said. "If you run into any problems, I'll have my cellphone handy all day – at least until quitting time."

"I'll be fine," Stephanie assured her. "You're gonna be gone till Monday?"

"No. We got a hotel for tonight and Saturday. We'll be back on Sunday."

"I can't believe Brick's letting you out of his sight all weekend," Stephanie joked.

"This is the first trip I've taken without him since the wedding." Korah chuckled. "He told me to stay out of trouble. We'll see about that..."

"Alright, Mama. Have a nice time. And don't worry about things here. Enjoy yourself."

"Okay, honey. Keep it professional," Korah said before disconnecting.

Stephanie left her office and returned to Malcolm's desk. He could tell by the smile on her face that she was excited about her first Korah-free day.

"Well, look at you," he said. "You're ready for some responsibility."

"I am," Stephanie said. "Did Mama give you a to-do list?"

"Yes," Malcolm said, lifting his planner. "I have it here."

"She wants me to work on getting a Human Resources department started," Stephanie told him. "Can you add that to your list?"

"Okay," Malcolm said as he scribbled. "Did she tell you we need to hire two construction workers?"

"Yeah. Do you have some applications for me to look at?"

"Yes. We have about thirty of them online. I went ahead and looked them over already. I printed out ten for you. I think these are the best candidates." He handed her a file folder.

"Thanks." Stephanie could see why her mom loved Malcolm so much. He was always on top of things, usually two steps ahead.

"Hey, girl!"

She turned and saw Yolanda in the doorway. Stephanie thought their bookkeeper looked adorable, with her baby bump making her dress protrude.

"*Hey*! How far along are you? You're gonna be in here waddling in a minute."

"Going on six months," Yolanda told her. She reached to rub the small of her back. "I think I'm waddling already. I know my feet are swollen."

Stephanie looked down and noticed her pink house shoes.

Yolanda followed her gaze and said, "I got my pumps in there, in case somebody important stops by."

"Don't even trip," Stephanie said. "I wouldn't have worn pumps at all, if I was you."

"So, how you feeling about being in charge today?" Yolanda asked. Her smile was nearly as radiant as Stephanie's.

"It's no big deal." Stephanie tried to keep from cracking up but couldn't.

"Yeah, right. I know better than that," Yolanda said. "Have you decided how you're going to start off your day?"

"I think I'm gonna go sit behind Mama's desk for awhile," Stephanie said. "Kick my feet up. Enjoy a cup of coffee."

"How would you like that coffee?" Malcolm asked. "Do you want donuts or anything to go with it?"

"We have donuts?" Yolanda and Stephanie asked simultaneously.

"No, but I can get some from the shop down the street."

"Yep," Stephanie mused. "This is gonna be an awesome day..."

● ● ● ● ● ●

The morning started off great, but the good times didn't last long. The logistics of their new Human Resources department created more questions than answers. Where would the new office be? Who would run it? Who would be responsible for collecting all of the files for their current and future employees? Currently all of this information was divided between Yolanda, Malcolm and Priscilla. Stephanie didn't think it would be right to bring in a new person until they got the information consolidated.

She had a better time with the new hires for Devin's construction team. After speaking with ten men and setting up four interviews for later that day, Stephanie decided she preferred interactions with people over paperwork. Thankfully the CEO position at Texas Builders required more of the latter. Korah usually delegated the invoices and payroll to Yolanda and Malcolm, while she met with clients, shook hands and attended meetings.

By lunchtime, Stephanie was eager to get out of the office. She wanted to go to a sandwich shop, and Malcolm was all for it.

"Want us to bring you anything?" they asked Yolanda, who had to stay back to hold down the fort.

"No, I'm good," she told them. "I brought a salad. I'm trying to watch my weight. I don't wanna put on any extra pounds with this one than I have to."

"Alright," Stephanie said. She was somewhat grateful that she declined, because she didn't want to head right back to the office. "But don't be starving my niece," she added. "I want that baby to be fat and happy."

"Don't worry," Yolanda said, subconsciously rubbing her belly. "Doctor said everything's looking great. See y'all later."

When they got outside, Malcolm insisted on doing the driving. This was another unexpected perk for the CEO of the day.

"Are you sure?" Stephanie asked. "I wanna check out a few sites after we eat."

"Yes, Ms. Stewart. I'm sure."

They ate well, but Stephanie made sure she didn't let her lunch get her to the point of lethargy. She and Malcolm had a lot of driving to do. She didn't want the long stretches of highway to put her to sleep.

"Where to first?" Malcolm asked when they returned to his SUV.

"Irving," Stephanie said right away.

He frowned. "I don't think we have anything going on in Irving, Ms. Stewart."

"Isn't that where Baron is? He's working on a car dealership."

"Yes, but that's not one of our sites. That's—"

"I know it's a Brick House site," Stephanie told him. "But Baron is our employee. I think we should check on him, to make sure everything's going okay."

"Oh, um, okay. But I don't have the address for that site."

"I do." Stephanie produced her phone and found the note she saved. She gave Malcolm the information.

"Alright. Irving it is," he said as he plugged the address into his GPS.

A few moments later they were on the road again.

"Did Mama ask you to report back to her, let her know everything we do today?" Stephanie wondered.

Malcolm smiled slightly. "No, Ms. Stewart. She asked me to let her know if we have any problems and to make sure we did everything on her to-do list."

"So you don't have to tell her we went to Irving?"

"Not unless she asks directly. But I don't see why she would."

"I'm not asking you to keep a secret," Stephanie clarified. "I'm just curious about how much you're required to tell her."

He nodded but didn't respond to that.

"Like at my graduation party," Stephanie continued. "Did you tell her that me and Baron were talking?"

"No, Ms. Stewart. It never came up."

Stephanie thought she was pretty good at reading people. She didn't think he was lying.

"Whatever you've got going on with Baron is really none of my business," he said.

"What do you think I have going on with Baron?"

He shrugged. "Honestly I have no idea. I know you like him."

"What about him?" she asked. "If you know so much, how does he feel about me?"

He shook his head. "I don't spend enough time around him to know that. He's hard to read."

"Tell me about it."

"I don't think your mom wants y'all to go out."

"Yeah, she's a hater."

Malcolm got a laugh out of that.

● ● ● ● ● ●

Fifty minutes later they pulled into an unpaved lot of what would soon be a beautiful Mitsubishi dealership. The lot was filled with work trucks and personal vehicles. Ahead of them was an even larger swath of land that had been cleared of vegetation, but no structure had been erected yet. This was the area where most of the activity was taking place.

Stephanie spotted more than twenty men; all dressed similarly in work boots, hardhats and Brick House tees. Some drove tractor backhoes. Others manned excavators. Many were on the ground pushing wheelbarrows. They appeared disjointed, but Stephanie knew they were all united with the task of preparing the land for electric, plumbing and the building's foundation.

"You want me to call him?" Malcolm asked as he put his car in park.

"No," Stephanie said. She unbuckled her seatbelt. "I think I can find him." She scanned the makeshift parking lot until she spotted the only vehicle with her company's logo on the side. "There's his truck, so I know he's here somewhere."

"I know you're not gonna go out there with those shoes on," Malcolm said, looking down at her heels.

Stephanie hadn't considered it, but he was right. The land had been turned over to the point that her shoes were bound to get stuck in the muck after only a few steps.

"I have some of your mother's work boots in the trunk," Malcolm offered. "There's a hardhat back there too."

Stephanie didn't want to wear a hardhat. She knew her hair looked great, and she wanted Baron to see it. But even though this site didn't have a roof yet, OSHA required everyone on the premises to wear a hardhat. Being an acting CEO didn't give her the authority to skirt that rule.

"Okay. Thanks."

A few minutes later she was ready to find her lead foreman. She wore a skirt that day and had already accumulated a few stares when she changed shoes in the parking lot. The number of eyes on her doubled when she entered their work area.

The sun was bright in the cloudless sky. With only a few days left in May, the ferocious summer heat had yet to turn the site into a blistering hellhole. The temperature that afternoon was 91 degrees – not *great* for construction, but most blue-collar workers in Texas would agree that it wasn't too bad.

Stephanie loved the sounds and scents of the heavy-duty construction vehicles. She knew the foggy plumes of smoke billowing from their exhausts was probably not good for the environment, but the smell excited her as much as the scent of blood did for a prize fighter. She didn't think there was anything better than construction. If she had one shot at a time machine, she'd bypass the dinosaurs and great wars just to see how the pyramids were built.

Even with work boots on, her feet sank into the soft soil with each step. It took a bit of effort to pull them out again. Before she made it too far, a forklift with wheels caked with soot began to rumble in her direction. Stephanie felt like she was about to break out in a sweat, so she waited for the driver.

"Afternoon," the worker said when he pulled alongside her. "Can I help you with something?"

"I'm looking for Baron Grant," she told him. "I'm Stephanie Stewart, from Texas Builders."

His confusion transitioned to surprise and then respect within a second. "Oh, yes, ma'am. He's here. You, you wanna climb aboard? This ground's not too good for walking."

The driver was a handsome blonde. Stephanie noticed he had so much dirt on his boots, you couldn't see the soles.

"Yeah, that would be great," she told him. She grabbed the frame of the forklift to help herself up. The worker reached and pulled her other hand.

Seconds later they were rolling on terrain so bumpy, Stephanie felt like they were in a dune buggy. She was just starting to enjoy the ride when the driver came to a stop in front of a group of men. The tallest of them had dark skin and a chiseled jaw line. Despite the grubby environment, he wore a white collar shirt tucked into a pair of jeans that fit him nicely.

Baron's eyes narrowed when he looked up and saw Stephanie in the forklift. He approached the vehicle on her side, taking in her appearance as he came. His gait had an unintentional swagger that made Stephanie's heart skip a beat. Her nipples tightened when he spoke with his deep, southern accent.

"How you doing, Ms. Stewart?"

"I'm fine." She didn't mean to bat her eyes. It just sort of happened.

Baron looked back at his workers, who were very interested in the visitor. Rather than question her in front of them, he told the forklift driver, "Say, let me borrow your wheels for a second."

"Yes, sir," the man said and hopped out.

Stephanie watched Baron walk around the vehicle to the drivers' seat. His shirt concealed most of the muscles in his upper body, but his ass looked awesome in those jeans. He sat next to her and gave her another inquiring look before he got the forklift rolling.

"What brings you out here?" he asked when they were a safe distance away from his nosey crew.

"I just came to check on the site," Stephanie said innocently. "How's everything going?"

Baron's grin told her, *You're full of shit*. Stephanie read it perfectly and had to fight to keep from laughing.

"Where's your mother?" he asked her.

Stephanie checked her watch. "Either on her way to Oklahoma, or she's there already."

"She told you to come out here?"

Stephanie nodded. "She told me to check on our sites."

"This isn't one of your sites."

"We have a lot invested in this dealership; time, resources. This job is just as important as our other projects."

Baron rolled his eyes slightly. Stephanie noticed he was driving her back to the lot out front. When he parked and turned to stare at her, she stared right back.

"Are we done here?" he finally asked.

"Uh, you haven't given me a progress report," she stated.

"You're some piece of work."

She nodded. "I try to be."

"Alright," he said with a sigh. "As you can see, we haven't gotten very much done yet..."

He told her how things were going with the land clearing, how he was getting along with Brick's crew and what his expectations were for the next few weeks. None of the information was earth-moving or even very interesting, but Stephanie enjoyed hearing and watching him talk. She loved being this close to him.

When he finished, he said, "I could've told you all of that over the phone, saved you a trip out here."

Considering all she'd gone through to make this meeting happen, Stephanie was starting to feel emboldened.

"Phones are so impersonal," she commented. "Sometimes it's better to see people face to face."

Baron nodded skeptically. "Yeah, I suppose that's true. But for this particular update, your resources would've been better utilized if you'd picked up the phone instead."

"I wouldn't have been able to see you, if I picked up the phone."

His eyes narrowed again. "Yeah, I'm thinking that's probably your *only* reason for coming out here."

"You should feel at least a little responsible for that."

"Me? How you figure?"

"Because I told you I wanted to see you outside of work, and you said no."

"Yeah, I don't think that's a good idea," Baron agreed.

"You got a woman?"

He shook his head. "No, it's not that."

"You think we're incompatible?"

He watched her mouth as she spoke. Stephanie's lips were full and enticing, even without lipstick. He appreciated her skin tone and her figure. Given that they both worked in construction, he was sure they had a lot in common. But, "There's a lot more to consider than whether we're compatible or not."

"Like what?" Before he could respond, she said, "Better yet, I think we should discuss this over dinner. You busy tonight?"

He laughed. Even his amusement oozed masculinity. "You're pretty damned persistent, I'll give you that."

"And *you* need to get back to work," she said. "The sooner you agree to dinner, the sooner I'll get out of this forklift."

He gave it some thought before shaking his head again. "It ain't a good idea."

"What's the worst that can happen? We decide we don't like each other, and we feel a little self-conscious when we see each other at work for a while? We're both adults, and we're both professionals. I think we'll get over it, and everything will be just fine. I would never do anything to get you in trouble. And I know you wouldn't up and quit over one bad date. So what's the big deal?"

The look in her eyes said it wouldn't be that simple at all. Baron knew she wouldn't let it go until she finally got her way. But if he told her he still wasn't interested *after* their little date, she would have to respect that.

"Alright," he said. "Call me around five, and let me know where you wanna go."

Her eyes brightened. "Cool." She hopped off the forklift with a new spring in her step.

"You need my number?" he asked.

She shook her head and smiled. "I got all your numbers, Baron."

He smiled too, despite himself. He tried not to check out her ass as she walked away, but it was impossible not to take at least one glimpse. Her skirt wasn't tight, but it was snug enough for him to see that she still had a nice bubble. It had slimmed down, just a little, since she started losing weight. But not enough to make him lose interest.

He'd been checking out Stephanie's physique for several years now. He realized how close he was to actually touching her, but he knew that would be a bad move.

"How'd it go?" Malcolm asked when Stephanie got back in his car.

"I don't know if I should tell you," she said, though her smile said it all. "I'm starting to think Mama got you spying on me."

"That's not true, Ms. Stewart. But you can believe that if you want. Anyway, it looks like I'm not the one who's gonna tell her about your trip out here..."

Stephanie noticed his change of tone as she followed his eyes. They were glued to a vehicle that had just entered the parking lot. Not only was it another Brick House truck, but the size and luxury of the vehicle told her who the driver was before he got close enough for them to see.

Sure enough, Brick eyed them suspiciously before coming to a stop directly in front of Malcolm's SUV, effectively cutting off their means of escape. Korah's husband kept his eyes on them as he put his truck in park and exited the vehicle. Stephanie thought

Baron had swagger, but Brick's stride was top dog all the way. He solidified his importance with every step.

He approached Stephanie's side of the car and waited for her to lower the window.

"Howdy!" he said, his grin as big as Texas.

"Hey, Brick."

He looked from Malcolm to Stephanie. "What brings y'all 'round these parts?"

Like Korah, Stephanie once found Brick's cocky demeanor annoying. But in the two years he'd been married to her mom, she grew to love everything about him.

"We just stopped by to check out your site," she told him, "to see how Baron's doing."

He leaned, with both arms on the doorframe. He shifted a toothpick he'd been chewing on from one side of his mouth to the other. Despite the rugged atmosphere, she noticed Brick smelled wonderful. He said, "This is a little out of the way, for you to be stopping by, ain't it?"

"Nothing's out of the way, when it comes to our company and our employees," Stephanie told him.

He continued to smile at her. "So, how are things going?" Brick was so handsome, she didn't mind that he was being condescending.

"Everything's going great," she said. "Baron says they're right on track. Are you happy with the work he's doing?"

"I sure am. Baron's a hard worker. A great leader. Wish I had ten more just like him."

Unlike everything else he'd said, she could tell he answered that question with complete honesty.

"That's good," Stephanie said. "Don't try to steal him from us again."

He laughed at that. "No, ma'am. Wouldn't do that. I appreciate having him here, and I wouldn't want to ruin the rapport our companies have."

Stephanie liked that he was being professional, despite their personal relationship. He made her feel like she really was the boss.

"Okay, we gotta get going," she told him. "Got some more sites to visit before we head back to the office."

"Sorry. Didn't mean to hold you up," Brick said. He backed away from the car. "Enjoy the rest of your day, Ms. Stewart."

He returned to his truck and waved at them before moving out of their way. They waved back, and Malcolm exited the parking lot.

"What do you think?" Stephanie asked.

"I think he's on the phone with your mother right now," Malcolm guessed.

"Yep. That's what I think too."

Sure enough, Stephanie's cellphone rang five minutes later. She laughed when she heard the ringtone she assigned to her mom.

"Hey, Mama."

"Hey, sweetie. Enjoying your day?"

She looked over at Malcolm, who found all of this hilarious. "Yes. We got a lot done." Stephanie started to tell her about the office work, but of course Korah wasn't concerned about that.

"I tell you to check on our sites, and you head straight to Irving?"

"You didn't want me to come out here?"

"That's not our site, dear."

"I thought you'd want to know how Baron was doing, Mother."

"I'm pretty sure Brick would have the best information, don't you think? It is *his* project..."

"Oh. Yeah, I guess I didn't think about that." Stephanie had to put her mom on mute for a second, so she wouldn't hear her laughing.

"I can see you're not gonna take my advice, so let me just say this," Korah said. "If you do anything to cause Baron drama, or, God forbid, make him want to quit, that's your ass. I'll stay on as CEO until I'm *seventy*. And then I might just pass the position on to Yolanda, when I'm ready to retire."

Without being able to see her face, Stephanie wasn't sure how serious her mother was. The threat sounded too harsh to be real. But Korah had always been very protective of Baron.

"You don't have anything to worry about," Stephanie assured her.

After a few beats, Korah said, "You better hope I don't," and disconnected.

CHAPTER NINE
WHO ARE YOU?

> *She configures*
> *Dates and numbers*
> *Times and places*
> *To fit her need*
> *She can control*
> *The flow of income*
> *The rise of towers*
> *The power of dreams*
> *No problem exists*
> *Without a solution*
> *No bridge to build*
> *Without a plan*
> *But for the life of her*
> *She's perplexed*
> *By the complexities*
> *Of a man*

Stephanie chose Olive Garden for dinner because it wasn't too fancy, but with the menu options and wine selections, they could enjoy a gourmet meal if they chose to. She arrived at the restaurant ten minutes after seven and was happy to see her date waiting on one of the benches outside. He stood as she made her way to the entrance, her heels clicking on the sidewalk.

She was pleased with the way Baron spiffed up for the occasion. He wore a dark blazer with a baby blue button down. His jeans weren't baggy, and he opted for loafers rather than sneakers. Overall, Stephanie thought he was as fine as ever. It was hard to read the look in his eyes as he gave her a once over when she drew nearer.

For her part, Stephanie knew she might only get one shot at this, and she hoped to appeal to all of his senses. He'd seen her dress smartly at work, but he had never seen her in a dress like the one she picked tonight. It was sleeveless and short, running out of fabric midway down her thighs. The dress wasn't too tight, but it clung nicely to her curves. The neckline dipped precariously. Stephanie didn't know if he was into boobs or ass. Either way, his eyes would be rewarded handsomely tonight.

When they were face to face, she noticed that even with four-inch heels, he was nearly a foot taller than her. Stephanie loved to look up at her men. She liked them tall and strong. Skin tone had never been a determining factor, but she appreciated Baron's dark brown complexion. He reminded her of her father, in a lot of ways.

"Good evening," he said as he opened the door for her.

"Hi. Sorry I'm late."

She didn't wear a lot of perfume (her mother always told her less is more), but she wore enough for him to detect an enticing fragrance as she stepped past him. She hoped he'd think she smelled sweet, like honey. Maybe he'd want to get closer and possibly kiss or taste her neck and chest.

She realized she may be expecting too much, but it had been almost three years since Devin first brought Baron to their team meetings at the office. Since then she had been pining for him, furtively and openly, as of late. After repeatedly failing to make this date a reality, she was starting to doubt her allure. But, as usual, her determination paved a way.

"You're not that late, Ms. Stewart."

She looked back, hoping to catch his eyes glued to her backside. But no, she got direct eye contact instead.

"Don't call me Ms. Stewart."

"Sorry. Old habits die hard."

"You know I'm not your boss."

He frowned at that.

She said, "I'm just in training."

"Your training is only a formality," he replied. "Everybody knows that."

"Are you saying you can't call me Stephanie? That's gonna make this night weird."

He nodded. He almost said, *Yes, ma'am*, but he caught himself.

"But then again, it's kinda sexy when you call me Ms. Stewart," she teased.

He didn't take the bait. "Okay, Stephanie."

"Spoil sport," she mumbled.

• • • • • •

They got a table towards the middle of the restaurant. It wasn't nearly as cozy as Stephanie had hoped for. Baron declined their waiter's offer to bring them a bottle of wine, and Stephanie found his conversation lacking throughout most of the meal. As she ate, a voice in the back of her mind repeatedly told her, *He's just not into you*. But Stephanie was reluctant to accept that. She knew Baron had put up a wall between them. It felt impenetrable, but she was dead set on knocking it down.

She didn't want to talk about work, but that was one thing she was certain he enjoyed. Hoping to loosen him up, she asked, "How are things going at the dealership?"

Sure enough, a smile appeared in the corner of his mouth. But his reply was still terse. "Not too much has changed since you saw it earlier."

"What about Brick?" she asked. "Is he treating you good?"

Baron nodded slowly. "Brick's a good man. He understands the business, and he knows what it takes to get things done."

Stephanie sighed quietly. So far all of his responses were predictable. She felt like she was interviewing him for a job. "I hope he doesn't try to steal you away from us," she joked.

Baron thought about the bonus Brick promised him, and his smile widened. All told, the bonus would come out to $12,000; two thousand for each month he was on the site. That was in addition to his regular salary. That kind of bread made him wish he got loaned out more often.

"What?" Stephanie said, noticing his smile. "Did he already try something slick?"

Baron shook his head. "That's your step-father. Don't you trust him?"

"I don't think I've ever referred to Brick as my *step-father*."

"How come?"

"'Cause I've never lived in the same house with him. He never made me breakfast or gave me a ride to school."

"He's still your step-father, technically."

She nodded. "You're right. But I don't see myself giving him a Father's Day card."

"You didn't say if you trusted him," Baron noticed.

"Of course I trust him. I think Brick's great. He keeps my mom happy. But what about you? You didn't answer my question either."

"I wouldn't leave Texas Builders – not for Brick House anyway. That would be way too messy, with him and your mother and all. Plus me and Devin are cool. I wouldn't do your brother like that."

Their waiter returned; still eager to add to their bill (and his tip). "Did you guys change your mind about wine?"

"We'll take a bottle," Stephanie said before Baron could object again.

"Excellent. Did you want the Moscato?" That was the selection he had offered them earlier.

"Yes," she said. "That'd be fine."

Baron gave her a look when the waiter walked away. "I told you I'm not trying to drink tonight."

"You can have one glass," she insisted. "Or you can let me drink the whole bottle by myself and worry about me driving home."

"You're too much," he said with a shake of his head.

Stephanie had heard that many times, and she was inclined to agree. The waiter returned with their wine and poured a glass for both of them.

When he stepped away, she asked, "Did you know my brother before you started working with us?"

Baron shook his head. "No. I met Devin on a site. One of your guys came to a temp service I was working at. He picked me and a couple more cats; took us to a building Devin was working on."

"You started as a temp?"

"It was actually a day labor place," Baron recalled.

"Day labor?"

Picking up on her tone, he said, "Yeah. What you know about them places?"

She frowned. "I know we don't use them anymore. Mama said a lot of those guys are crackheads and alcoholics. They don't really wanna work. They just show up, hoping to make enough to get high for the day. The next morning they're dead broke again."

Baron took a sip of his wine. At least Stephanie thought he was taking a sip. Instead he continued to turn his glass up until it was completely drained. He placed it on the table and reached for the bottle the waiter had left. As she watched him fill the glass again, Stephanie wondered if they had, in fact, picked up an alcoholic from the day labor center.

"Your mom's right," Baron said when he set the bottle down. His expression was contemplative now. "Those day labor places are filled with crackheads and alcoholics; at least the ones I've been to. You gotta get there at five in the morning, to put your name on a list. Some of the guys who've been there for a while, they have contracted jobs, and they can come in a little later. But everybody else has to be there by five.

"After you get on the list, you sit there and wait, hoping someone will come in looking for a crew. Some of the workers chug coffee to stay up. Some of them take a nap on the floor. Some are still drunk from the day before. You can smell it on 'em – not just their breath, but their clothes and hair. They smell like they *sweat* liquor. And then you got the crackheads who haven't been asleep all night. It's like the Night of the Living Dead up in there. Everybody looks like they're homeless."

Stephanie became aware of her increased heart rate. She was nearly in shock as he reminisced on the bad, old days. She was glad she ordered the wine, because it certainly loosened his tongue. But damn, this might be more than she wanted to know.

"What's the matter?" he asked her. "You didn't expect to hear that I came from a place like that?"

Stephanie didn't want to be rude, but there was no denying that type of lifestyle was foreign to her. Her mom struggled a bit, when their company was in its infancy. But in all of her childhood memories, their family had been well off.

"Were you, um, on drugs?" she dared to ask.

He gave her a long, hard stare. Stephanie didn't realize she was holding her breath. But then Baron chuckled.

"Nah. The thing about those day labor places is for every twenty addicts who only want to get high, you've got one hard worker who's trying to get on his feet. But you don't end up in a place like that because you've done right all your life. My problem was, after five years in the pen, I had to wear that *convicted felon* label. That label says a lot about what you can and can't do in this country, where you can and can't work."

Stephanie swallowed, a little too hard. She was pretty sure he heard her.

His eyes narrowed. "Oh, you didn't know about my record?"

She shook her head slowly. She brought her glass to her lips and drank a good portion of it, much like he had done.

He continued to smile. "I figured since you've been going out of your way to hook up, you'd at least done your homework. I know you have access to my files."

Stephanie continued to shake her head, wondering why she *hadn't* looked into his background a little more. She realized much of her attraction was based on Baron's looks and the overwhelming praise he received from others. Now she wondered why everyone was so enamored with a convicted felon who used to hang out with alcoholics and crackheads.

His gaze intensified. "I like that; the way you're looking at me now."

Stephanie tried to neutralize her expression. "What do you mean?"

"You're finally looking at me like you don't have the upper hand, like I threw you for a loop."

She rolled her eyes at that and finished her wine. She pushed her empty glass towards him. "Gimme some more."

Baron didn't budge. "That doesn't sound like you're asking me to pour you a glass. Or am I still on the clock? That's why you feel comfortable bossing me around?"

Stephanie's eyes widened. What the hell was going on? Who was this man sitting across from her? Baron looked to be about six-foot three, 230 pounds. There was no way the small amount of alcohol he consumed had affected him this profoundly.

"I'm sorry," she said. "Could you pour me some more wine – please?"

"Sure." He filled the glass halfway.

"A little more," she said.

He chuckled as he poured a little more.

She felt composed by the time he was done. She asked him, "What were you in prison for?"

There were so many wild scenarios running through her mind, she was almost relieved when he said, "Dope. I got caught selling crack one too many times."

None of this vibed with the Baron she knew. Stephanie tried not to react to these revelations.

"When I got out, your brother was one of the first people who saw something in me," he said. He stared in her direction, but Stephanie felt like he was looking past her, possibly at a distant memory.

"I worked with him for two weeks straight," Baron said. "We talked, a lot. He never had the kind of problems I had, but he seemed to understand what I was going through. He decided to hire me. He said nobody at the office would question my record, if he told them I was straight. He had to buy out my contract from the day labor people. That wasn't cheap. He used to tell me I wasn't only a good worker; I was a natural leader. Your brother is the reason I am where I am today."

Stephanie was increasingly impressed as she listened to his story. She loved Devin, but she never would have characterized the moves he made on the work sites as *life changing*. For some people, a job is no more than a means to pay the bills.

For others it could mean the difference between remaining free and getting caught up in the high rate of prison recidivism for young, black men. She knew where Baron was today. Knowing where he had come from added a layer of admiration that was missing before.

• • • • • •

The conversation remained fluid as they finished their dinner and the rest of the wine. Stephanie stumbled upon another level of Baron's personality when she inquired about his relationship status.

"I'm not looking for a woman right now. I'm good."

"You're good? How long have you been single?"

He thought for a second. "It's been a minute."

"I know you gotta have *someone*," she pressed. "You're too fine to be all alone. I don't believe it."

The flattery brought a smile to his face. Stephanie loved all of the small nuances of his lips. As much as she enjoyed the time they were spending together, she looked forward to the conclusion of this date. Hopefully he wouldn't be opposed to a little kiss.

"I'm sure there are stranger things out there than me being single," he replied.

She shook her head. "No, I don't think there are."

"I like sticking to myself," he explained. "Way less drama that way."

"It's not like every girl out there comes with drama."

His jaw dropped. "What? I can't, I can't believe you fixed your mouth to say that."

"What do you mean?"

"You, *of all people*, should know what I'm talking about. You're the queen of drama."

"*What*?" Stephanie tried to appear offended, but she couldn't stop smiling. "Why would you say that?"

"The boss' daughter follows me around, forcing me to go–"

"*Forcing*? Really?"

"Yes, *forcing* me to go out with her," he continued. "*Forcing* me to drink liquor..."

She laughed. "Okay, now I know you tripping."

"Not by much."

She folded her arms over her stomach. "If you don't wanna be here, you can leave right now."

"And you're spoiled too."

She waited, but he did not stand up to leave. He shook his head and laughed. She did too.

"Do you have any kids?" she asked.

"No," he said right away.

"And how have you managed that?" she wondered.

She thought his expression darkened for a moment. Or maybe she imagined it. His smile went away, that much was certain.

"Why should a man have a child in this day and age?" he said. "Just to give a woman one more thing to have power over?"

His comment gave Stephanie pause. "A child is for the man, as much as it is for the woman," she said.

He smacked his lips. "Yeah, right. Since when has that been the case? Women use babies as pawns. They have complete control over where it lives, what it eats, what it wears. Even if you're married, they can up and leave any time they want. And guess what, they're taking that baby with them."

His outlook on children was surprisingly gloomy. It was hard to believe those words were coming from someone who had never been a father. She wanted to question him further, but she sensed his reason for feeling that way might dampen the mood more than her original question had.

Instead she asked, "What do you like to do in your spare time, on the weekends?"

"I have a boat," he said. "I like to go out to the lake."

That was another shocker. Young, black men who went to prison for drug pedaling didn't usually grow up and buy a boat.

"It's nothing major," he said, "just a little motor boat; a two-seater."

Stephanie had been on much bigger watercraft, but her eyes lit up as if he could show her something new. "Ooh, will you take me out on the water some day?"

He watched her for a moment before nodding slightly. "Maybe. We'll see."

• • • • • •

By the time they left the restaurant, the sun had completely faded. The night sky was filled with stars, moonlight and hopefully romance. Stephanie began to doubt if she'd made a love connection when Baron didn't put his arm around her as they headed for the parking lot. But she wasn't ready to throw in the towel until she heard it from his mouth.

Careful what you wish for.

"You know I'm not gonna touch you."

They had reached her car. Stephanie lingered there, rather than hop inside. She was hoping she'd get a chance to taste the lips she'd been staring at all night. Baron's comment appeared to close the door on that scenario.

"What do you mean, you're not gonna touch me?"

He chuckled. His teeth were bright, in contrast to his dark skin. Now that they were standing again, Stephanie was reminded of how wonderfully tall he was. She wanted to climb him like a beanstalk.

"I'm still not sure that's a good move," he told her.

"Uh uhn." She worked her neck playfully. "I just bought you dinner – *and wine*. Nah, brother. You owe me."

That brought more laughter.

He said, "I didn't ask you to pick up the check."

"You didn't stop me."

"I tried to." He couldn't believe she was trying to flip the script. "The man put it on my side. You're the one who damn near climbed the table to grab it."

"You let me grab it."

"I wasn't gonna fight you for it, not with all those people watching."

"It's all good," she said. "But I'm thinking that dinner was worth *at least* a kiss. The wine, well, you gotta let me grab your ass for that."

"What the..." He assumed she was kidding, but it was hard to tell with this woman. Since she was pulling a role reversal on him, he decided to play the same game. "Is that all you want me for, my body?"

They both laughed.

"Come here," he said.

Stephanie's heart fluttered when he reached for her. But instead of a kiss, he pulled her in for a hug. It wasn't even a full body hug. It was a side-to-side, friendship hug; with his hand on her shoulder, rather than around her waist. Stephanie couldn't hide her disappointment when he backed away.

"What's wrong?" he said.

Rather than respond, she reached for his chest and grabbed a fistful of his shirt. She pulled him forward, giving him no choice but to come closer or lose a button. Despite the aggressive move, she didn't kiss him squarely on the lips. She kissed the corner of his mouth, catching only a portion of his bottom lip.

But the kiss was slow and as sensual as she could make it, considering she didn't get much participation. The brief contact sent a warm, pleasant wave of energy down her body.

When she let him go, Baron blinked a few times before rising to his full height. He didn't say anything, and that was fine by her. She wanted him to take some time to digest everything that had happened tonight.

She turned to open her car door. She looked back and caught him glancing down at her booty.

Thank God!

She would've been sorely disappointed if her freakum dress didn't elicit at least one dirty thought.

"Goodnight," she told him as she slid into the bucket seat of her Benz.

"Goodnight, Ms. Stewart."

Instead of closing the door, she glared at him until he corrected that.

"I mean *Stephanie*," he said with a chuckle. "Goodnight, Stephanie."

CHAPTER TEN
A BIG MESS

On Sunday afternoon Baron was enjoying his day off. He was at home with the only girl who could stay there fulltime; his West Highland terrier, Pearlie. He had nearly a dozen boxing and MMA matches stored on his DVR. With his work schedule, which usually didn't allow him to make it home before sunset, watching TV for hours at a time had become a luxury. Baron was happy to binge on the fights and satisfy his bloodlust. He frowned when his cellphone rang. His expression didn't improve when he saw the name on the Caller ID.

"Hello."

"Hi," Stephanie said. "You busy?"

They hadn't spoken since their date (which Baron would prefer to call a *meeting*) at the Olive Garden on Friday. He could tell by the background sounds on her end of the line that Stephanie was currently on the road.

"Not really," he told her as he returned to his recliner. He turned down the volume on the fight but kept his eyes glued to the screen.

"I was wondering if you'd like to have lunch."

After a noticeable pause, he said, "When?"

"Today. Right now."

Baron checked the clock on the cable box. It was a few minutes past one. He hadn't eaten since breakfast, but the microwavable burritos in his freezer sounded like a better alternative than getting caught up with the boss' daughter.

"I'm good," he told her. "I appreciate the offer, though."

"Oh. Okay." Before he could hang up, she said, "Actually there's something I need to talk to you about. That's why I wanted to have lunch."

Baron remained wary, but he knew he hadn't done anything that could get him in trouble. "What do you wanna talk about?"

"I need help with a project at home," she said. "It's construction work."

Out of all of the bizarre things she could've said, that had to be at the top of the list.

"You need... That doesn't make sense."

"I know it sounds weird," she acknowledged. "But I'm serious. I can send you some pictures, if you want. I was wondering if you could come take a look at it. I'd like to hire you to complete the project."

A few seconds passed while Baron tried to come up with a response.

"I can't go to Devin," she said. "And I can't talk to Mama about it either. I kinda got myself in a little trouble. I need help. I mean, I *could* tell Devin, but I don't wanna hear his mouth. He'll never let me hear the end of it."

Her explanation helped, but Baron still found the request peculiar.

"It's a *job*," Stephanie stressed. "I'll pay you. You can do it on the weekends or after work during the week, if you get off early enough. I'm not in a rush to finish, but I need to get it done without my brother finding out. I promise it'll be worth your while. Can you please help me?"

Baron was torn between sitting on his ass all day and getting involved in whatever nonsense she had going on. As usual, money was a great motivator. He did pretty good with his salary at Texas Builders. The bonuses Brick promised him for his work at the dealership would make his bank account look even sweeter. If he could pull in even more money from Stephanie's project, he might be able to pay off his new truck by the end of the year, rather than the three years he still had left on the loan.

If it turned out Stephanie didn't really have a project, and this was simply a ruse to get him to her house, Baron decided he'd look her straight in the eyes and tell her to leave him alone. She was a fine woman, no doubt. Smart and successful too. But getting with her was too risky. Too many things could go wrong.

"Alright," he said. "What's your address? What time you want me to be there?"

"I'm on the road," she said. "I don't mind picking you up."

Baron gave it some thought and decided he didn't have a problem with that. He was determined to put an end to this if her *project* was a bunch of baloney, so it didn't matter if she gave him a ride. "That's fine," he told her.

"Okay. Text me your address."

● ● ● ● ● ●

Twenty minutes later Pearlie rushed to the front door. When Baron looked in that direction, the doorbell rang. He answered wearing a white tee-shirt with athletic shorts. Stephanie had never seen his bare legs before. She couldn't see much of them now; the shorts were so long they concealed his knees. But she saw that his calf muscles were slightly larger than normal, and his dark legs had a thin coat of hair.

More impressive was his upper body. Without a collar shirt or long-sleeves to spoil the view, Stephanie basked in the glory of his biceps, forearms, and his muscular shoulders and traps. His arms looked so nice, her eyes moved to his chest as an afterthought. His swollen pecs made her stomach tighten. She wondered if he worked out a lot when he was in prison. She doubted if his work schedule allowed him to hit the gym every day, but his body was remarkably fit.

By comparison, Stephanie looked conservative in a long skirt and blouse that was buttoned all the way up. Baron thought she was stunning, as always. Even though her outfit reminded him of a middle school teacher, her sex appeal was undeniable. Each time he saw her, Baron wanted to throw caution to the wind and wrap his arms around her. He longed to touch every part of her body. He prided himself for the restraint he'd shown thus far.

"Hey," he said. "Where you on your way from, church?"

"Yeah," she confirmed. "I went with Mama this morning."

"How's Mrs. Avery doing?" he asked as he stepped out on his porch and locked the door.

"She's fine." Stephanie turned and headed down the sidewalk. She looked back and admired his home. "This is a nice house. Have you lived here long?"

He dropped his keys in his pocket and followed her. "Kinda, but I just bought it a couple of years ago. Had to get it renovated; from the ground up. The foundation was terrible. Paint chipping, windows that were installed in the sixties. It wasn't much to look at when I first started."

Stephanie didn't doubt that. On the way there, she noticed his neighborhood left a lot to be desired. Baron's house was not only the best-looking one on the street, but it was the most beautiful within a ten-mile radius.

She opened her car and slid behind the wheel. A second later, Baron took a seat on the passenger side.

"Why'd you pick this neighborhood?" she asked, still admiring his two-story masterpiece.

"I grew up here," he revealed. "Not full-time, but I spent almost as much time here as I did at my house. My mom lives a few blocks away. This was my granny's house," he said, looking out the window. "When she passed, her kids; my aunts and uncles, started acting a fool. You know how some folks get when they find out a little money's headed their way. Granny didn't have a will, and everybody wanted a piece of this place. They didn't want to live in it. It was too messed up for that. They just wanted whatever came from the sell.

"But Granny didn't want us to sell her house. She told me that before she passed, and I know she told them too. It was disrespectful, the way they were acting."

A dark cloud settled over him. Stephanie regretted asking about the property, but it was too late to back out of the conversation. It didn't appear that Baron minded discussing it, even if the story was disconcerting.

"When I saw a For Sale sign in front of Granny's house, I was furious," Baron recalled. "I called the realtor. She said they had a couple of offers already. They were only asking for 60 grand. I offered 70, and we closed two weeks later. My aunt wasn't happy when she first heard I was the buyer. By then, I think she realized she was doing wrong. But they didn't back out. I guess money means more than family these days."

Stephanie nodded. "Not always – but I can see why you were upset. How long did it take you to get it fixed up?"

She noticed the windows were all new. The doors were too. The paint was perfect, as were the storm drains. Even the front lawn was greener and more robust than any house on the street. Stephanie recognized the grass as St. Augustine.

"It took over a year," Baron said. "The inside needed just as much work as the outside. Electric, plumbing..." He shook his head, grinning. "Let's just say they don't make pipes like that anymore. Had to repaint everything. When I was little, I never knew about the hazards in Granny's house. But there were plenty. Lead-based paint, no surge protectors, a raggedy stove with old gas lines. It's a wonder this place didn't blow up years ago."

His smile was endearing.

"Looks like a good investment," Stephanie said. "This house could go for $200,000 now."

Baron nodded. "And it'll be in the family forever."

Stephanie wondered who he planned to leave the house to, since he didn't have any kids. She didn't ask, because the last time she brought up children, his mood became pessimistic. He had nothing but negative things to say.

Instead she told him, "I would love to see what you've done to the inside."

He looked her in the eyes. "Maybe one day. Anyway, what's up with the project at your house?" he asked, changing the subject.

"I, um... You really need to see it for yourself," she said as she pulled away from the curb.

Baron nodded and settled in for the ride.

● ● ● ● ● ●

Stephanie's affluent neighborhood was in stark contrast to Baron's. Her streets were all clean and neat, with nary a pothole or trash bin that had been left on the curb after collection day. You couldn't even enter her gated community without getting clearance from a security guard posted in a booth out front.

When they pulled into the driveway of what Baron would consider a small mansion, he couldn't help but marvel at the fact that this house was owned by a twenty-two year old woman. Her home, car and her assured position as CEO of the family business helped explain why Stephanie was so spoiled. Outside of graduating college, she had done nothing to deserve any of it.

Baron caught himself, realizing he was being judgmental. Just because no one in his family (or any of his friends' families) was wealthy enough to leave an inheritance for their children didn't mean it was a bad thing. Who said there should only be heirs in rich, white families? The black communities in America would be in much better shape if each generation didn't have to start from scratch.

"Your house is amazing," he said as they pulled into the garage.

"Thank you," Stephanie replied. "But you haven't seen my problem yet."

Once inside, she kicked off her pumps in the kitchen and carried them with her as she led him further into the home. Baron had been trying to keep his mind free of dirty thoughts, but he found himself watching the sway of her hips as he followed her. He realized he should've changed into jeans before she picked him up. Stephanie hadn't even done anything explicitly sexy, but she was on the verge of giving him a stiffy. Jeans would've concealed his arousal a lot better than–

What the hell?...

All sexy thoughts evaporated when they turned the corner, and he encountered a scene he would describe as *total destruction.*

"This is my problem," Stephanie said. She stepped aside and allowed him to enter the room.

Baron stepped slowly, not fully believing what he was seeing. He didn't know how many bedrooms there were in the house, but the one he was looking at was a catastrophe. Technically he was looking at *two* bedrooms, because the wall between them had been torn down, mostly. The carpet in the first room was ripped up, leaving portions of the original concrete floor exposed. Someone had started removing the carpet in the second room, but they didn't get more than halfway done.

The furniture had been removed from both areas. That was the only bright spot Baron could note. The floor was littered with clumps of sheetrock. The gigantic hole in the wall exposed electric wires and insulation. There were paint buckets and random tools scattered everywhere. When Baron's eyes returned to the woman of the house, she stood sheepishly, with her church shoes in hand.

"I can explain."

Baron shook his head slowly, knowing this would be one hell of a story.

A minute later they sat at the kitchen table. She still had her church outfit on, minus the shoes. Baron still wore a look of disbelief.

"Okay, so what happened was…"

He laughed.

"What?" she said.

"No story starting with '*What happened was*' has a good ending."

"Well, my story is going to have a good ending," Stephanie predicted. "That's why you're here."

"Okay," he said, leaning forward in his chair. "Let's hear it."

"Do you want a beer or something?"

He shook his head.

"Alright, so what happened was," she continued, "I wanted to tear down the wall between those two rooms, so I could turn them into a home theater. I already have the theater chairs picked out. I bought a projector. It's gonna be beautiful. You'll see."

Baron didn't doubt that. She certainly had the means to make it happen.

"When I asked Devin to help," she said, "he told me to wait a couple of months. He was tied up with work stuff, and he didn't have time. I asked if he could do it on the weekends. He said he would, but things kept coming up. Yolanda says he spends time with her and the baby on the weekends – and that's cool. I talked to Mama, and she said I should wait for my brother, to make sure it was done right."

"I take it you decided not to wait," Baron deduced.

"Devin's not the only contractor out there," Stephanie said. "The problem is a lot of the other contractors in the city know my family, so I couldn't go to them. I didn't want word to get back to Mama that I was using someone else. I went to Home Depot a few weeks ago, and I ran into a guy who seemed pretty official."

Baron started shaking his head. Even if he hadn't seen the mess, he knew where this story was headed.

"He had a crew," Stephanie went on. "His work truck looked professional; had his company information on it, lots of tools. I checked his website while we were in the store. As far as I could tell, he did quality work. So I went ahead and hired him."

Baron took a deep breath and let it out slowly.

"I guess you can tell things didn't go as planned," Stephanie said. "We didn't have problems in the beginning. He and his crew showed up on time and got started on the work. It looked like everything would work out perfectly. But over the next week, they became less and less reliable. They wouldn't show up when they said they would. They would leave trash and stuff everywhere. One of them tracked dirt all the way through my living room. They weren't even supposed to be going through the front. I felt like they weren't listening to me.

"You saw how they pulled up the carpet in the first room, but they didn't finish in the other one? They were supposed to pull up *all* of the carpet first. I started getting into arguments with them. I felt like they didn't respect me, always coming with bullshit excuses.

"The last straw was when the contractor asked for more money. I told him he hadn't done anything. What the hell did he want more money for? Plus, after the half-ass way he was leading his crew, he didn't deserve the money I already gave him. I was so pissed, I kicked them out of my house and told them not to come back. I guess they figured that since I'm a woman, and I'm living alone, they could pull a slick one on me. But I ain't the one."

Baron agreed they probably did take her for a fool. Not only was she a woman living alone, but judging by her home and the nice things inside, Stephanie appeared to have money to burn.

"So now I'm stuck between a rock and a hard place," she said. "I could tell Devin what happened and let him come finish the job. But I don't wanna hear his mouth. I already know what he's gonna say. And I don't want Mama to know what happened, because it's not a good look. How am I supposed to run the company one day, if I can't even get a home theater built in my own house? That's what she'll say."

Baron thought that was an accurate prediction. He also understood the sibling rivalry she had with Devin. He was a great foreman, but to Stephanie he would always be a big brother, first and foremost. The teasing would never end, if he saw the predicament she got herself in. Twenty years from now, at Christmas dinner, he'd still be laughing at her.

Hey, you remember the time that contractor got over on you?

But above all else, "You too damned spoiled," Baron told her.

"*Spoiled?*"

"Yes, spoiled. Devin told you to wait, but you wouldn't. Now you got your house all tore up, and you can't even go to your family for help."

"I don't see how your '*I told you so*' is going to help anything."

He laughed. Stephanie adored the sight and sound of his amusement. She wished she was a comedian, so she could keep a smile on his face.

"Will you help me or not?" she asked, smiling herself.

"You need a whooping," he decided. "Somebody needs to lay you across their lap."

Stephanie's eyes brightened. The thought of him spanking her heated her whole body.

Baron realized his comment could be taken as a sexual innuendo, and his face warmed. He noticed how intense her gaze was. He had to look away.

"How can I help you without anyone finding out?" he wondered.

"Easy," she said. "Just like you came over here today without them knowing, you can come next weekend, or any day you get off early enough and feel like working."

"What about the crew?"

"We can find a crew anywhere," she said. "There's guys hanging out at the Home Depot all the time. If you pull up in a truck and yell '*Trabajo!*' they'll hop right in, no questions asked. I'll pay them, and I'll pay you. I'll buy whatever equipment you need."

The more Baron considered it, the more it sounded like her crazy plan was doable. He wasn't fluent in Spanish, but every construction site he'd been on had plenty of Hispanic workers. Oftentimes they were the majority. Over the years Baron had learned enough Spanish to lead them and make sure the job got done expertly. Another thing he liked about Mexican laborers was their work ethics. They were humble, and they didn't ask for a break every thirty minutes.

"Okay," he said. "You want me to come on the weekends–"

"You don't have to come *every* weekend," she said. "If you can only do a Saturday or Sunday, that's fine. And if you want a whole weekend off, that's cool too."

"I don't think I can come after work on most days."

Stephanie's pulse quickened. It sounded like he might help her. "That's okay. Whenever you can make it is cool with me. Just give me an hour's notice, so I can go pick up the workers and have them here by the time you get here."

"How much are you paying?"

"How much you want?"

"You're asking *me*? You supposed to be the boss."

"I don't want to take advantage of you," Stephanie said. "I already feel stupid for what happened with the other guys. I know how hard you already work. I want you to feel like this is worth it, and it's not wearing you out. I can work with you on the price. That's the least of my worries."

● ● ● ● ● ●

They returned to the rooms in question, and Baron took his time inspecting them. Things looked bad, but the work wasn't as daunting as he originally thought. Even working only two days a week, he was pretty sure he could complete the job in less than a month. That would include setting up the furniture and other amenities she wanted in the theater.

The extra money was enticing, but more importantly Baron found that the gentleman in him couldn't refuse a damsel in distress.

He told her, "Alright. I'll do it."

"Thank you!" Stephanie's face lit up. She threw both arms around him and squeezed tightly.

Up close, he thought she smelled very nice. Her boobs pressed against him made his blood run hot. He kept his arms to his sides and willed himself not to become excited. The last thing he needed was for her to back away and notice an erection.

Thankfully his willpower prevailed and his manhood remained flaccid. She backed away, smiling brightly.

"Wanna get something to eat before I take you home?"

He looked her up and down. "You must be talking about a drive-through, 'cause I'm not going nowhere with you looking like that, and me looking like I just rolled out of bed."

She laughed. "No, I don't mean a drive-through. I can go put on some shorts or something. We'll go somewhere casual."

She took off before he had time to reject that.

Baron returned to the kitchen and tried to get his mind off whatever was going on in her bedroom. After a minute, he imagined she was down to her bra and panties – and that was exactly the kind of stuff he *didn't* want to think about.

He wondered if he'd made a mistake by agreeing to help. Regardless of his good intentions, Stephanie was TEMPTATION personified. He'd agreed to spend multiple days in the lioness' den. He knew he was a fool, because rather than shaking in his boots, he was starting to look forward to it.

CHAPTER ELEVEN
ALL WORK AND NO PLAY

Dark brown nipples
Sweet like berries
Tongues like swords jab and parry
One touch is enough to spark the flames
Of desire
So reckless
Impossible to contain
Her panties, suddenly uncomfortable
They feel like restraints
He frees her
His mouth quickly takes their place
Her hips rise into him as he eats his fill
She vocalizes her pleasure
Not a drop is spilled
Her eyes roll back
Then flash open
When he penetrates
Her throat catches
He sinks deeper
Flesh to flesh
Face to face

Over the next week, the remodeling work at Stephanie's house progressed a lot smoother than she expected. Baron called on Tuesday afternoon and told her he'd be getting off early that day. Stephanie was in her mother's office at the time. She excused herself to take the call.

"What time do you think you can be there?" she asked Baron.

"We're leaving here at five. I can be at your place by five-forty-five."

She grinned. Only a construction worker would consider that *early*. "You don't have to rush right over. I know you'll be tired after working all day."

"No, it's not a problem," he said. "I don't think your project is gonna take as long as we predicted. I wanna hurry and get started, so we can knock it out."

"Okay. I'll be home at five-thirty."

"Do you want me to pick up the workers?"

"I thought I was going to do that."

"Yeah, but I've been thinking about it. I don't know how safe it is for you to pick up strangers in your car. They'll see your Benz and your house... If you get home before I make it there, they might decide to do something stupid, with you being a woman and all."

Stephanie had considered that, but, "I think I can handle myself."

"I'm not saying you can't, but–"

"I have a license to carry, and I'm a good shot."

"Okay. That's great. So *I'll* pick up some workers on the way there."

That statement gave her pause. Stephanie was not accustomed to her employees overriding her decisions. Apparently it was no longer up for discussion, so she told him, "Okay. I really appreciate it."

"Cool. See you at five-forty-five."

When she returned to her mother's office, Korah asked, "Who was that?"

"Just some guy I'm talking to."

Korah nodded, having no reason to doubt her story.

"What time are you leaving today?" Stephanie asked.

"No later than five," her mom replied. "Why? Got a date?"

Stephanie nodded. Her smile was almost sinful.

Korah shook her head. "Girl, you're playing the field more than Devin did at your age. Looks like you're gonna wait until you're in your thirties before you settle down."

"I don't know," Stephanie said. "I might not wait that long."

"No rush. You're young and beautiful. Take your time. Enjoy life. Your carefree days will be over before you know it. Just be careful. A lot of weirdos out there."

Stephanie found it interesting that two people had warned her about weirdos within five minutes. That was a sign that she should listen to them. "I am careful, Mama. Don't worry."

"I know, honey. You've always been strong and independent."

"More than Devin?"

Korah rolled her eyes. "And *competitive*, almost to a fault..."

● ● ● ● ● ●

At 5:50 Baron showed up at her home with three men piled in his truck. He didn't look tired, but Stephanie felt a little guilty about adding more work to his schedule. Thankfully Baron didn't have to do much manual labor. He gave instructions to his crew, and they took care of all the grunt work.

Stephanie had heard great things about his leadership skills, but this was her first time witnessing it up close. She was impressed with everything about him, from his Spanish speaking, to his knowledge of the project and even the way he stood tall and directed the men.

The laborers were grateful for the opportunity, so they probably would've responded similarly to whoever was in charge. But from Stephanie's perspective, Baron earned their respect with his posture, tone and his willingness to get down on all fours and work alongside them.

That night they ripped up the remaining carpet from the bedrooms and dismantled the trim. There was a constant train of people moving in and out of her house as they took the old carpet and other debris to Baron's truck. Stephanie didn't have a lot of one-on-one time to speak with her foreman. Not as much as she'd like. But they met in the kitchen towards the end of the night to discuss a few details about the job.

Before he returned to his workers, Baron asked her, "How do you plan to keep your family away from here until we're done?"

"I see my mom every day," she reminded him. "She doesn't visit me here that often. Usually I'm the one going to her house."

"What about Devin?"

"He's got a pregnant wife and a baby at home," Stephanie said. "I can't remember the last time he showed up unannounced. That's not something we have to worry about."

Baron nodded. That day he wore a Texas Builders tee with jeans that were a little soiled from his work at the dealership. Stephanie *loved* to see him in tee shirts. His chest was so big and pronounced. She hoped he'd ask to use her shower before he took off. The thought of him stepping out of her hydro massage tub with just a towel wrapped around his waist made her heart sigh. She knew the chances of that happening were around zero percent, but a girl can dream, can't she?

"Can I make you dinner?" she asked him. "I know you must be hungry."

"I appreciate the offer, but I'm alright," he said. "I stopped by Burger King on the way over here."

"That was hours ago. I'm sure you could eat again. A big guy like you needs some home cooking, not Burger King."

He watched her for a moment before saying, "You can cook?"

"Of course I can cook. What kind of woman do you think I am?"

The kind who probably grew up with a maid and a chef in the house, he thought, but his lips remained sealed.

"When my dad died, I had to do a lot of the cooking at home," Stephanie informed him, as if she'd read his mind. "Mama was busy trying to keep the company afloat."

Baron nodded. He was so used to seeing her as pampered, it was easy to forget the hard work she, Devin and Korah had done to make their family business a success.

"You wanna make dinner for me *and* the guys?" Baron asked.

Stephanie was so focused on the man standing before her, she had forgotten the other hardworking men in her home. "No, just you," she told him.

Baron shook his head. "I can't sit at your table and eat dinner while they're working their asses off."

Stephanie didn't appreciate his response, but she knew this was one of many characteristics that made Baron an effective leader. "I can make them some sandwiches," she offered.

"If you wanna make *all of us* sandwiches, we'll be happy to have them," he said with a smile.

That wasn't the romantic dinner Stephanie had in mind, but if Baron wanted a sandwich, she'd certainly oblige. She'd make him the best damn sandwich he ever had.

"You want ham or turkey?"

"Turkey," he said. "But we're leaving in a few minutes, so we have to take them to-go."

Again Stephanie was miffed that she wasn't getting her way. But she made the sandwiches and even put them in sandwich bags. She also handed each man a Coke and a small bag of chips on their way out. Baron was the last to leave.

"Thank you," he said. "I'll call you tomorrow and let you know when I'll have time to come again."

"Okay."

Stephanie hoped for a hug or a kiss before he left. She didn't realize how foolish that was until he exited the house without another word.

• • • • • •

Wednesday was no good for Baron, and neither was Thursday. On Friday he called at four o'clock and said he and the crew could stop by. Stephanie cleared her schedule to make time for him.

The crew worked for three hours that day. That was long enough for them to finish clearing the floors and demolish the remainder of the wall that separated the two bedrooms. Stephanie was glad to have Baron's expertise, because the workers had to be careful with the electrical wiring that was already in place. Baron told her she didn't need to hire an electrician for the new wiring needed for the theater.

"I can reroute all of this," he assured her. "Save you a pretty penny."

"Really? Thanks."

Stephanie was even more grateful when one of the workers (the only one who spoke English, as far as she could tell) told her they could work the following day, if she wanted. Stephanie called Baron over and the three of them discussed their plans for Saturday.

"I'd like to make some real headway," Baron said. "I don't have any plans, so we can put in a full eight hours, if that's okay with you."

Stephanie nodded. "That'd be fine."

"The reason why I asked," the worker said, "is because I have a truck, and I can bring my guys with me. You don't have to pick us up," he told Baron. "Just let me know when you want us to get here."

"Uh, let me get back to you on that," Baron told him. When the worker walked away, he said, "I don't know about that."

"Why?" Stephanie asked him.

"We don't really know these guys. I'm not sure if it's safe for them to come here on their own."

"You worry more than my mother does," she replied. "What do you think they're gonna do?"

He shrugged. "Anything's possible. Maybe they'll come back another day to rob you."

"They already know where I live," she argued. "If they want to come back another day, that's an option right now. But they can't even get on my street without going past security. We might as well let them come on their own. That way you don't have to worry about picking them up or dropping them off."

"I don't mind."

"You're doing enough already. You don't have to do *everything*."

"Alright," he conceded. "But I wanna get here before they do. Under no circumstances do I want you home alone when they show up."

She smiled. "You sure are protective." She took a step forward, until there were only a few feet between them. "Is it because you like me?"

"Um, either that or I don't want to be held responsible if something happens. Your mother would have my neck."

She moved closer still. "Why can't you admit that you like me?"

He grinned. "I do like you. I think you're swell."

With her next step, her boobs pressed against him. He looked down at her cleavage and tried not to react.

"Is that all?" she asked. "You think I'm *swell*?"

"You're, um…" He took a step back. His eyes remained glued to her chest. "Those things are pretty swollen."

She giggled. She liked his pun, but more than that, she appreciated that he was acknowledging her sexiness. She didn't chase him across the room, but she asked, "Why you running?"

He looked around. "It's not like we're home alone."

Stephanie continued to watch him closely, like a cat stalking her prey. "That's your excuse?"

He nodded. "I think it's a good one."

Stephanie felt her heart kick into another gear. She knew she was close, yet still far away.

"Do you guys want some more sandwiches before you go?"

His eyes brightened. He nodded. "Yeah, that would be great. We really liked them."

"Alright. I'll have them ready in a few minutes."

● ● ● ● ● ●

On Saturday the crew showed up at nine am and planned to work till five. Baron arrived first, but he only beat the other guys by ten minutes. That wasn't enough time for Stephanie to have a private moment with him, but she had bigger plans for later.

That day the workers finished the last of their demolition and began the process of restoring and renovating the two rooms, which was now one huge room. Baron wanted to complete the electrical wiring and get started on the new floor.

Stephanie left the men to their work and got caught up on her housekeeping. She checked with them at lunchtime to see if everyone was okay with her making burgers and fries. They all thought that sounded great.

When she was done cooking, Stephanie inspected her new theater while they ate. Everything was coming along nicely. She couldn't get over how fortunate she was to find a random group of laborers who turned out to be among the hardest working men she'd ever met. But it was Baron who received the bulk of her praise.

He was confident and knowledgeable, easy going, yet assertive enough to keep the crew on task. At times he had all three men working on separate assignments. They never lost focus, complained or loafed. But that wasn't to say they weren't enjoying themselves. Baron brought a radio that was always tuned in to a Spanish station. The men were very talkative, usually when Stephanie wasn't around. As she tended to her chores, she was delighted by the amount of laughter in her home. It took a special kind of leader to keep his crew happy and productive hour after hour.

At four pm, about an hour before the men called it a day, Stephanie went to the kitchen to start dinner. She didn't always wear an apron while cooking, but she donned one that afternoon. That was a clear indication that she meant business. Forty minutes later, the house was filled with delectable aromas. The workers were obviously interested in the meal, but they didn't say much. They just smiled as they passed through.

The one who spoke English was nearly salivating when he told her, "Mmm. You're cooking up a storm in here. Sure smells good!"

"Thanks," Stephanie said, hoping he wouldn't think his crew was in for a treat that night.

Baron was more outspoken when he approached her. That day he wore a tee-shirt with jeans and work boots. Stephanie's kitchen was huge, but Baron seemed to fill the room when he walked up behind her.

"What you got going on here? Chicken?"

His deep voice on the back of her head singed Stephanie's skin. "And green beans," she said. "Corn, mashed potatoes. Some cornbread."

She turned in time to see his eyes widening.

"Damn," he exclaimed. "You expecting company?"

She smiled and nodded. "Yeah."

She thought his eyes registered jealously for a moment, or at least curiosity. But maybe not. He inhaled deeply, his chest growing even larger as he savored the smell of her dinner. "If you have any leftovers, you should hook me up, next time we come."

"Okay." She nodded before turning back to the stove. She could feel him standing there for a second longer before he backed away and exited the room.

Stephanie was done cooking, by the time the men started packing up their tools. She disappeared for a while and emerged from the bedroom with a new outfit; tight jeans with a sleeveless blouse. She walked into the kitchen as Baron was seeing the men out.

Their spokesman said, "We could work tomorrow, if you need us. I know it's Sunday, but it's okay with us."

"That would be fine with me," Baron said. "I'll talk to the lady of the house, to see if it's okay. I'll call you."

"Okay, Mr. Baron."

Baron turned and was surprised by her appearance. His eyes traipsed down Stephanie's body, taking in her slim waist and full hips before returning to her face.

"You, um, you wanna see what we've done?" he asked.

"Sure."

She backed into the hallway and then followed as he led the way into the theater. She was happy to see the crew had smoothed and repaired the area where the wall had been. The new sheetrock was placed perfectly. The only thing needed was a couple of coats of paint to bring the rooms together. They had also completed a portion of the raised floor. Overhead Baron had installed chrome, flush mounted lights. He flipped a switch to show her they were functional.

"I can't believe you're almost done with the floor," she said as she crossed the room in his direction.

"Yeah." He surveyed the area. "The guys were wanting to know if we could work tomorrow. I know it's Sunday, but–"

"It's fine," she said. "I go to church with Mama sometimes, but I get home at one."

He looked into her eyes. "Are you sure? I know we've been taking up a lot of your time."

"I'm sure. You know I wanna get this done as soon as possible."

"You said you had some seats in mind?"

"Black leather recliners," she confirmed. "The ones I'm looking at are connected, with a console in the middle. You can open it to hold snacks and drinks or fold it all the way up, if, you know, you wanna snuggle."

His eyebrows rose.

"I want two rows of four," she said. "One for down here and the other set on the raised floor."

He nodded. "That's gonna look real nice."

"You should come and watch a movie with me when we're done."

"We'll see."

"It's always '*We'll see*' with you," she said with a smack of her lips.

He chuckled. "Alright, well I'd better get going, before your date gets here."

"No, you don't." She stepped to him and hooked her arm around his. "He's already here."

Baron laughed as she led him out of the room.

"I had a feeling something was up."

"Are you hungry?"

"Yeah. But I've been working all day. I wouldn't want to have dinner with you, smelling like this."

"You smell fine," she said. "It's not like you've been working outside. But you can take a shower, if you want."

He laughed again. "Nah, that's alright. Let me go wash my hands, at least."

● ● ● ● ● ●

Dinner was as marvelous as she had planned. Stephanie hadn't cooked for a man in over a year. Her ego got a boost as she watched Baron clean his plate, muttering pleasing expressions like, "*Mmm,*" "*Man,*" and "*Dang this is good.*"

His smile was ear to ear when he pushed his plate away and wiped his hands on a cloth napkin.

"You sure you found the right calling?" he joked. "I know construction runs in your blood, but you could open a restaurant and make a killing."

"I'm not that good," she said modestly. "I just have a few dishes I'm good at."

"You can tell that lie to someone else," he said. "Don't worry. I'm not gonna come knocking on your door every night, to see what you got for dinner."

Damn, I wish you would, she thought. Before she let her mind take her any further than this was actually going, she asked him, "Do you still think it would be wrong for us to see each other outside of work?"

He grinned before responding. "To tell you the truth, I don't too much know what's right or wrong anymore."

She rose from her seat and walked slowly around the table, her eyes locked on his. "But you gotta decide," she said softly. "I'm at the point where I'm willing to back off, if you want me to."

Ironically, she did the opposite of back off as she spoke. She walked closer to him, until her body pressed against his shoulder. She placed a hand on his back as he looked up at her. Neither of them was smiling now. Her hand moved up his spine, to the back of his neck. His skin was warm, his muscles hard and primed. Her breaths were slow and shallow.

He turned towards her. Her legs impeded him, so she backed away for a second. When he faced her, she stepped between his spread legs. He reached slowly and placed both hands on her hips. Stephanie stared down at him. Her breaths were quickened now. She tried to maintain composure, but the realization that he was finally touching her made her head spin. Her skin quivered beneath his fingers.

Finally he said, "I don't want you to back off."

A fire blossomed in her chest, but she surprised him by backing away.

"I'll be back in a second."

She turned and walked out of the room. With her back to him, she sighed silently and tried her best to keep from stumbling. Her legs didn't feel steady at all.

● ● ● ● ● ●

Baron remained at the table for three and a half minutes. He wore a look of uncertainty that transitioned to surprise when Stephanie returned. Now she wore a red, satin robe. It was short and not tied closed. She held it together loosely with one hand. Baron couldn't stop his jaw from dropping. Stephanie's eyes were dark, her expression serious.

She simply said, "Come here," and then turned and left the room again.

Baron remained frozen in place for a few seconds before he shot to his feet and followed her. When he made it out of the kitchen, he saw her disappear into a bedroom at the end of the hallway. He followed, his jeans growing more stiff with each step.

114

Stephanie's bedroom was huge. It looked professionally designed. The lady of the house was not in the room when Baron crossed the threshold. Straight ahead he saw patio doors standing open. Unless she had slipped into the closet, Baron knew that was the direction Stephanie had gone. He continued his pursuit.

He'd seen many amazing things at her home in the short time he'd been there. Baron was stunned once again when he stepped through the patio doors and saw that she had an indoor Jacuzzi. The new room was circular, with floor to ceiling windows that were currently shuttered. The hot tub had a marble design with faux candles along the rim. The lighting in the room was soft. The sound of bubbling water was soothing, though Baron was growing more excited by the second.

Stephanie did not look back at him as she approached the water. She peeled the robe off her shoulders and let it fall to the floor. Baron thought she might be nude, but her bathing suit was just as alluring. He inhaled sharply when he saw that the bottom was a thong. Her bare cheeks were as luscious as he'd imagined. The hot tub was floor level, so she stepped smoothly into the water, rather than climb in.

Baron wondered if she was purposefully moving as seductively as possible as she entered the water. If so, she pulled it off perfectly. She glided to the other side of the hot tub and turned to face him before she spoke.

"I know you don't have any trunks. You can wear your boxers, if you want. Or you don't even have to wear those."

Baron didn't fancy himself a breast man, but the way Stephanie was spilling out of her bikini held him in a trance. He pulled his tee-shirt over his head and began to unbutton his pants, without taking into account that he still had his work boots on.

Stephanie admired his bare torso as she made her way back across the water.

"Here, let me get your boots."

He stepped close enough for her to reach and untie them. She even loosened the laces and held the boots down, so he could easily step out of them.

Baron pushed his jeans down his hips and debated whether he should go skinny-dipping or not. At that point, he didn't think it mattered. He was so hard, the bulge in his boxers left nothing to the imagination. Stephanie's smile was back as she stared at his package. Baron opted to leave his drawers on, for now, since the host remained somewhat clothed.

He slipped off his socks and stepped into the warm water and into her arms. They stood quietly for a while, holding and watching each other. Baron felt he should say something, but his yearning to kiss her was more powerful.

They gave in to their carnal desires simultaneously.

He pulled her closer. Stephanie moaned her approval when their lips came together for the first time. A glove of electricity enveloped her as she sucked first his top and then bottom lip. His tongue sought hers as his hands moved quickly to her ass, gripping both cheeks without hesitation, as if it was something he'd been waiting years to do. He pulled her hips even closer, until she could feel his wanting; hard and hot between her legs.

Stephanie's head rolled back, and she moaned again. His kisses became sensual sucks that trailed from her mouth to her neck. He pressed forward, backing her against the smooth rim of the hot tub. Her legs spread easily, and he grinded between them. Their mouths reunited, and her eyes slipped closed. The thundering in her chest matched the lightning in her mind. Flickering lights swarmed behind her eyelids.

Her hands moved freely up and down his sides. As they kissed, she couldn't resist reaching between his legs. She wrapped a hand around his manhood. The feel of his virility caused a shudder to roll down her legs. Her body responded to him so fiercely, she wondered if it was possible to climax with no penetration. He grunted in response to her caress, and his mouth broke away from hers. His eyes were low and dark with desire. Stephanie continued to squeeze his manhood, but it wasn't enough.

She reached with both hands and tugged at his boxers. "Take these off."

His hands left her body, and he complied. If he noticed her doing the same with her bikini bottoms, he didn't acknowledge it.

Their kiss was even more voracious when they came together again. He sucked her tongue so pleasingly, Stephanie thought she might go blind. She ran her hands up and down his chest, loving the strength and raw power as his muscles flexed. He drove his hips forward and realized there was no longer a barrier impeding his progress. His eyes flashed open, and his nostrils flared. His hand left her waist and moved between her thighs.

Stephanie's breaths came in shudders as he stroked her with his fingers. She cried out when the longest one slipped inside. The sensations from the water and his long, stiff finger made her thighs tremble.

She threw her head back and whispered, "Yes, Baron. *Yes.*"

His hands moved again. He grabbed hold of her top and yanked it up her chest. Her breasts fell into his awaiting hands. He wrapped his lips around her left nipple and sucked while he fondled her right breast. He jumped to the other nipple and gobbled it up just as greedily. Stephanie's hands moved to the back of his head. She urged him forward, encouraging him to suck harder.

"Oh, baby. Yes!"

He continued to grind between her legs as he pleased her with his mouth. Rather than penetrate, he rubbed the bottom of his shaft up and down between her labia. The friction against her clitoris propelled her even closer to an orgasm, but she wanted him inside her.

She needed it.

"Wait." She pushed him away breathlessly. "Bedroom," she managed. "Let's go to the bedroom."

He followed her lead as she climbed out of the hot tub. The sight of her bare ass made his dick throb. He pursued her like a dog in heat. As she walked, Stephanie reached back to undo her bikini top. By the time they entered the bedroom, they were both completely nude. Stephanie rummaged through a dresser drawer until she found a condom. She handed it to him and took a seat on the bed. She admired him fully, from head to toe, as he tore the package open.

The way his dick jumped with each one of his heartbeats made her wish this wasn't their first time. If it wasn't, she would've been on her knees at that moment. The thought of deep-throating him made her walls clench powerfully. She clasped her legs together and tried not to squirm while he rolled the condom down his shaft.

When he was ready, she scooted back to the center of the bed. Within seconds he joined her. Stephanie felt like she was dreaming when she looked up and saw his massive body hovering over her. Baron maintained eye contact as he lowered his hips, until his manhood was reunited with her slick opening. He entered her slowly. Stephanie's eyes slipped closed. Her breath caught as he filled her inch by inch. When he was completely submerged, her eyes fluttered open. She saw that he was watching her.

He lowered his body and kissed her, very softly. He began to stroke her so sweetly, she thought she might cry. Her muscles gripped him pleasantly. Within seconds the throbbing of her clitoris surpassed her heart rate. The trembling in her legs converged in her wet center.

"*Shit*," she moaned. "*Baron, I'm finna cum.*"

"It's only... seven o'clock," he said as his strokes increased in speed and pressure. "You, kicking me out sometime soon?"

She tried to respond, but her budding orgasm stole her breath. "*Uh-uhn*," was all she could get out.

He stood on his arms, so he could look her in the eyes again. "Then cum," he encouraged her. "As long, and as many times as you want."

She was thrilled to hear that. But the pressure was building so mightily, and his dick felt so good, she feared that any climax after this first one would pale in comparison.

Fortunately she was wrong about.

Her orgasm hit her like a pedestrian versus an 18-wheeler. She wrapped her legs around Baron's waist as her flower blossomed, imploring him to go harder and deeper. He obliged with long, hard strokes that blessed her with full penetration and constant clitoral stimulation.

When she exploded, Baron muttered something. But between the freight train sound of blood rushing in her head, the bubbling of the hot tub, and her own cries of pleasure (which were much louder than she intended), she scarcely heard him.

But what she thought he said was, "Damn, baby. I feel. *Shit, I feel you.*"

CHAPTER TWELVE
COME CLEAN

Mr. Fix it
With his work boots
And his tool bag and his cool swag
With his rough hands
And his big chest and his slim waist
And his briefcase
Please come over
To inspect my pipe work
My sheets are wet
I've sprung a leak
Take off your boots
Leave them by the door
Sorry, I just had my carpet cleaned
I'll take that shirt
Don't be shy
Here, let me help you out of those jeans
Hurry, Mr. Fix It
The problem's right here
In my bedroom
Come fix me

On Sunday, the crew showed up at one o'clock as planned. They completed their work on the floor, including the raised portion. Baron sent two of them to pick up the new carpet, while the remaining men got started on painting. They returned with the carpet a short time later, but Baron wanted to finish painting before they laid it.

With four men painting at the same time (Baron included), the crew was able to paint the whole theater in one day. Stephanie loved the color. It was dark enough to give visitors an authentic movie experience when the lights were off but still appealing when the lights were on.

For lunch, Stephanie drove all the way to Hemphill. This was one of several areas in Overbrook Meadows that fully catered to the Mexican community. Even the billboards there were all in Spanish. She had a complicated to-go order, including meats she couldn't pronounce, but she made it home without a hitch. The men were so grateful for the meal, they were still smiling when quitting time came at seven.

Stephanie wanted Baron to stay after the workers left, but she could tell he was tired. Plus she was past due for her Sunday nap. Before Baron took off, they walked through the new theater. Stephanie was proud of how well everything had come together.

"Do you want a ramp here?" he asked, referencing the step down from the raised floor in the back. "We could have a slow incline, so it ends all the way down there," he said, pointing to where the lower seats would be.

"No, it's just one step," she said. "Plus we got the other doorway. Anyone in a wheelchair could go that way."

He nodded. "Okay. Looks like all we have left is to lay the carpet, bring in the furniture and mount the screen. I can probably mount the screen myself, save you some money with the crew."

"Oh–" She yawned unexpectedly. "Excuse me. Okay."

"I'ma let you get some rest," he said.

She placed a hand on his chest. Looking up at him, she smiled. "Thank you. For everything."

"Thanks for lunch," he said. "If you decide to eat any of those leftovers, watch out for the light green salsa. Looks innocent enough, but..." He sucked in air, still trying to soothe his mouth. "Muy caliente."

They both laughed. They walked to the door and kissed briefly, longingly, before he left her alone.

● ● ● ● ● ●

On Monday, Stephanie arrived at the office feeling fresh and upbeat. Her mother surprised her by asking if she'd like to run the team meeting. This was one of few occasions when the front office staff met with the lead foremen to discuss their current jobs and projections for the week.

Baron was not in attendance, but Devin was there along with Monte and Larry Merchant. Stephanie stood and took the lead at the meeting. She told Devin to expect Kevin and Wallace, two new workers she hired last week, to show up at his freeway expansion site. Devin informed the group that he was still on track for completion next month.

"The mayor wants to meet with you this week," he reminded Korah.

Korah turned to Malcolm and said, "Make sure you give his people a call and set it up."

"Yes, Mrs. Avery," the young man said.

Stephanie poked her head out of the conference room and asked Beatrice to join them for a second. Moments later a middle-aged woman, clearly not a friend of the spotlight, reluctantly entered the room.

"This is Beatrice Olsen," Stephanie announced. "She's in charge of our new Human Resources department. Beatrice graduated from the University of Georgia and has worked for several reputable corporations; most recently a contracting firm in Louisiana. Her husband's work recently brought her family to Overbrook Meadows. This is her first job since they've been here. Beatrice has been an asset to every company I contacted. We're grateful to have her expertise at Texas Builders."

The new-hire's face reddened. "Please, call me Bea."

Everyone welcomed her to the fold.

The meeting concluded a few minutes later. Stephanie thought things went well, considering it was her first time leading the discussion. Yolanda and Priscilla told her she did a great job before they returned to their desks. When Korah asked her daughter to come to her office, Stephanie expected more praise.

But her mother's expression was less than approving when she asked her to close the door. Before Stephanie had a chance to sit down, Korah asked, "Have you spoken to Baron? Why wasn't he here this morning?"

The questions seemed to be laced with booby traps. Stephanie decided to answer the more innocent of the two.

"He might think he didn't need to come today, since he's not working on one of our sites."

"Did you talk to him? Did he tell you that?"

Again Stephanie chose to respond to the question that was less likely to arouse suspicion. "No, he didn't tell me that."

"Baron is still our employee," Korah complained. "Just because he's not working on one of our sites doesn't mean he's lost in the wind for six months, or however long it takes him to finish that dealership. If he's having trouble over there, resources he needs, of course Brick is his direct supervisor. But we need to be in the loop as well."

"I went to check on him last week, and you didn't seem happy about it."

Stephanie realized her mistake immediately. Where was a two-second time machine when she needed one?

"That's because I'm not sure of your motives," Korah said, her eyes bunched together in disapproval. "Did you go over there for work, or were you flirting with that boy?"

Stephanie's mouth was constantly putting them at odds, so she remained silent this time.

"Have you talked to him since then?" Korah asked, not letting her off the hook.

Stephanie understood there was a big difference between delivering half-truths and flat out lying to her mother, which was something she hadn't done in a while. She decided to come clean. She girded herself for the backlash before telling her, "Me and Baron have gone out a couple of times."

Korah registered disappointment, but it was obvious that wasn't a complete surprise.

"Girl, why would you do that? I told you – *more than once* – that it wasn't a good idea."

"Mama, I think you're overreacting. You said Devin and Yolanda–"

"Stop throwing that in my face, like they're the torchbearers for office romance. Even if they did work out – and, trust me, I'm extremely happy for them – you know that's not the way it usually goes. Statistically speaking, it's more likely to end in disaster."

"What about you and Brick?"

"Girl, that doesn't even count. We don't work for the same company. The most that could've gone wrong with us is I would end up hating a competing contracting business. As I'm sure you know, I already hate *plenty of them*. Don't tell me Devin and I are the models you choose to live your life by, because you've always been a renegade. You don't look to other people to decide which way to go, so why now?"

"I'm not..." She lowered her head and took a moment to gather her thoughts. "Okay," she said, looking up at her. "It's not because of you or Devin. It's because I like Baron. That's it. And he likes me too."

"Whether you like someone or not isn't reason enough to jeopardize your family's livelihood."

"Mama, I'm not going to jeopardize this company."

"Oh really? What about conflict of interest? The way this company is structured, you're his boss. I guess sexual harassment doesn't seem like something that could hurt us." Before she could respond, Korah said, "Fox News just settled a harassment lawsuit for twenty million dollars."

Stephanie shook her head. "He's not gonna sue us for sexual harassment." Considering the level she and Baron had taken their relationship to, that was almost laughable. But Stephanie dared not crack a smile at that moment.

"What about your *reputation*?" Korah pressed. "I know you've heard of construction workers whistling and catcalling women who walk by their site. You think that's something that only happens on TV? No, Stephanie. That's *real life*. Those men have nothing to do all day but work and gossip and talk about women. What about when rumors get out that one of them is sleeping with the boss? You don't think they're gonna talk about that?"

Stephanie opened her mouth and then closed it without responding.

"What about when some of them decide they might have an easier time on the job, if they could be the next one to hook up with you?" Korah said. "How you gonna feel when you go check on a site, and all the guys are giving you eyes, some going as far as flirting with you?"

"Mama, you're overreacting. That's not gonna happen."

"Yeah, I know you got it *all* figured out. Or *maybe* you're making selfish decisions, thinking only of yourself, even though the outcome could affect a good number of people. You wanna be the boss? That's not what bosses do."

That last jab hurt. Stephanie couldn't hide the sting. She sighed. "I'm sorry if I disappointed you, Mama. But it's not like you're saying. I like Baron. I have for over two years. I haven't been drooling over any of the other 250 men working for us. Baron is smart and sweet. He's a strong leader, and we get along really well. If I made a mistake with him, I'll deal with it personally and professionally. And I promise it will never happen again. Even if you hire *Shemar Moore*, I won't bat an eye."

Korah rolled her eyes. "I was ready to believe you, until you mentioned Shemar."

Stephanie giggled. "Okay, but you get my point."

Serious doubt remained, but Korah realized things had already progressed further than she had hoped. All she could do now was pray that her daughter didn't screw things up. "Fine," she said. "What's on your agenda for the morning?"

"I'm gonna help Bea get her office set up and help her with the mainframe. She mentioned some things... Things they do at other companies that we may want to implement here."

"Any specifics?"

"Yes. Most of it sounds good. The only thing I wasn't sure about is a mandatory ban on hiring convicted felons."

"She can screen them, but Devin has the last say on whether that's an issue or not," Korah said. "If he says they're good, I trust him."

Stephanie nodded. "That's what I thought." She started to leave the office, but then turned back and said, "I met some guys at Home Depot who were looking for work. You don't have a problem if they don't speak English, do you?"

Korah frowned. "What? Are they here legally?"

"I think so."

"As long as they have a social security number, they can fill out an application," Korah said. "But why would you want to bring in some randoms? You don't even know if they're any good."

"Oh, I can tell they are," Stephanie said with a smile.

Her mom didn't know what to think of that, but she had too much on her plate to care. "Whatever," Korah said and then turned to her computer.

● ● ● ● ● ●

By quitting time in Irving, Baron felt good about another productive day at work. The big boss had called earlier, announcing his plans to stop by and check on the site. Some of the men were apprehensive about Brick's visit, understandably. They went out of their way to straighten up and make sure anything that drew the owner's ire wasn't directly their responsibility.

Baron didn't share their anxiety when Brick's humongous King Ranch truck rolled onto the premises. He hopped on a forklift and made it to the parking lot just as Brick exited his vehicle.

"Afternoon."

The two men shook hands.

"How's it going?" Brick asked him. "You haven't called, so I'm guessing there's no trouble."

"Not a bit," Baron assured him. "I couldn't have asked for a better site or a better crew. Wanna take a look around?"

"That, I would."

The men boarded the forklift, with Baron behind the wheel. They talked jovially as Baron gave him a tour of the site. It was still relatively rough. A portion of the steel frame for the main building and a few of the smaller ones had been planted. There were over two dozen sturdy beams jutting towards the sky. None of the floors were in place, but Brick knew the blueprints as well as his lead foreman did. Other than Baron, he was the only person on the site who knew where the service center and showroom would be.

While Brick took note of his foreman's work, Baron couldn't help but notice the way the crew responded to Brick. There were levels of respect that rose with the corporate ladder. The way the men reacted to Brick could be described as *reverence*. Some couldn't hide their surprise, and there was even trepidation deep in their eyes. Baron had seen the same behavior when Korah visited her sites. Baron wasn't a terribly ambitious man, but he had to admit it would be nice to yield that much power.

After riding for nearly thirty minutes, getting off the forklift several times for more detailed inspections, Brick had seen enough.

"You can run me back to my truck," he told Baron. "I see you got everything under control. I was a little worried about Pellum," he said, referring to their crane operator. "I heard he takes his partying too far sometimes; letting it drag into the work week. He hasn't been late or anything?"

Baron was surprised that Brick could be so far removed from the rank and file, yet still have his finger on the pulse of his crew members.

"He tried that two Mondays in a row," Baron confirmed. "I had a talk with him. We're good now."

Brick grinned and didn't ask about the specifics of that conversation.

When they got back to the parking lot, Baron was surprised to see another truck he recognized. This one bore the Texas Builders' logo on the side. The company's shining son sat behind the wheel. Devin got out of his truck and met the men as they exited the forklift.

"Hey, what's going on?" His smile was genuine as he gripped the men's hands separately and pulled them in for a bro hug.

"What brings you by these parts?" Brick asked. He was all smiles too.

"Came to holler at my man," Devin said, patting Baron on the back.

"You're not getting him back," Brick joked. "Not till we finish what we got going on over here."

"Nah, you're good," Devin told him. "Just don't try to drag him to the dark side, while you got him all up under your wing."

"Why does everyone keep saying that?" Brick wondered.

They both laughed. Baron stood between them, feeling proud that he was so valuable.

"How much money did Mama lose in Oklahoma?" Devin asked Brick. "She won't tell me."

"Won't tell me neither," Brick said. "And I guess that's telling *both of us* something!" They laughed again. "Me and you, we need to take us a little trip," he told Devin. "You're about to have your hands full with another little one. We need to have some fun, before that baby is born."

"You're right," Devin agreed. "My house is already like a carnival, and I just got one kid running around. I'd love to get away for a weekend. We should go to Vegas. Hey, you should come too," he said, turning to Baron.

"Unlike you gentlemen, I got no wife or children at home," Baron said. "So whenever y'all ready, I'm down."

"Lucky man," Brick said, and they laughed again. "Well, I'ma hit the road. *Somebody* promised me meatloaf," he bragged.

"Oh yeah?" Devin said. "What time should I be there?"

"I'll tell your Mama to put some in Tupperware. You can pick it up tomorrow," Brick said. He patted Devin on the shoulder before turning to his truck. "Y'all take it easy. Be safe."

They offered their goodbyes.

"So, what's up?" Baron asked Devin as Brick rolled out of the dirt parking lot. "You come to get a tour too?" He didn't mind showing off his work, but Baron was expected to oversee the crew at Stephanie's house tonight.

"No. Actually I came to see you," Devin said. "How come you weren't at the Monday meeting?"

"Oh, did I need to go to that? Sorry. I thought since I was over here–"

"It's cool," Devin said. "That's what I figured. What time do y'all usually start work?"

"The crew shows up at nine. But you know I like to be the first one here," Baron stated.

Devin knew he wouldn't be able to accomplish that, if he had to be at the main office in Overbrook Meadows at eight. "If you can make it, Mama would appreciate it," he said. "But if you can't, I'll let her know why."

"I'll try to be there from now on," Baron said. Then, "I know you didn't come all the way over here to tell me that. What's up?"

"We haven't kicked it in a while," Devin said. "Let's go to Hooters, get some beer and wings."

"Oh, uh..." Baron couldn't come up with an excuse off the top of his head.

"You got a date?" Devin guessed. "That's cool."

"Nah, it's not that."

"I mean, if you just don't wanna hang out with me, I guess that's alright." Devin scratched his head, looking back at the freeway. "Not like I drove an hour to see you, or nothing like that..."

He met Baron's eyes and laughed. After a moment, Baron joined him. The guilt trip may have been a joke, but it worked.

"Alright. Let me put this forklift up. I'll be back in a second," Baron told him.

"Cool. You can follow me in your truck. We'll stop somewhere on the way back to town."

"Bet."

As he watched him return to the forklift, Devin felt a little guilty about forcing the issue. It looked like Baron had something else planned tonight. He hoped it wasn't anything important. Devin wished his mother hadn't sent him on this information-gathering mission. But when it comes to family, you gotta do what you gotta do.

CHAPTER THIRTEEN
T & A

I've been here from day one
Since then, you've never left my dreams
I was there when you were hurting
We stayed up all night when you couldn't sleep
I applauded when you grew stronger
I'd give my last breath, so you could breathe
No one was more proud to see you
Bounce back from that defeat
How could all this time be wasted?
You knew I was waiting
I've been very patient!
But now that you got your strength back
You're ready to move on to better things?
What about the one who's been by your side?
Goddamn you!
What about me?

On the way to the restaurant, Baron called Stephanie.

"Hey, I gotta cancel today."

"Why? What's up?"

"Your brother just showed up at the site, wants to hang out for a while."

Stephanie wasn't suspicious of that. She knew Devin had been to Baron's house a number of times. They hung out at least once a month.

"Why didn't you tell him you had a date?"

"I should have," Baron agreed.

"Oh well. The crew is still on standby. I'm gonna call Fred and tell them to come on and start laying carpet tonight."

Fred was the spokesman for the crew that had been working there. By then Baron trusted the men, but, "I told you I don't want them there when I'm not around."

"It's okay," Stephanie said. "I'll call a couple of my girlfriends over, so I won't be alone. Nobody's gonna try anything if I have company. Plus I got my pistol. Stop worrying about me."

"A gun in your nightstand won't help you, if you're in the living room."

"I'll wear my shoulder holster," she promised. "Would that make you feel better, baby?"

That was the first time she had called him *baby*. Baron decided he liked it very much. And he knew he couldn't control her. Far as he could tell, no one could.

"You don't have to wear your gun in plain sight," he conceded. "That would probably freak them out. But don't you think I need to be there to supervise them?" It was a last ditch effort. He already knew what she would say.

"If I can't get carpet laid at my own house, I don't deserve to run a contracting company. Y'all have fun. I'll talk to you later."

Baron waited fifteen minutes, until they passed through Bedford, before he called Fred. He wanted to make sure Stephanie had a chance to speak to him first.

"I'm gonna be late tonight," he told him. "You guys got a handle on what you need to do until I get there?"

"Yes, Mr. Baron," the man said. "Your girlfriend, she told us you wouldn't make it tonight. Everything will be okay. We'll start on the carpeting. It's okay."

Baron never referred to Stephanie as his *girlfriend* when he spoke to the men. He guessed it was their natural chemistry that tipped them off. "I *will* be there," he said, contradicting him. That was a lie, but there was no harm in having Fred think he might show up at any second. "I'm gonna try. I'll be there as soon as I can."

"It's okay," Fred repeated. "All of us, we know how to lay carpet."

Baron didn't feel like he was being overprotective. He'd be worried about any woman inviting a crew of workers into her home at nighttime; especially strangers she met at Home Depot.

● ● ● ● ● ●

When he got to the restaurant, it was easier to get his mind off things. The hot and fresh wings were delicious. The eye candy was too. Their waitress had it going on in the front and the back. Her skimpy outfit made the men grin each time she returned to the table to see if there was anything else she could get them.

Over the next two hours, the guys talked about work and family. Baron told Devin about one of his aunts who was impressed with the work he'd done on his grandmother's house and had mentioned that she regretted selling it. Baron wasn't sure what her angle was, since there was no way he would sell the house back to her. He thought it was something that may cause strife down the road.

Things at Devin's house were great – if you considered a pregnant wife and a rambunctious two-and-a-half year old who'd recently harnessed the power of crayons *great*. To add to the madness (or beauty, depending on the day), Devin let Yolanda talk him into adopting a puppy from the animal shelter. They were still housebreaking *Popcorn*, so it was not uncommon to find a cold, soggy surprise on the carpet, at two in the morning, when Mother Nature called and your eyes were still half-closed as you stumbled down the hallway.

Baron laughed at Devin's anecdotes. The stories made his life seem dull by comparison. He enjoyed spending time with his friend. Unlike the women in Baron's life, homeboys rarely came with drama.

"What about you?" Devin asked, as they sipped their second and last beer. Both men had to drive home, and neither was irresponsible enough to hit the road while buzzed. "Has Stephanie left you alone, or is she still on the chase?"

Baron didn't think the question was the reason for the outing, but he knew it would come up sooner or later. Stephanie's bold pursuits had become a topic of discussion for them.

He sighed. "I think I, uh…"

Devin watched him for a moment and then laughed. "You finally went out with her," he guessed.

In his defense, Baron said, "Yo, man, you know it was pretty hard to say no."

"Yeah, I know," Devin agreed. "She wasn't gonna let it go."

"I hope it's not something I'm gonna regret," Baron revealed.

"Why you say that?"

Baron frowned, as if suddenly realizing he was talking to Stephanie's brother.

"You know I'm not gon' trip," Devin said. "She's my sister, but you my boy. You know I'm not gonna run back and tell her what you said."

That was only half of the problem. Baron was also careful not to say anything that might make Devin jump to his sister's defense.

"You know it could go bad," Baron stated. "If something happens between us – she says it won't affect my job. But I'm still worried about it. I mean, she's my boss. Or she will be one day, right?"

Before Devin could respond, Baron's phone rang. He removed it from his pocket and saw that it was Fred calling. He told Devin, "Excuse me for a second," and turned away from the table.

Fortunately Fred's question wasn't too complicated. He wanted to know how they should lay the carpet around the raised portion of the floor; whether Baron intended to put trim around it. He answered him and ended the call. He wished he could've asked a few questions of his own, like whether Stephanie's girlfriends had really come over or not. But with Devin sitting right there, he didn't risk it.

"You working on a project?" Devin asked when their eyes met again.

"Just a little home improvement gig for one of my cousins," he said vaguely.

"Is that what you had to do tonight?" Devin asked. "Man, you should've told me. We could've hung out any time."

"It's alright. I got some guys over there laying carpet tonight. They can handle it without me."

"But I don't wanna keep you from getting paid. Your work comes first. You should've told me," Devin repeated.

"It's cool," Baron said. "Trust me, I'm getting paid regardless." He smiled.

Devin grinned too. "I see you. I didn't know you were moonlighting. Looks like you're making money hand over fist. Who's, um, who'd we say was paying for this here meal?"

They both laughed. "Nah, I got it," Devin said. "But, um, back to what you were saying about Stephanie... You know I wouldn't let nothing happen to you, as far as that's concerned. She'll never be able to fire you or talk down to you. Plus she won't be in charge of the company for at least a year. By then whatever happens between y'all will be done happened. Either she'll be over it by then, or, by some miracle, y'all might still be together."

"*By some miracle...*" Baron chuckled. "Is that what it takes to make your sister happy, an act of God?"

"Naw." Devin grinned. "Just because I've never met the man who can do it, doesn't mean it's impossible."

Baron nodded and sighed.

Not wanting to throw his sister under the bus, Devin said, "I'd say you got a better chance than most, because she's been after you for so long. Plus the things she likes about you, it's on a different level than some cute guy she runs into at the mall. She likes you for who you are, your work ethics and integrity."

Baron gave that some thought. It felt good to hear it, especially from Stephanie's brother. Devin had always kept it straight with him.

"But you do need to be careful though," Devin continued. "She is a barracuda. Everybody knows that."

Baron's eyebrows rose.

"She's my sister, and I love her," Devin said. "But when she was in high school, she'd have boys calling the house, straight *crying!*" He laughed. "I'd want to tell them, '*Nigga, quit snotting up your pillow and go find somebody else!* **Damn**. *Done let this girl take all your manhood!*'"

That cracked Baron up, but he took heed to Devin's warning.

His phone rang again. This time it was his friend Lisa.

Baron didn't turn away when he answered. "Hey, what's up?"

"Where are you?" she asked. "You at home?"

"No. Lemme call you back."

"Wait. I – can we talk for a second?"

"Not right now," Baron said. "I'll call you later." He disconnected before she could say anything else.

When he looked up at Devin, he felt guilty for taking a call from another girl while they were discussing Stephanie. He felt even worse when his phone rang *again*, almost immediately. Baron wanted to put his cell on silent when he saw it was Lisa calling him back. But he had to be available to take calls from Stephanie or Fred; in case there was an issue at her house.

"Sorry, I gotta take this," he told Devin as he stood and left the table. He headed towards the restaurant's lobby. His frustration made him look menacing. The hostess was about to tell him, "Have a nice day," but the words got stuck in her throat.

"Girl, what is it?" Baron snapped as he answered the phone.

"What is *wrong* with you?" Lisa sounded like she was near tears.

Baron's expression softened. "What do you mean?"

"Are you avoiding me?" she asked. "Why do you get an attitude every time I call?"

Baron was not a fan of women who used absolutes whenever they got upset. You could take them out to eat every Saturday for months, but if you got tied up two weekends in a row, they'd tell you, "You're *always* too busy. *You never take me anywhere!*"

"I'm not avoiding you. I've been busy with work," he explained.

"You found a girlfriend?" she guessed.

That was another issue Baron had with Lisa. Over the past year she'd been involved in a few relationships, but she made it clear those men were poor substitutes for the man she'd much rather be with. She'd only accepted her friendship status with Baron, because that was all he would offer. He repeatedly told her he didn't want to be with *any* woman. At times he felt Lisa was itching to catch him in a lie.

"Listen," he told her. "You're bugging right now."

"Why won't you answer the question? We're supposed to be friends. Why can't you talk to me?"

"I'm at a restaurant." He tried to speak calmly, but it wasn't easy. "I'm with my supervisor. You can't keep blowing up my phone, making it look like I got a fucking stalker."

"I just wanna know why you can't talk to me." Her voice was growing shrill, steadily on the rise. "Do you have a girlfriend? Just tell me."

Baron knew answering *yes* to that question would make things worse. She was liable to break down crying. He'd have to hang up on her again, and that would make him feel like a dick. And who's to say she wouldn't call him right back?

Ultimately, he realized this was his own fault, for trying to keep a woman in his life as a friend when she clearly had other plans for them. The solution was painful but simple: He had to cut Lisa off. Considering they'd been friends for two years, he owed her the decency of telling her face to face.

"I can stop by when I leave here."

She sucked air between her teeth. Her response came in a shuddered breath. "When?"

He checked his watch. It was 7:30. "We should be out of here by eight."

"Alright. You'll—"

"I'll call you when I'm on my way." He disconnected and tried to neutralize his expression as he made his way back to the table.

Devin appeared concerned, rightfully so. "You're a popular man tonight."

That statement wasn't a request for information, but Baron needed to discuss his dilemma with someone. He knew Devin wouldn't relay any of this to his sister.

"You remember that girl I was telling you about, Lisa?" he asked as he took his seat.

Devin nodded. "Yeah. She's, like your best female friend, but she's always making a play to get back in your bed."

"That's the one," Baron said, lifting his beer. "She's not gonna wanna hear that I'm with Stephanie now..."

The men talked for a while longer. After hearing his side of the story, Devin agreed that Baron would have to cut Lisa out of his life, if Stephanie was the one he wanted. But he surprised Baron with a nonbiased opinion.

"That's *if* Stephanie is the one you want," he said. "But it sounds like Lisa's a good woman. Y'all get along well, and she would do anything for you. Stephanie comes with some drama — as you know or will soon find out. A lot of unseen variables. I'm not dissing my sister. I'm just saying, coming up, she broke a lot more hearts than I did."

Baron took all of that into consideration as they paid the tab and left the restaurant.

Outside, the moon was on the rise in the starry sky. They were both eager to get home, but Baron had to make at least one stop first.

"I'm glad you showed up today," he told Devin in the parking lot.

They clutched hands and embraced briefly.

"No problem," Devin said. "Anytime you wanna talk, you know I'm around."

When he got in his truck, Devin considered the information his mother wanted him to obtain from this meeting. He learned more than either of them had expected, but now he regretted his position as a spy. He couldn't be Baron's friend if he betrayed his trust.

Before he backed out of his parking spot, he texted Korah.

Sorry. Didn't get much. He confirmed he's dating Stephanie, that's it.

She responded thirty seconds later.

Okay. Thanks. Guess we'll hope for the best. Love you.

Love you too Mama

● ● ● ● ● ●

Baron debated calling Stephanie before he stopped by Lisa's house. He decided against it. Visiting a friend he'd known for years shouldn't be a problem, at least not in any relationship he wanted to be a part of. But he would be asked to explain himself, and Baron wasn't in the mood for that. It was bad enough Lisa was showing out in the first place.

When he rang her doorbell, Lisa answered wearing shorts with a tank top. Even in his state of irritation, Baron couldn't help but notice how attractive the long-legged beauty was. If she went out more often, men would fight over the opportunity to buy her a drink. The problem was you couldn't get Lisa's looks without the attitude that came with it. It was like bringing a Great Dane pup into a small apartment. Sure everything is warm and fuzzy at first.

But it wouldn't take long before you realized you were about to have a big-ass problem.

Lisa was already in full distress mode. Baron could see it in the smudged mascara around her eyes as they made their way to her couch. He'd experienced this scenario several times, but it was always Lisa's latest boyfriend who had broken her heart. Baron didn't think it was fair that he was responsible this time, simply because he had moved on with his life.

When they were seated she said, "So, you got a girlfriend?"

He frowned. He didn't like how she made him feel caged in and defensive. "We're not going together. Why you sound like you trying to check me, or something?"

"You didn't answer the question."

He and Stephanie weren't in an official relationship, but Baron would claim anyone at that point. This was getting ridiculous. "Yeah. So what if I do? *You and I are not together.*"

Right on cue, she started to fall apart. "But you said you didn't want to be with anybody."

Her lips were trembling. Baron knew her attempts to fight back tears were futile. She was holding on to a ghost of a relationship, had been for a long time.

"That's right," he said calmly. "I said I didn't want to be with anybody. And then I met somebody. And now I'm with somebody."

"That fast, huh?"

"Lisa, I'm being pretty damn patient with you, mostly because, when you're not acting a goddamned fool, you're a pretty good friend. But you need to tell me what my relationship status has to do with you, since *we are not together*," he repeated.

"I just... I was thinking, I don't know." She ran a hand through her hair, moving it away from her puffy eyes. "I guess I always thought that when you were ready, it would be me. I'm right here. I've always been *right here*. Why would you look somewhere else?"

She managed to hold back her tears until she finished the sentence. Baron knew she'd been biding her time, hoping he'd change his mind about them being together. But this was the first time she admitted it. It put him in an awkward situation, but her behavior wasn't all that nefarious. There were plenty of guys stuck in platonic relationships. If given the chance, some would love to swoop in and be their *friend's* knight in shining armor.

"I'm sorry you feel that way," he said. "But just because I didn't want to be with anybody didn't mean I was gonna turn to you when I decided I was ready. I'm pretty sure I told you that before."

"But I was hoping..."

When she didn't finish, he said, "I get it. Trust me, I understand. I've been there. I've..." A memory brought an embarrassed smile to his face. "Shit, there was one girl I *begged* to go with me."

Lisa couldn't believe it. "When?"

"In high school. Her name was Stacy Henderson."

"That doesn't count," she said. "That was so long ago. I bet she wouldn't turn you down now."

"Who knows," he said with a shrug. "It wasn't meant to be for me and Stacy, just like it's not meant to be with us."

Lisa sighed and wiped her eyes with the back of her hand. "You gotta keep driving that message home, don't you?"

"At this point, yeah." He nodded. "Need to make it perfectly clear."

"But can you tell me why? Is it something wrong with me?"

"I'll tell you the same thing I tell you whenever you have it out with one of your boyfriends: Men are stupid. They don't know a good thing, even when it's staring them right in the face. And, yeah, maybe that includes me too."

"Is that rank and file answer supposed to make me feel better?"

His expression became serious. "No Lisa. Only *you* can make you feel better. You won't ever find true happiness, until you understand that."

● ● ● ● ● ●

They talked for a while longer. Lisa's mood mellowed out and even began to improve. Baron was able to get her to giggle at some of his corny stories, which served no purpose but to put a smile on her face.

When his phone rang, he was surprised by the time showing on the bright display. He meant to leave Lisa's house thirty minutes ago. Seeing Stephanie's name on the Caller ID, he almost didn't answer. But he hadn't stopped worrying about the men who were working in her house. Stephanie said she'd invite friends over, but who could say if she had really done it?

Baron shot Lisa a universal look that said, *This is my woman calling. Don't say nothing.* She blew him off with a roll of her eyes. He took that to mean, *Boy I'm not gon' say nothing. I'm not stupid.*

Baron accepted the call. In retrospect, that decision would forever live in infamy.

"Hello."

"Tell me you're not still with my brother."

Baron was relieved to hear women speaking in the background. Stephanie had not lied about protecting herself with company.

"Is that her? Is that why you're treating me like this?"

Baron's eyes grew as big as doorknobs. A part of him, a very desperate part, initially thought those words had come from his phone. He wanted to believe that. But deep down he knew it wasn't Stephanie's voice. Plus the statement wouldn't make sense coming from her.

As his attention moved to Lisa, he literally could not believe what was happening. He stared at her, with his mouth hanging open, as if a double rainbow had just deposited a leprechaun and a pot of gold on the couch next to him.

"Is that her?" Lisa asked again, raising her voice this time. A moment ago her expression was normal. Now her eyes were filled with unexpected malice. "***Is that your girlfriend?***" she nearly screamed.

On the other end of the line, he imagined Stephanie's expression resembled his. She asked him, "Who's that?" Before he could respond, she spoke again. Stephanie's voice was low now. It had become dark and bitter, in a matter of seconds. "You just slept with me *two days ago*, you dirty ass nigga."

"It's not what you think," Baron managed. His nostrils flared. He never laid hands on a woman, but at that instant, the restraint it took to keep his hands to himself made the veins in his neck stand out. His muscles trembled as he stared death at Lisa.

For her part, Lisa didn't have sense enough to recoil in fear. Instead she held her head high, as if daring him to commit an act of violence.

This chick is bat shit crazy, he finally realized. Tragically, the other woman in his life was just as belligerent.

"It's not what I think?" Stephanie mocked. "Boy, that's the most *tired* shit you could've said."

"I'll call you back." Baron jabbed the END button before she or Lisa could add more fuel to the fire. He shot to his feet, hovering over Lisa with a countenance that would've made the average man piss his pants. ***What the fuck is wrong with you?*** he bellowed.

Lisa's expression cracked again. The tears were back, in the blink of an eye.

"Why not me?" she screamed. ***"Why you pick her over me??"***

At that moment Baron had a million great reasons why he (and every other man on earth) should avoid a relationship with this witch at all costs. But he wasn't about to spend another moment entertaining *crazy*. He'd tried to do the right thing. He was there for her, *once again*, in her time of need. And what did it get him? She betrayed him by trying to sabotage the first glimpse of love he'd had in years.

As much as he hated Lisa at that second, the pity he felt was just as strong. This was truly a lonely, desperate soul. She was a rusty anchor; trying to pull him down with her. He should've put his phone on silent the first time she called tonight.

He took a deep breath, which calmed him only a little, before turning and leaving her house. Lisa continued to cry loudly, at first begging him to stay and then cursing him for leaving. Baron ignored her and got into his truck. The relief he felt as her house became a memory in his rearview mirror was hindered by the reality of what she had done. Knowing Stephanie, she wouldn't believe his story, even if it was the truth. But he had to try.

This time the ladies in the background were quiet when she answered her phone. Baron imagined they were crowded around her, waiting to console her when the man of her dreams turned out to be a run of the mill *dog*.

"You slept with me two nights ago," Stephanie breathed as a greeting. "And you're at some other bitch's house tonight. Why'd you even bother calling back? What makes you think there's anything you can say to make this right?"

Baron took a slow breath, again cursing himself for trying to do the right thing for a friend who turned out to be a psycho.

"I've known Lisa for years," he explained. "She's had plenty of boyfriends during that time. We're just friends. She was feeling down tonight, so I stopped by, because she needed somebody to talk to.

"I don't know why she yelled that when I was on the phone with you. Well, I do know why. I guess she wants to get with me – but she already knows that's not happening. I didn't know she was crazy enough to try to mess up something I got going on, but now I know. I won't talk to her anymore. I'm sorry she disrespected you."

Okay. He'd told the truth. That's what women wanted, right? If Stephanie didn't believe him, that said a lot about her too. She had no reason to doubt that he was being honest.

When she spoke again, she was completely stoic. Her change in demeanor was unexpected, almost frightening.

"Okay, Baron. If you want me to believe that, I will."

A wave of relief washed over him.

But it was short-lived.

"Just answer one question," she said.

"Okay. Anything."

"Have you ever slept with her?"

Baron's heart sank to the pit of his gut. His body grew numb. *Shit*. It would've been easy to lie. Lisa wasn't around to contradict him. But if he and Stephanie were to have a relationship, a *real* one, it had to be built on honesty.

"A long time ago," he admitted. "When we first met. But since then, we've only been friends."

He couldn't hear Stephanie's heart break or confirm that his words caused tears to spill from her eyes. But that's how Baron imagined it. He saw her pained soul on the freeway ahead of him; glowing as brightly as the streetlights that led the way home.

"Then she's not just a friend," Stephanie said, still eerily calm. "But that's cool. Go ahead. Do your thing, boo."

Baron didn't try to respond before she hung up on him.

CHAPTER FOURTEEN
LET'S PLAY

Let's play a game
***Thirst** is the name*
Lotion in your hand
Scrolling Instagram
See her showing that ass crack
She posting pics
You liking them
You full of sin
She's full of sin
Now you hopping in her DM
She'll respond
But she got a man
Seems reckless
But she got a plan

On Tuesday Baron wasn't surprised when he reached out to Stephanie, but she wouldn't take his call. He knew she had her girlfriends with her last night, and although a support system was generally a positive thing, in certain instances your homegirls can hype you up and lead you to make the wrong decision. Even if Stephanie wanted to hear him out, she would've lost face if her friends were watching and shaking their heads in the background.
Girl, hell naw!
Don't let him do you like that.
Baron left her a voicemail when he took his lunch break.
"Hey, it's me. I know you're upset about last night, but you got the wrong idea. I would never disrespect you like that. Call me back."

He tried to get her off his mind for the rest of the day, but it was nearly impossible. Baron found himself checking his phone every thirty minutes or so, wondering if she'd called back, and he didn't hear it ring. The worksite was so noisy, that was a real possibility. But none of the messages or missed calls he received were from Stephanie.

He called her again near the end of his shift.

"Hey, it's me again. If you don't wanna talk about what happened, could you at least call to let me know if you need me and the crew to come by today? It's not fair to keep them on hold, just because of what happened with us."

Stephanie did respond that time, but not how Baron expected. She sent him a text message a few minutes later:

I talked to Fred. I don't need you today

Baron was glad she didn't ignore him completely, but her message left him more frustrated. He didn't like that she was dealing with Fred directly, even though it was her home, her project and she had every right to do so. He also didn't like that she sent a text message, rather than call. It was clear she didn't want to give him a chance to explain himself, but he tried anyway.

Okay, thanks for responding, he typed. **Did they finish laying the carpet last night?**

No response.

This is childish, he typed angrily. **We need to talk**

No response.

Baron waited an hour, until he'd made it all the way home, before he tried again. The long drive did little to alleviate his angst. If she didn't want to discuss their relationship status, at least she could give him more information about the theater.

He typed, **You hired me to do a job. I need to know where we stand on that**

Despite the lack of communication he'd experienced all day, he was surprised when she still didn't respond. After waiting ten minutes, Baron was so upset he almost threw his phone across the room. He had to remind himself that if he allowed a woman to take away his self control, it would be a tremendous failure on his part.

Instead of fretting over Stephanie, he continued his normal routine. He tried to convince himself that it felt good to be off work and have nothing else to do.

●　●　●　●　●　●

On Wednesday Baron got a call from a furniture company. They informed him that the theater seats he ordered for Stephanie's project were ready for pick up. Baron had planned to rent a large U-Haul and hopefully get all of the chairs to Stephanie's house in one trip. He didn't want to rent the truck until he spoke to her.

When he called at lunchtime, and she didn't answer, he got so upset, he didn't bother leaving a message. Stephanie was only 22, which probably meant this was all a game to her. Baron didn't want to play his part, but he was an unwilling participant nonetheless. If he went off on her voicemail, it would reveal his frustration, and that would be a victory for her. Even though this was all very immature, Baron did not want that to happen.

On Thursday morning, he tried her phone again. When she didn't answer, he decided he didn't care about the game anymore. What difference did it make if he won or lost? He was a grown man. If Stephanie wanted to behave like a spoiled brat, that was her problem. If he continued to play this out on her terms, he'd be sinking to her level.

With that in mind, he made the move she didn't expect. Malcolm answered immediately when he called the main office.

"Thanks for calling Texas Builders. How may I help you?"

"Is Stephanie in?"

"Who's calling?"

"This is Baron."

"Oh. Yes, sir. One moment."

After thirty seconds of hold music, Stephanie came to the line.

"What do you need?"

Baron tried not to let her attitude get to him. His nostrils flared when he said, "You didn't get any of my messages?"

"I responded to you," she quipped.

"You responded to one out of ten messages I sent you. What about the other ones?"

"I've been busy."

He hated that she sounded so freaking *normal*, while his world was turning upside down. How could she do this to him? Why did he allow it to happen?

"Are you not going to talk to me about what happened?" he asked.

"Not right now," she said. "I'm at work. I don't have time for that."

"I know you're at work," he growled. "Don't you think I know what number I called?" He caught himself. *Wait, slow it down.*

Stephanie didn't speak while he attempted to calm himself, as if she could hear his inner struggle.

"Alright. That's cool," he said. "Can we talk about the theater at least?"

"What about it?"

"I need to know what's going on with the work. The furniture place called me yesterday. They said your chairs are ready."

After a pause, she said, "You want to finish the job?"

"Yes," Baron breathed, hoping they'd reached a breakthrough. "I want to finish every job I start."

"They laid the rest of the carpet on Tuesday," she revealed. "The only thing left is the seats and the screen. When do you want to bring the chairs?"

Baron was upset that she'd brought the crew in twice without his involvement, but he didn't mention it. "I can come today after work."

"Okay. At five-thirty? Six?"

"Probably six, since I have to rent a truck and pick up the chairs first."

"Okay," she said. "I'll make sure the workers are there by then, so they can help you unload them."

Her statement seemed innocent enough, but the hidden message was not lost on Baron. Apparently she didn't want him to communicate with Fred and his crew directly. Taking that power away from him was her way of reinstating her position as the leader of the project. In some regards, it wasn't a big deal. But considering Baron's title at work was *lead foreman*, it was a well-placed jab.

If she expected him to argue the point, she'd be sorely disappointed. He didn't take the bait.

"Fine," he said. "I'll see you this evening."

• • • • • •

Baron had to leave the dealership at 4:30 in order to meet the timeline he had given Stephanie. Generally he preferred to be the last man on his sites, because workers sometimes left tools out or didn't remove the keys from the construction vehicles. But Brick's men hadn't shown themselves to be that irresponsible, and Baron trusted the number two man on the site.

He told Rick, "Can you make sure everything's secure before you leave? I gotta take off a little early."

"Sure thing," Rick told him, "I'll check everything before I go."

Baron went to pick up the U-Haul first. He left his vehicle there and drove off with the biggest truck they offered. To ensure he wouldn't have to make more than one trip to the furniture store, he also rented a flat trailer and had it hooked to the back of the truck.

When he got to the furniture store, the trailer turned out to be a good idea. Due to the height of the theater seats, he could only fit one row in the back of the U-Haul. He and two men from the store secured the second row of chairs to the trailer, and Baron hit the road again.

He arrived at Stephanie's gated community at ten minutes till six. His heart began to kick uncomfortably when the guard checked his ID and allowed him entry. He rounded the corner and saw Fred's truck parked in front of the house. He backed the trailer into the driveway and knocked on the back door.

He was greeted by Fred and the other two workers. If they were concerned about whatever was going on with him and Stephanie, they were smart enough not to ask. They seemed as jovial as ever. They went outside and began to undo the ropes Baron used to tie the chairs down on the trailer.

In the meantime he went to the living room to let the lady of the house know he had arrived. But Stephanie was nowhere in sight. Baron suspected she was in her bedroom. He stared down the hallway but couldn't get his legs to move in that direction, even though she had invited him to the room on Saturday night. That was five days ago. Things were undoubtedly different now.

Ten minutes later the crew was ready to bring the chairs into the house, but they encountered a problem. Each row of seats had four chairs that were connected. Individually the chairs would fit through the back door, but as a set they would not. Separating them and putting them back together once inside would add at least an hour to their work time, but they had no choice. Fred and his crew were getting paid by the hour, so of course they didn't mind at all.

After they separated the first chair, Baron helped one of the workers bring it into the house. In the hallway leading to the theater, they ran into Stephanie, who had finally decided to make an appearance. Baron nearly dropped his half of the chair when he saw her. Not only did Stephanie look *amazing*; with her hair and makeup recently done, but she was busting out all over the place. Her dress was short and barely there, with spaghetti straps and a plunging neckline.

Her boobs were always nice, but tonight they looked *massive*. Baron felt his body heating as he recalled sucking on her breasts in the hot tub. Even now he could make out her nipples beneath the dress' thin fabric. Stephanie didn't have long legs, but her heels added several inches to her height. Her creamy, chocolate thighs were enticing. Baron remembered when she wrapped them around his waist during her climax.

Thoughts from that night, combined with the current visuals, caused beads of sweat to appear on his forehead. He looked from Stephanie to the man helping him carry the chair. The worker had been as lost in lust as Baron was, but he averted his gaze when Baron caught him staring. There was not enough room for Stephanie to pass through the hallway, so she took a couple of steps back, so they could enter the theater.

"Oh, excuse me, boys," she said with a smile.

Baron didn't think she'd ever looked more appealing, but he knew this was a trap. She wanted him to see what he was missing out on, by being a no good dirty dog. He would've thought that knowing what kind of trick she was trying to pull would allow him to avoid getting caught up, but that wasn't the case. He saw what he was missing out on, and he wanted her. *Badly*. He was ready to apologize again, even though he hadn't done anything wrong.

Stephanie stood in the theater's doorway, as Baron and the worker placed the chair in the appropriate spot on the lower level. He watched her the whole time, just as she watched him. Baron wiped his hands on his pants and started to approach her.

Just then the doorbell rang. Stephanie's smile grew wider.

She said, "Hey, I'm gonna step out for a while."

Baron couldn't stop his face from falling.

"Do you mind watching my house while I'm gone?" she asked him. "Shouldn't be more than a couple of hours."

Baron wanted to ask where she was going, who she was wearing the outfit for and what the hell he was supposed to do if they finished the work before she returned. But it was hard to get his thoughts together with his face still crumbled on the floor.

"Thanks, boo," she said, without waiting for him to respond.

She turned and gave them a glimpse of her world-class ass before disappearing down the hallway. Baron was so curious about who she was leaving with, he almost ran after her. But that would've been worse than the way he was drooling over her dress a moment ago.

He had to accept that he couldn't beat Stephanie at this game. She had home court advantage, she had nothing to lose, and she seemed to be making up the rules as she went along.

He shot his worker a mean glare, and the man lowered his gaze once again. Baron didn't mean to take any of this out on him, but he'd be lying if he said he didn't feel like punching something or someone. The two of them returned to the kitchen to retrieve another theater seat.

● ● ● ● ● ●

Two hours later Baron was alone in the house. He walked slowly through Stephanie's theater. With all of the chairs placed, it was almost complete. All that was left was for him to install the projector screen in the front of the room. Stephanie already ordered the screen and gave the store Baron's contact information, so they could call him when it was ready for pick up. He expected to hear from them any day now.

Baron checked the new seats as he surveyed the theater. They were all lined up perfectly. The chairs were big and soft, a little smaller than recliners. He took a seat in one of them, thinking it would be nice to watch a movie there. But it didn't have to be a movie. The projector Stephanie purchased was similar to a smart TV. With a Wi-Fi connection, she could pull up anything on it, from Netflix to Hulu.

As he sat quietly, Baron tried to get his mind off how horrible he felt. It wasn't working. He felt like he had the word **"FOOL"** tattooed on his forehead. This wasn't the first time he'd been treated unfairly by a woman, but he hadn't been played this thoroughly in years. Stephanie was young, but when it came to mind games, she was masterful.

Why the hell am I still here? he wondered. The answer to that disgusted him: Somehow Stephanie had gained complete control. She knew he would stay until all of the workers were gone, because he did the same thing on all of his worksites. She knew he wouldn't steal anything because, first of all there were security cameras everywhere, and also because she was his boss; on this job and at work. If he did anything out of line, it could cost him his career.

Baron didn't have a key to lock up her home, but that wasn't the real reason he stayed. Stephanie lived in a safe neighborhood with a security guard watching the only entry, which was also the only exit. He could walk out of her house and leave the front door wide open, and nothing would come of it.

Baron had to accept the fact that he was still there because he wanted to know what was going on. He wanted to see Stephanie when she returned. He wanted to know who she had left with. He wanted to know if she would bring a man home with her. If so, would she tell Baron to leave, so she could make love to someone else? These questions were sickening, but there was no way Baron could move on until he had the answers.

"Fuck this," he grunted and rose to his feet. He went to the kitchen, planning to leave through the back door, but his legs stopped moving when he got there.

Who the hell did she leave with?

Why did she have to wear that dress?

As much as he hated it, Baron knew that he had to play his part till the bitter end. He walked to the fridge and opened it

angrily. He sighed. *Well, at least there's beer.* He pulled a bottle
of Bud Light from a six pack and took a seat at the kitchen table.
He twisted the cap off with a strong hand that was rough and
calloused on the palm.

He stared straight ahead and drank his beer and waited.

He thought about his dog at home. He left Pearlie alone at
seven am. It was now after eight, and it didn't look like he'd get
home until ten. His baby didn't deserve this. Dogs are pack
animals. Since Pearlie was his only pet, Baron was the only pack
she had. He should've been there with her. She loved him more
than anyone else, and look how he was treating her.

Ten minutes later he returned to the fridge for a second
beer. He took this one to the theater, where the seats were more
comfortable and there was a console between them that had cup
holders and a place for snacks.

Twenty minutes after he finished his second beer, Baron
finally heard the sound he'd been waiting for. Someone entered
the house through the front door. He heard voices in the living
room when he rose from his seat and stepped into the hallway.
One of the voices was female, and though it was soft spoken, he
recognized it as Stephanie's. The other voice was a male. He
spoke in low mumbles, while she giggled flirtatiously.

Baron was not surprised at the sight he was treated to
when he rounded the corner and stepped into the living room. In
the well-lit foyer, Stephanie stood with a man Baron recognized. It
was the same guy she had brought to her graduation party. He
wore jeans with a tee-shirt, while she outshined him in her tight
dress.

Baron's stomach turned. He clenched his teeth and fought
to keep the contents of his stomach down as he watched them.
The man had Stephanie backed against a wall. His hands moved
down her sides to her full hips. He tried to kiss her, but she
pushed him away coyly; turning her head so that his lips brushed
her cheek and neck.

"Boy, stop."

As she turned away from her date, her eyes found Baron.
Rather than express surprise or even guilt, Stephanie's eyes
remained locked on his while her date attempted to transition
from first to second base. Baron's eyes glazed over with white hot
fury. His muscles tensed, and his fists balled subconsciously. He

knew what was happening, and he still let her do it – *again*! His lips parted, baring his teeth. He sucked in deep, slow breaths. The air only fueled the fire burning in his soul.

Stephanie's eyes widened slightly when he took a step towards them.

"Stop," she told her boyfriend. But she was smiling, and he still hadn't noticed they weren't alone. The boy was oblivious to the impending doom standing no more than thirty feet away.

Baron caught himself before he did the unthinkable. If they were on one of his worksites, he would've mopped the floor with Stephanie's boy toy. The fool never would've seen it coming. But this wasn't a construction site, it was a beautiful home. It was his *boss'* house. If things turned violent, he could end up in jail – or worse.

More important than that was how obvious it was that this was exactly what she wanted him to do. He could tell by the conniving look in her eyes as she continued to stare straight at him. Everything he'd done tonight had played right into her hand. Baron cursed himself for being so predictable and simple-minded.

He turned and left the room without falling for her tricks this time, but it was too little too late. He had already reacted; wearing his pain and resentment on his sleeve for her to see and savor her accomplishment.

When he reached the kitchen, he heard her date ask, "Is someone here?"

He didn't hear Stephanie's response before he exited through the back door. His heart continued to pump adrenaline laced with fury through his bloodstream when he got into the U-Haul.

At that point, Baron wanted nothing more than to retreat to the sanctuary of his home, to comfort his dog, as Pearlie comforted him with her everlasting love and faithfulness.

But thanks to Stephanie, he couldn't even do that. He still had to drive all the way to Arlington to return the U-Haul before he could pick up his own truck and head back to Overbrook Meadows.

CHAPTER FIFTEEN
MONDAY MEETING

The weekend passed dreadfully slowly. Baron did not attempt to contact Stephanie, and she made no attempt to reach out to him.

On Monday morning, Korah was not happy to see that Baron was not present for another meeting. After discussing Texas Builders' progress and goals for the week, she dismissed the group but asked her son to hang back for a minute.

She asked him, "Did you talk to Baron about our Monday meetings?"

Devin nodded. "I did. I told him you wanted him to come."

"What did he say? Did he give you a reason why he couldn't make it?"

"He said everyone gets to the site at nine, but he likes to get there before them. He won't be able to make it to Irving in time, if he has to be here at eight. But he said he'd make an exception on Mondays."

"Doesn't look like he made an exception today."

"I don't know what's going on with him," Devin said. "Want me to call him?"

Korah shook her head. "No. I'll call him myself."

On the way to her office, Korah passed her daughter, who was standing next to Yolanda's desk. She and Stephanie locked eyes for a moment. Korah's eyes narrowed, and Stephanie averted her gaze. Korah wore a look of annoyance when she made it to her desk, but her voice sounded normal when she dialed Baron's number.

"Hello?" he answered.

"Hi, Baron. This is Korah."

"Oh," he said, his tone shifting from neutral to enthusiastic. "How's it going, Mrs. Avery?"

"I'm fine, Baron. We missed you at the meeting this morning. Did you have trouble getting here?"

"Oh, um, no, ma'am. I'm on my way to the dealership in Irving. I didn't think I'd make it to work in time, if I had to stop by the office first. I talked to Devin about it."

"I did too," Korah said. "He said you told him you'd make an effort to be at our meetings."

"I know, ma'am. I..."

She waited.

"I'll be there from now on, Mrs. Avery," he said.

"Are you having any problems?" she asked. "Anything you want to talk to me about?"

"At the site? No. Everything's great."

"Not just at the site," she said. "I mean *in general*. How are you doing? I don't get to see you as much as I'd like to."

"I'm fine," Baron stated.

She hoped he'd add more to that, but there was only silence. Korah wished they were having this conversation face to face. She'd be able to judge his disposition better, if she could look him in the eyes.

"Okay," she said. "Brick says you're doing great work over there. We're all very proud of you."

"Thank you, Mrs. Avery. I appreciate that."

When she got off the phone, Korah's irritated expression returned. "Stephanie," she called into the hallway. "Come here, please."

Her daughter couldn't hide her guilt as she appeared in the doorway. "Yes, Mama?"

"Come in. Close the door."

Stephanie swallowed before doing as she was told. She nibbled on her bottom lip as she took a seat across from her mother.

"What happened with Baron," Korah asked bluntly.

Stephanie's eyes widened. "Wha, what do you mean?"

Korah's nostrils flared. Her eyes slipped closed as she took a slow, deep breath. She opened her eyes and frowned at her baby girl. She did not repeat her question.

Stephanie cleared her throat. "He tried to play me."

Korah pursed her lips. Her frown intensified. "Explain yourself."

Stephanie didn't tell her they made love. Instead she said she and Baron got "*really close,*" and she caught him at another woman's house two days later. Stephanie also left out the part about bringing Theo home to aggravate Baron. Korah didn't need to hear the full story to come to a conclusion.

"I told you to leave that man alone. This is *your* fault. You're the reason he didn't come to the meeting today."

"Mama, he cheated on me," Stephanie complained.

"How the hell did he cheat on you, if you're not even in a relationship?"

"We kissed, Mama. I thought it meant something."

"Well, maybe it meant more to you than it did to him. I don't know, and frankly, I don't care. The bottom line is you went after him, after I told you not to. And now things have turned out just like I said they would!"

"But, Mama–"

"Be quiet!" Korah snapped.

Stephanie recoiled and blinked back her tears.

"*You* caused this problem," Korah said, "and you're going to fix it. Do you hear me?"

Stephanie wanted to stand her ground, but she nodded slightly.

Korah stared her down for a few more seconds before saying, "Go! Why are you still sitting there?"

Stephanie slowly rose to her feet and commenced a walk of shame out of her mother's office. Malcolm and Yolanda, whose desks weren't far enough away to avoid hearing the berating, averted their attention as the heiress made her way to her own office.

• • • • • •

Stephanie waited until lunchtime before she called Baron. By then she had gotten control of her emotions, and her mother didn't seem as upset as she was earlier that day.

When he answered, Stephanie heard construction vehicles in the background, so she knew he was taking his lunch on the site, rather than go to a restaurant or café.

"Yeah," he grunted.

"Hey," she said.

After a tension-filled pause, he said, "What?"

Stephanie wasn't accustomed to their staff speaking to her that way. She tapped a pencil on her desk and tried to keep her cool.

"So, um, why weren't you at the meeting this morning?"

"What?" He smacked his lips. "Man, I already talked to Devin *and* your mama about that. I told them I would be there from now on."

Stephanie felt her temper rising. She began to tap her foot in additional to the pencil. "Okay. No need to get an attitude."

"Is that it?" he asked. "I got work to do."

"Aren't you at lunch?"

"Somebody brought me a burrito. I'm good."

Stephanie sighed. "Look, we need to talk."

"About what?"

"About everything. I'm sorry for what happened last week."

"A lot of shit happened last week. What are you sorry for?"

Really? She couldn't believe he wanted to do this the hard way. "For bringing that guy over," she said, "when y'all were working on my theater."

He grunted. "I ain't worried about that. Just kids being kids."

"You need to stop saying that. You're not that much older than me."

"Yeah, but you the one playing childish games."

"Don't make it sound like you're totally innocent. You went to some chick's house right after we..." She shook her head. She realized she had gone from tapping the pencil to squeezing it in her fist so tightly, she thought she'd break it. She put the pencil down and wiped her eyes. She didn't realize she was starting to tear up.

"I told you I didn't do anything," he said. "She was just my friend."

"Yeah right."

"Why you think I'm lying to you?"

"You said you had sex with her."

"I told you that was a long time ago."

"Then why'd you go to her house?"

"Look, I went over there because she's my friend, and she needed to talk. I didn't mean to hurt you. But I bet you can't say the same about that mess you pulled. You wanted to hurt me. And you wanted me to hurt that boy."

"No, I didn't."

"That's your boyfriend, ain't it?"

"No. We're just friends."

"Mmm hmm. I guess you gon' tell me y'all haven't had sex?"

Stephanie did not enjoy having the script flipped on her. "I said I was sorry for inviting him over."

"Alright. Whatever. So we're good then, right?"

"I don't know. Are we?"

"Yep. Far as I'm concerned," Baron said. But she could hear the aggravation in his voice. Despite her apology, they were anything but *good*. "I gotta get back to work," he told her.

She blew out a pent up breath. "Alright. Enjoy the rest of your day."

● ● ● ● ● ●

Korah texted her husband before she left the office at five.

Headed home soon?

In about thirty minutes, he replied.

She was glad to hear that. You never knew when Brick's work would keep him tied up past nightfall.

How was your day? he asked.

Not great

Sorry to hear that. Guess I'm not getting a home cooked meal tonight

She grinned. **I can pick up some Boston Market**

Get baked, he typed. **I'm trying to watch my figure**

That brought another smile to her face. She also enjoyed watching his figure.

She had time to pick up the food and get things ready at home before he arrived. Brick wore jeans with a baby blue button-down that day. He sported real cowboy boots, rather than the steel-toed ones he used for work. The boots were ostrich skin. He walked into the kitchen with a dark-colored Stetson in hand. If they were on his ranch in Lewisville, she would've thought he had just pulled up on his favorite Palomino, Roscoe.

He smiled first at his wife and then at their dinner. He approached her and slid an arm around her waist. He pulled her to him and kissed her slowly. Her whole body came alive for him.

"How was your day?" she asked when he stepped back.

He shook his head. "I don't wanna talk about my wonderful day, after you said yours wasn't so good."

"It's alright." She smiled. "Why was your day so wonderful?"

"Well, it started with *me* being so wonderful, and everything fell into place from there."

She laughed. "I can totally see how that could happen."

While they dined, he regaled her with his latest contracting heroics. Today he rescued two bids from the brink of defeat. With the second one, Brick admitted that a female investor couldn't get enough of him when he showed up at her office for a meeting. She even asked if he wanted to go out for drinks tonight, to discuss their bright future together.

In response to him telling her he was happily married, she replied, "I am too." And, "I won't tell if you won't."

Brick declined her offer but still got the contract signed. According to him, that was something only an extraordinary contractor could pull off.

Korah didn't mind hearing about other women's inescapable attraction to her husband. Brick had always been very cavalier; willing to use all of the talents God blessed him with to his advantage.

Before they met, she derided the fact that Brick was so arrogant, he posted his own portrait prominently on the first page of his website, whereas most contracting companies offered a glimpse of their designs. Now she bore the debonair cowboy's last name. Waking up to him every morning was incredible.

In addition to scoring two big contracts, Brick also accomplished more mundane feats today, like cutting two months off the completion of a Sam's warehouse and getting a skyjack started after nearly every capable man on the site had given it their all and swore it needed to be sent in for repair. Much to the chagrin of the workers, Brick's handyman skills allowed them to complete their shift, rather than knock off two hours early due to faulty equipment.

After dinner, Korah told him, "I think I'll take a long, hot bath."

Brick stared at her across the table. "Can I join you?"

Their tub was huge, so there was no problem there. She nodded. "I'd like that."

"You go ahead. I'll straighten up this mess," he said, looking down at the table.

"Thank you." She bent to kiss his cheek before she left the room.

Ten minutes later the bathtub was filled and bubbly. Korah stripped down and stepped into the soothing water. She took a seat and leaned against the back of the tub. Brick joined her in the bathroom a minute later. He wore only his boxers. His bronze skin looked beautiful beneath the soft bathroom lights. The muscles in his chest and arms held her gaze, but she noticed he'd brought a bottle of wine and two glasses.

Her heart melted.

"This is the best sight I've seen all month," she told him.

"Me or the wine?" he wondered.

"The combination."

He placed the wine and glasses on the rim of the tub before pulling his boxers down and stepping into the water. "Let me get behind you."

Korah checked out his package as she slid forward and made room for him. With Brick now occupying the position she'd had, she slid between his legs and reclined against his powerful chest. Their bathtub was ten feet long, so she could still straighten her legs fully.

She poured wine for both of them.

"What happened at work?" he asked as he took a sip.

She told him about Baron not coming to their weekly meeting and how Stephanie was most likely the cause of it. She relayed the conversations she had with Baron and her daughter.

"She didn't say they slept together, but I think they did," Korah informed him. "Why else would she be so upset about him seeing another woman? But if they did sleep together, then she's right to be offended by what he did, I suppose."

Brick put his glass down and wrapped his arms around her torso. His hands didn't stop moving for the next twenty minutes. He caressed her stomach and her breasts. Korah's center began to pulse, making it hard to keep her mind on what they were talking about.

"That doesn't sound like Baron," Brick said. "But obviously I don't know him that well. Did you talk to Devin about it? Don't they hang out sometimes?"

"Devin took him to a bar last week," Korah confirmed. "But that was before any of this happened. I didn't ask him if he knows about this other girl."

"I saw Baron today," Brick said. "I went to the site around one. He didn't seem upset about anything." He continued to massage her breasts, tweaking her nipples until they perked up for him.

"This is Stephanie's fault," Korah said with a sigh. "I told her to leave that man alone."

"You said the same thing about Devin and Yolanda," Brick reminded her. "You didn't want them to hook up either. But things worked out."

"Not you too."

"What?"

"Stephanie keeps throwing that in my face. But you know they're not the norm. I celebrate Devin and Yolanda's marriage every day. I love my grandbaby." Her eyes slipped closed as she thought of the beautiful child. "I can't wait till the next one gets here. But most workplace romances don't end like that."

"What about us?" Brick said. His hands moved between her legs. He rubbed her opening with his fingers. Her legs parted for him.

"We never worked together," she hummed.

His fingers were smooth and stimulating. He parted her lips and slipped deeper into her warmth.

"But you thought I would cost you that contract, if you went out with me," he said. "Everyone told you I was nothing but trouble."

Korah's heart thumped pleasantly as she considered the high school contract that brought them together. That job was small potatoes, compared to the buildings they were erecting now. But back then, it would've been the biggest contract for either of them.

"Still not the same," Korah breathed.

"I don't know," Brick said. His voice was soft and warm next to her ear. "The heart wants what the heart wants."

Two of his fingers penetrated her. She moaned and arched her back, spreading her legs even further apart. Brick stroked her inner thigh with his other hand.

"My goodness you're wet," he commented.

She chuckled. "That's the water, sir."

"Some of it is," he acknowledged. "But some of it ain't. I know my woman when I feel her."

She moved away from him. In addition to its length, their bathtub was wide enough for her to turn around and straddle him. He stared into her eyes as she repositioned herself. His chest rose and fell slowly. When she began to lower her body, he reached to guide himself in.

"Oh *mmm*." Her eyes slipped closed as he pushed in deeper and deeper. She braced herself with a hand on either side of his neck. She leaned forward and sucked his bottom lip when they became one. He was right. She was very wet, and it wasn't just because of the water. But her walls were still nice and tight around him.

He kissed her and said, "If things *do* go bad, I could take Baron off your hands, if you need me to."

Korah was not so far gone that she couldn't open her eyes and tell him, "Not on your life, buster."

CHAPTER SIXTEEN
WORK ETHICS

Around the time Brick and Korah were enjoying their cozy dinner, Stephanie was surprised to hear her doorbell ring. No one could get past the security guard posted at the entrance of her community unless they were one of the thirteen people on her approved visitor's list. None of those people had called to say they were coming over.

Her eyes widened when she went to the door and checked the peephole. It was Baron. Stephanie got home an hour ago and had already changed into an unflattering *home-for-the-night* outfit. She had even washed her face and put on an oatmeal based facemask that was supposed to help with exfoliating.

"Uh, just a minute!" she shouted before she turned and took speedy steps towards the bathroom. Once there, she quickly washed her face and checked her appearance in the mirror. Her hair was pulled back in a ponytail, and she thought her face looked pale with no makeup.

Who the hell comes to your house without calling? She didn't want Baron, or anyone else, to see her like that.

But then again, what did it matter what Baron thought of her appearance? She only needed them to get along well enough to behave cordially at work. Whether he still found her attractive or not was no longer relevant.

She returned to the front room and checked the peephole again. Baron stood, waiting patiently. He didn't look irritated or angry. A bit sheepish maybe. She opened the door, and they looked each other in the eyes. He broke the gaze; his eyes rolling up and down her frame before returning to her face. Stephanie felt like he was judging her. Even though she had decided his opinion didn't matter, his powerful gaze made her feel uncomfortable and unsure of herself.

"Evening," he said. Baron wore khakis today, with a teal button-down tucked-in neatly. "Sorry to show up without calling," he told her. "I got a call from Carlton's today."

Stephanie knew that was the furniture store they purchased the theater seats from.

"They said your screen was ready," Baron announced. "I went ahead and picked it up when I got off work. Got it in the back of my truck. I can install it for you, right now. Or if you're busy, I can leave it, and you can–"

"Oh, um, no, I'm not busy," she said. She couldn't hide her confusion. "I didn't think you wanted to come back here. I know you were upset..."

He nodded. His expression remained unreadable. "If I start a job, I like to finish it," he explained. "Unless you fired me..."

She frowned. "I didn't fire you. If you want to install the screen, that would be great. Did you bring the workers with you?"

He shook his head. "It's only a screen. I'm pretty sure I can handle it on my own."

Stephanie didn't know about that. The screen she purchased was eleven feet long and six feet tall. And it wasn't one of the pull-down varieties. She thought it would take two men just to bring it inside the house, let alone set it up. But if Baron thought he was capable, she wasn't going to argue with him. She'd seen him topless, and he certainly wasn't lacking in strength.

"Okay, if you're sure you don't need any help," she said. She looked past him and didn't see his truck parked in front of the house.

"I'm in the driveway," he said. "If you open the back door, I'll bring it in that way."

"Alright."

She closed the door and went to the kitchen to meet him. Baron had his truck backed in. She saw her screen in the bed. It was so long, a few feet were hanging over the tailgate. Baron had wrapped it in a thick blanket and secured it with ratchet straps.

"You sure you don't need help bringing it in?" Stephanie asked again. She didn't think she'd be any help, but maybe one of her neighbors wouldn't mind.

"I'm good." Baron didn't look her way as he began to undo the straps.

• • • • • •

While he worked, Stephanie slipped into her bedroom to spruce herself up. She changed out of her shorts and put on jeans. Her tee shirt wasn't too frumpy, but she replaced it with a stylish one anyway. She traded her house shoes for sneakers, in case Baron changed his mind about needing her help. She also applied a little makeup before she went to the theater to check on his progress.

By then Baron had the screen inside and unwrapped. Stephanie was surprised by the magnitude and beauty of it. She was also impressed with Baron's solution for working alone. He had brought in two six-foot ladders that were holding the screen up; one on each side. He had attached the ratchet straps from the truck to the ladders. Presumably he could use the straps to raise and lower the screen, but Stephanie would be lying if she said she understood how he had it all configured.

Baron had his back to her, as he worked on the wall mounts. Stephanie still hadn't shaken her unease as she stepped closer.

"Do you want something to drink?" she asked.

He looked over his shoulder and stared at her for a moment before responding. "No. This won't take long." He returned his attention to the wall mounts before he asked, "You finna take off?"

"No. I'm not leaving."

He didn't ask why she'd changed clothes, but he told her, "You look better without makeup."

Stephanie was taken aback. It was always nice to hear that from a man, but she thought he was too upset to throw a compliment her way. "Thank you. You, um, I'm gonna make dinner. Do you want something to eat?"

She thought it took an enormous amount of time before he responded.

"Yeah, that'd be fine."

"Is there anything you want me to make?"

He shook his head. "Whatever you're making for yourself is fine. I'm no vegetarian, vegan or Muslim. Can't say I ever turned down a hot meal."

Stephanie smiled at that. She left him to his work and went to see what she had in the kitchen.

● ● ● ● ● ●

Baron finished setting up the screen before Stephanie pulled her spaghetti casserole from the oven. He took the ladders to his truck and washed his hands before taking a seat at the kitchen table to wait for her.

For the second time that evening, Stephanie felt uncomfortable with his eyes on her. That was probably because he was just staring, without speaking. The tension in the room was so thick, she could've served it as a side dish. Instead she made a salad and garlic bread. She stole glances at Baron ever so often and found him looking at his cellphone. But she felt like he was glaring at the back of her head each time she looked away.

By the time she finished their dinner, her forehead was moist with sweat. She wished she could blame it on the oven. She dabbed the sweat with a kitchen towel before taking their plates to the table.

"Here you go."

Baron nodded approvingly as he slid his plate closer. "Thank you. Looks great. Don't you wanna check out the screen first?"

"No," she said as she took a seat across from him. "I'll go after we finish."

Stephanie didn't realize how nervous she was until she reached for her fork and noticed her fingers were trembling. *Jesus.* She sighed and looked up at him. After a moment, Baron did the same.

"Something wrong?" he asked.

"You're not saying much," she replied. "I don't know how you feel right now. You're making me nervous."

He frowned. "I don't mean to. I'm sorry. I appreciate you making dinner for me."

"No," she said, shaking her head, "I'm the one who needs to apologize – for what happened the last time you were here. What I did was wrong."

He scooped up a forkful of casserole. "It's okay. You were upset about what happened with Lisa."

Now that they were speaking, Stephanie felt composed enough to start eating. "You never really said who she was," she commented.

"You never gave me a chance," Baron noted. "Just went from zero to a hundred; making your own conclusions."

Stephanie didn't like to hear that she acted so impulsively, but she nodded. "You're right." She ate a little more and then asked, "So, who is she?"

Baron grinned. "It still matters at this point?"

She nodded. "Yeah. I wanna know."

"An ex-girlfriend," he said. "But we were always better at just being friends. The whole time I've known her, we were only in a relationship for two months. The rest of the time, I guess you could say I was her confidante; the guy she would call when one of her boyfriends broke her heart and she needed a shoulder to cry on. She called me when she wanted to get a male's perspective on things."

Stephanie understood that. She didn't have a man in her life who filled that role, but some of her friends did. "She always wanted to get back with you?" she deduced.

Baron didn't want to acknowledge that, but he nodded. "For the most part, I would say no. We were just friends. We kicked it, watched TV, went out to eat. But sometimes when she had a bad breakup, she'd start thinking about us getting back together. I'd tell her no, and she'd usually get over it in a day or so.

"The shit she pulled when I was on the phone with you, that was the first time she ever did anything like that. When it happened, I looked over at her like she was crazy. She literally tried to sabotage my, um, you know, whatever we had going on."

Whatever we had going on? Stephanie wished he had a better description of their fledgling relationship, but she didn't say anything.

"That's when I knew how far gone she was," Baron continued. "I mean, I guess I always knew. A part of me did." He shrugged. "Maybe I was in denial. I wanted her to be happy. I put up with a lot of stuff, to try to make her happy. But what she did to me..." He shook his head. "It's inexcusable. I would bend over backwards for her, but when she saw I had something to be happy about, she tried to rip it away." He sighed. "That's the worst kind of person."

His explanation told Stephanie a lot. Inwardly she was ecstatic to know that she was the reason Baron *had something to be happy about.* She hated that those feelings were now past tense. She didn't understand why Lisa would want to steal his joy, if he'd been so good to her.

Before she had a chance to ask, Baron said, "What about your boyfriend? I kinda feel like you played me from the start."

Her eyes widened. "What? Why do you say that?"

"I know that was the dude you brought to your party," Baron stated. "If y'all been together since then, why was I even in the picture? What'd you come after me for?"

Stephanie shook her head. "No, you got the wrong idea about him. *Completely.*"

Baron shrugged as he lifted his fork again. "I'm only going by what I saw."

"Okay," Stephanie said, realizing how convoluted things may appear from his perspective. "Theo and I have dated on and off, but he was never my boyfriend."

"Just somebody you have sex with?"

Stephanie was caught off guard by his bluntness. She wanted to deny it, but he'd been honest with her, and he deserved the same. Was that all Theo had been? She cocked her head to the side, her eyebrows bunched together. Baron's expression remained blank as he waited for her to get her thoughts together.

"I, um, I can't say I've ever thought of him like that," she told him. "But, I mean, I guess that's kinda true. I could always call him whenever I needed a date, or something."

"Let me guess," Baron said. "He wants to be in a real relationship, but you don't wanna get tied down."

Stephanie hated the way he peeled back her layers and left her exposed. She wanted to blame him for the way she was feeling, but she understood he was only holding up a mirror; reflecting what was inside of her.

"It's not that I don't want to be tied down," she said. "I just didn't want to be with *him*, not long term."

"That's cool," Baron said. "Nothing wrong with that, especially if you make it clear that's how you feel, and he's okay with it."

Stephanie's lack of response made Baron grin.

"I take it you haven't explained it to him like that."

She lowered her eyes. "You make it sound like I'm the worst person in the world."

He shook his head. "No, that's how you tried to make *me* feel. But the difference is, I was honest with Lisa from the jump. I never told her '*Maybe, Let's talk about it later,*' or none of that. Every time she asked about us getting back together, it was always a flat-out '*No.*'"

"Theo knows I see other people," Stephanie assured him. "I'm pretty sure he wouldn't get all broken-hearted if I told him not to call me anymore."

Baron continued to eat his casserole. "If you say so. This is really good, by the way. I see you ain't scared to bust out the shredded cheese."

"Oh no," she said, looking down at her plate. "Did I use too much?"

"Too much cheese?" He scoffed at the notion. "You'll never hear that complaint from me."

Stephanie smiled. She loved that he was such a big eater, and he enjoyed her cooking. "The night I brought Theo over, I just want you to know we didn't do anything."

"Not my business."

"I brought him over here to make you jealous," she revealed, ignoring him. "That was it."

"Sure looked like things were headed for the bedroom," Baron stated.

"We didn't go past the foyer," Stephanie promised him. "As soon as you left, I made him leave too."

Baron rubbed his forehead. "So you're outright *using* him."

Stephanie hated the picture of her he was painting. She wished it wasn't so damn accurate. "I guess I never thought about it like that. But you're right. I'm going to tell him not to call anymore."

"Don't do that on my account."

Her heart sank. Did that mean there was no hope for her and Baron to reconcile? "I'm gonna do it for myself," she stated. "He's been hanging around for too long. I don't need him in my life. I should've been honest with him."

Baron shrugged. She couldn't tell if he was pretending not to care or if he really didn't give a damn.

"I wanted to ask you something about Lisa," she said.

He met her eyes.

"If you told her you didn't want to be with her, why did she get so upset when I called?"

He looked away, shaking his head. "That's a... That story's kinda depressing."

"More depressing than her wanting to get with you for years, but you kept rejecting her, forcing her to entertain other relationships that never worked out?"

He looked into her eyes and nodded. "Yeah. More depressing than that."

Stephanie was intrigued but also worried because of his somber tone. How bad could it be?

"I'll tell you after we get through eating," he said.

Stephanie thought that was probably for the best.

CHAPTER SEVENTEEN
A WOMAN'S CHOICE

Mama's baby
Daddy's maybe
Divorce court
Child support
Moving out
She gets the house
She gets the kids
You get the bills
Mortgage
Medical
Alimony
Day care
Damn, baby
Are we playing fair?

They were mostly quiet as they finished their meal. Stephanie offered him beer or wine afterwards. He declined both but accepted a bottled water. They went to the theater, and she saw the finished product for the first time.

Stephanie wasn't sure why she was so surprised by the result. She'd been in the theater plenty of times since they brought the chairs in. All Baron did today was install the screen. But for some reason the huge screen changed everything about the room as it brought her vision together.

Stephanie thought her home theater could rival anything she'd seen in person or in magazines. It was so large you'd feel like you were actually at the movies, yet cozy enough to remind you that this was really someone's home.

"I love it!" she told Baron. "This is exactly what I hoped for. I can't believe y'all got it done so quickly."

"Is the projector plugged in?" he asked, looking to where she had it mounted in the back of the room.

"I was playing with it yesterday," she said. "I got it programmed, but I'll probably have to adjust the picture for the screen."

"Where's the remote?" he asked. "Let me check it out."

She didn't need him to do that for her, but it felt good to have a man there who wanted to help with technical things. Baron turned the projector on and spent the next few minutes adjusting the placement, picture size and quality, until the visuals looked perfect on her new screen. He used the remote to open Netflix and started a random movie. Everything was great except the sound.

"I forgot to ask about your speakers," he said. "You said they're wireless?"

"I have them," she confirmed. "They're still in the box. I'll get to them this weekend."

"Don't you want them mounted?" he asked. "You don't want me to do that before I leave? It will only take a few minutes."

"No rush," she said. "I don't need it done today. Come here."

She took his hand and led him to the row of seats on the upper level. She sat down, and he took the spot next to her. Thanks to the raised floor, the view from there was not impeded by the chairs in front of them. There were no bad seats in Stephanie's movie tavern.

Baron leaned back and told her, "These chairs feel good. It would be nice to watch the Super Bowl here."

"You can," Stephanie said right away. "Consider this your formal invite to next year's Super Bowl party."

He smiled, but considering it was mid June and the Super Bowl wasn't until February, Baron wasn't ready to confirm those plans.

He told her, "We'll see."

Stephanie was hoping he'd loosen up more, but she knew she couldn't force it. They stared ahead at the projector screen. She had forgotten what movie he put on. It didn't matter, because she wasn't interested in it. She was glad the volume on the projector was mostly muted.

"You said you had a depressing story," she reminded him.

"I do," he said with a nod. "For the record, I don't like to talk about this. Lisa's the only woman I've ever told, outside of my family."

Stephanie felt anxious because he was willing to share something so private. But the look in his eyes took away any happiness she might have felt. As she watched him, her expression became as somber as his.

"Lisa came around at a low point in my life," he said. "It was right after Yvette. I told her I wasn't looking for a woman when we first met. She said that was cool. We could just hang out sometimes. Obviously that didn't work out too good."

Yvette? Stephanie had a few follow-up questions, but she remained quiet and let him tell the story at his pace.

"Yvette was the one who ruined me," Baron said with a grimace. "And that's something I hate to say. When I used to hear guys talk about how they were no good after *so-in-so* left them, I thought those dudes were soft. How you gon' let a woman determine how you feel for the rest of your life?

"But then it happened to me, and now, I don't judge those guys anymore. When someone tells me they gave up on women after their ex, I tell them, 'I feel you.' Because I know how that can happen."

Stephanie felt her eyes widening as she listened to him. This didn't sound like the Baron she knew. He always seemed like he was in complete control.

"I was with Yvette for a year and a half," he explained. "I had just got out of jail and was trying to get back on my feet. We were together when I started working for Texas Builders. With the steady income, I made enough to move out of my mama's house and get my own apartment.

"I bought a truck for cash. Nothing fancy. Yvette needed a ride too, so I paid down on a car for her. Made the payments too. I always put her ahead of me. She had two kids. I treated 'em like they were mine."

Stephanie nodded. Again she kept her questions and comments to herself.

"When I heard she was cheating," Baron said, "I didn't believe it. After all I'd done for her – and was still doing – it didn't make sense. What could she possibly want that I wouldn't jump through a ring of fire to get for her? But then I found out it was her baby-daddy she was hooking up with, and it made sense. He'd been trying his hardest to get her back. She had to see him all the time, 'cause of the kids. I always thought she was still carrying a torch for him. But she told me she would never go back; he wasn't a good father or provider.

"That shit she did, it hurt me, all the way to the core. Even still, I would've been able to move on. In this life, you gotta take your bumps and keep it moving, you know? A bitch is gon' be a bitch."

When Stephanie's lips parted, he said, "I'm sorry. I don't mean nothing disrespectful by that. I don't use that word to refer to all women. But just like some men are dogs; some women are too. By definition, that makes them a *bitch*. That's just, it is what it is."

Stephanie didn't say anything.

"What messed me up was, um..." He coughed. Stephanie was shocked to see his eyes glaze over. "I heard she was pregnant," he said. "She didn't try to find out if it was mine or her ex's before she went and got an abortion."

He became quiet. The *A*-word hung in the air like the stench of death. A dark chill spread over Stephanie's whole body. Baron stared straight ahead at the silent movie neither of them was watching. He turned and looked at her.

"You know what, I, um, I think I will take that beer."

Stephanie didn't want to leave him, but a part of her felt relieved when she left her seat and stepped out of the room. In the hallway she took deep breaths, her eyes wide and dilated.

An *abortion*? She knew that wasn't the worst thing in the world to do. A friend of hers had the procedure a few years back. But Stephanie had never met a man who was so broken up about it. When her friend made the decision, her boyfriend at the time was all for it. He even took off work that day, so he could give her a ride.

When she returned with the beer, Baron had gathered his composure. His eyes didn't look glassy anymore. Stephanie felt guilty for the thoughts she had a moment ago when she left the room. If he was experiencing emotional turmoil, she should've been there for him. Then again, Baron was the one who sent her out of the room. Maybe he did that on purpose, so he could have a moment to himself.

She handed him the beer and then realized she didn't pop the top.

"Oops. Sorry." She reached to retrieve it.

"That's alright. I got it." He was about to twist the top off by hand, but she took the beer away.

"I wanna try this," she said as she lifted the hidden console between their seats. The top portion had a bottle opener that worked as advertised. "Here you go," she said, returning the beer.

Baron grinned and said, "Thanks," but his smile faded just as quickly. He took a long drink and asked her, "Did you know a man has no rights, when it comes to something like that? Even if the father wants the child, is fully capable of caring for it and is willing to go to court to fight for it, there's nothing he can do. It's a woman's choice. She gets to decide."

Stephanie shook her head. She didn't know that, but she understood why it should be the case. No one should make a woman carry a baby for nine months, if she's adamantly opposed to having it. Sometimes women experienced complications during delivery, up to and including death. No law should force them to endure that.

But at the same time, she understood Baron's dilemma. She could imagine how horrible it must feel to *truly* want to be a father, only to be told that the mother is going to terminate the pregnancy. From the looks of it, he still hadn't gotten over it.

"This all happened in one week," he said. "Sunday I found out she was cheating with her baby-daddy. Tuesday one of her friends told me she was pregnant. I called Yvette, and she denied it. Friday I heard she had an abortion. When I called her that time, she said it was true. She told me, 'You don't even know if it was yours or not.'"

He became quiet for what felt like a long time. Stephanie knew his mind was stuck on that painful memory. Her heart bled for him.

"She was right," he said. "I guess I should be cool with it, you know, since I don't know if it was mine. But... It's hard for me to see it that way." He sighed. "That girl did me so wrong. Y'all complain about men; being deadbeat dads and whatnot. But sometimes y'all women are just as bad. I think some of y'all treat us *worse,* 'cause you got all the control. You decide if we get to be a father, when we get to be a father. And then you decide if we get to raise our child as a family, or if we only get them every other weekend. It's a damn shame, the way y'all do us."

His comments reminded her of something he'd said during their first date. Stephanie had asked why he didn't have any children, and the conversation took a dark turn.

Why should a man have a child in this day and age? Just to give a woman one more thing to have power over?

She noticed he seemed bitter at the time, but she never imagined he'd been through this much.

"As far as Lisa," he said, "I met her a few months after the dust settled with Yvette. I wasn't ready for a relationship. I didn't trust women. I told her about my ex, and Lisa said she understood. Turned out she was just biding her time, waiting for the day when I got over Yvette, so her and I could be together.

"Like I told you, we tried to give it a go a couple of times. But me and Lisa just don't click like that. She might think so, but I never did. And then you came along, and... I don't know. I guess that messed with her head. She was waiting on me for two years, and I turned around and told her I was with you. She wanted to know why I passed her up."

Knowing she was the one who finally broke down his walls filled Stephanie with warm, wonderful emotions. She would've told him how good he made her feel, if the conversation wasn't so solemn. She reached and took hold of his hand. She thought he'd pull away, but he didn't.

"I'm sorry," she said. "If I had known any of that, I never would've reacted the way I did."

He smiled at that and finished the last of his beer. "How were you supposed to know? We only went on one date. This whole thing feels like it was rushed, from day one."

Stephanie couldn't hide her guilt. "That's my fault. I didn't mean to rush you. It's just that, when I see something I want, I gotta go for it. I did wait for you, for as long as I could. You know I wanted to ask you out years ago."

His grip around her hand tightened. He stroked her fingers gently with his thumb.

She said, "You know, I've never met a man like you. Not only did you get out of jail and turn your life around–"

"*Prison*," he said, correcting her. "Jail's for short time. I did five years."

She nodded. "That's a long time. But you didn't let it keep you down. And how you took care of that girl and her kids... And you were ready to step up when she got pregnant. I – I wanna say that's *admirable* – but that doesn't seem like a strong enough word to describe you."

"I don't think it's admirable," he replied. "If a man wants to be with a woman who got kids, he has to be willing to put himself in the role of *father*. Even if the real father is still around, the kids will look up to you. They'll probably see you more than him, if y'all start living together. As far as me wanting to raise my own child, or at least a child I thought was mine, I definitely don't deserve praise for that. That's just the right thing to do."

"Admirable and humble," she said smiling. "You're a real man, Baron. I can't believe I treated you the way I did."

"Shit, I can't believe it either," he said with a chuckle.

"Since we're being honest," she said, "there's something else I have to tell you."

Baron's smile disappeared. He sighed and allowed her to pull her hand way.

"It's not bad," she said. "Not *that* bad."

His expression told her he would be the judge of that.

"You remember when I told you I had trouble with the contractor who was building my theater?" she asked.

Baron's eyes narrowed as he nodded.

"Okay, that wasn't true," she said. "But, come on. You had to know *something* was up. My family works in construction. Why would I bring in an outside contractor to do anything to my house?"

Baron reached to scratch the top of his head. "You said you got into an argument with Devin, or something like that."

"That wasn't true," she said. "I'm sorry I lied to you."

Baron shook his head in confusion. "Well, what the hell happened to those rooms?"

"I hired some guys to do that," she revealed. "I told them I was going to combine the rooms, and I needed them to pull up the carpet and start tearing down the wall. After two days I told them I ran out of money and couldn't afford them anymore. I said I'd call them when I had the money to finish."

Baron's mouth hung open as he listened to her.

"I knew you wouldn't come over and start the job from scratch," Stephanie explained. "The only reason you agreed to help me is because half my house was tore up, and I told you I didn't have anyone else to turn to."

He continued to stare at her for a few seconds before commenting. "Wow."

"Do you forgive me?" she pleaded, with her words and her eyes.

"You went through all of that, just to get me to come to your house?"

"Well, technically yes. But the plan to build this theater was real. I just wanted you to do it. You did an outstanding job, by the way. I'm gonna recommend you to all my friends."

He couldn't help but laugh at that. "I don't even know what to say about you."

"Tell me you forgive me."

She moved the console dividing their seats to the up position, so she could scoot closer to him. She laid her head against his chest and looked up at him with the best hound dog eyes she could muster. Baron shook his head, but he reached and wrapped his arm around her. Stephanie was afraid she'd never feel his embrace again. Her heart shuddered with relief.

"I forgive you," he said. "It's... As crazy as your plan was, I can't say I'm not flattered."

Stephanie's smile broadened. "My mama said if you really want something, you have to go after it, with your whole heart. You gotta do whatever is in your power to make your dreams come true. If not, you might as well take a seat while someone else takes over the world."

"Your mama said that?"

"Not in those exact words. I tweaked it a little. Made it mine."

He thought for a second. "With that philosophy, I know you'll be successful when you take over the company. Not sure if you should've applied it to me, though."

"It's not like you made it easy for me."

She placed a hand on his stomach and snuggled closer. He tried to sit up.

"Hey, watch out, now. I been sweating all day. You gotta get off me."

She held him tighter. "Maybe I like the way you stink."

"You're saying I *do* stink?"

With that, he pushed off the chair. Stephanie couldn't stop him from rising to his feet. She stood as well. She looked up at him, thinking about the moment she approached him at her graduation party. Despite all that had transpired since then, she had no regrets.

"I wanna get to know you better," she said. She wrapped her arms around his waist. His midsection felt strong and sturdy.

He folded his arms around her. The side of her face returned to the comfortable spot on his chest. Her eyes slipped closed as she smiled. Her (maybe) man wasn't funky at all.

He said, "I damn sure wanna get to know you better too. Gotta find out what I'm getting myself into."

CHAPTER EIGHTEEN
THE FINAL CHAPTER
GROUNDBREAKING

The meshing of souls is no easy task
Personalities conflict
We've all got a past
We've all got to ask if it's worth it to know
What's beneath the surface
The beauty
The glow
If I bare my soul
Could this be the spark
Of something beautiful?
Or is this the start of dark, lonely days
When you break my heart?
If you bare your soul
Your vulnerabilities and fears
Will I be the next man to bring you to tears?
Will I take what I want
Like a thief in the night?
Are we even compatible?
Deciding what's right and what's wrong
Seems impossible
A great mystery
Are you willing to try?
Are we meant to be?
The meshing of souls is not always perfect
But if you love me
And I love you
I know that it's worth it

On Tuesday, September 6th, Baron completed his work on Brick's Mitsubishi dealership. By noon that day, there were no construction vehicles left on the premises. The parking lot was clean, the windows were all spotless. Every floor surface was waxed and sparkling. Luxury cars began to converge on the sprawling structure, as the owners and investors met for the final walkthrough.

Brick, sporting a black suit and black Stetson, led the group of rich, smiling faces through the dealership. In the six months it took to erect the main building, service center and adjacent structures, he was only there a few hours a week. But he knew the place like the back of his hand.

Baron walked alongside him, taking mental notes on his professionalism. The Brick House CEO was knowledgeable and charismatic. He showed off the offices and showroom floor, pointing out minor and key details that made the dealership top of the line, head and shoulders above most of their competitors.

"People are going to love coming here," he told the group of twenty as they concluded the tour. "They'll love the cars. They'll enjoy relaxing in the lounge with their Wi-Fi and cappuccinos. They'll come here for service on their vehicles, even after their warranties expire. Because on top of everything else, you have a full-service restaurant. This place is gonna make a lot of money. I see nothing but money rolling through these doors."

The crowd applauded him. Brick took a moment to bask in their admiration before he told them, "The man you really need to be grateful for is this gentleman right here."

He reached and put an arm around Baron's shoulder.

"His name is Baron Grant," Brick said. "He's the lead foreman who oversaw every aspect of construction. Baron was here every day, from back when this was just a big, empty field. As the contractor, I get to take credit for the hard work he put in. But without him, we wouldn't have this beautiful dealership. He's the one who deserves your praise."

Brick turned, smiling. He reached to shake Baron's hand as the group continued to applaud. Baron grinned, a bit sheepishly, not accustomed to so much attention.

"I'm proud of you, son," Brick said as he shook his hand.

Baron nodded appreciatively. "Thank you, sir. It's been a pleasure working with you."

● ● ● ● ● ●

A few days later, on Friday, September 9th, Baron continued to experience growth in his professional career. He showed up at Texas Builders' main office at noon to pick up Stephanie, who would accompany him to the groundbreaking ceremony for a new medical tower at Jackson Memorial.

The Ed and Margaret Genders Cardiovascular Center would replace the hospital's current heart tower with an eight story architectural wonder. The new building will house over 80 beds, an underground parking garage, and a state of the art cath lab with interventional radiology on the same floor. Baron was tapped to lead construction on Texas Builders' newest contract. Stephanie would represent the company as the head contractor.

They were both thrilled. But for Stephanie, the significance of this assignment was more poignant. This would be her first time overseeing a project from start to finish. She was grateful that her mother trusted her with such an important contract, and she was eager to prove herself, not just to Korah, but to everyone in the company whose livelihoods would one day rest on her shoulders.

She knew they were all watching. She would show them that she could be as cost-effective as her mother and as thorough as her father.

Baron was greeted with adulations when he entered the office that afternoon. He wore a dark gray suit with a white shirt and red tie. His dark skin looked radiant under the florescent lights in the lobby. Malcolm smiled brightly as he welcomed him.

"Looking sharp!" he exclaimed. "Ready for your big day?"

"Ready as I'll ever be," Baron said. He reached to adjust his tie. "Don't think I'll ever get used to wearing suits, though."

"I don't know about that," Malcolm said. "The way your career is taking off, you might end up wearing one every day."

Baron grinned at that.

"*Stephanie*," Malcolm called into the hallway. "Your ride is here."

The Texas Builders' heiress emerged from her office wearing a skirt suit that (not coincidentally) matched Baron's. The cinched waist accentuated her curvy figure. She opted for flats rather than heels.

"Ooh, baby! You look *good!*" she said as she approached Baron.

She immediately reached to straighten his tie. Baron stood proudly, looking down at her. Stephanie wore her hair down with loose curls. Her highlights were faint, as was her makeup. She looked very professional and capable.

"You looking good too," Baron told her.

She wrapped her arms around him when she was done with the tie. "Baby, I'm so proud of you."

He continued to smile as Korah, Priscilla and Yolanda emerged from their offices. Yolanda had her second child two months ago and had recently returned to work, now a lot slimmer and quicker on her feet. She and Devin named the new child Cierra, after Yolanda's mother.

"Oh, look at you two!" Korah gushed. Her eyes sparkled as she watched Stephanie and Baron. "You're gonna do us proud! Way to represent!"

"Those suits are *nice!*" Priscilla said as the crowd converged on them. "Did you plan that?"

Stephanie nodded. "Yeah." She buttoned her sports coat and stood stately next to her man.

"That's how you do it," Yolanda said, smiling broadly. "Everyone is gonna stop and take notice of you two. We got the best-looking team in construction!"

Stephanie couldn't agree more. She slipped an arm around Baron's waist.

"Any last minute advice?" she asked her mother.

"Nothing you don't already know," Korah said. "Just smile and be yourself; confident, radiant."

"Don't shovel like a girl," Malcolm suggested, referring to the ceremonial shoveling Stephanie, Baron and members of the hospital's board of directors would perform during the ceremony.

Everyone laughed as they came together to hug and congratulate their representatives. Korah held Stephanie's hands, her heart filled with pride.

"This is it, baby; your time to shine."

"Thanks, Mama, for everything."

"Knock 'em dead," Korah said. She pulled her in for a big hug. "Make Mama proud."

• • • • • •

Fifteen minutes later Baron exited the freeway near the hospital district, with Stephanie in the passenger seat of his truck. In the past five months, she'd occupied the seat many times, when Baron picked her up for outings to the movies or out to eat and even to the marina a few times, where his boat was docked. Stephanie never considered herself an outdoorsman, but she was excited to explore new interests as she and Baron deepened their relationship and celebrated their love.

Since they'd been dating, she was happy to say she'd found a comforter and friend in Baron. More than just a handsome face and hot body, he was a complex individual who had been tested and pushed to the limit many times. He always emerged stronger and wiser. He was fiercely loyal to his family – even the ones who squabbled over his grandmother's house and didn't support him while he was in prison.

When Baron considered someone a friend, he was always there for them, for better or worse. This could sometimes lead to problems, as it did with Lisa. But Stephanie wouldn't change a thing about her boyfriend. Baron was a passionate lover, attentive and patient.

On her side, Stephanie was doing her best to subdue her spoiled tendencies, in general, and especially around Baron. He was four years older, and he deserved a mature woman by his side. Change wasn't as easy as flipping a light switch, but Stephanie already cleared the first hurdle when she separated him from the *boys* she was used to dating.

At the hospital, the Texas Builders' duo met with the president, the architect and the mayor of Overbrook Meadows, Kim Kearney. They also spoke with trustees and donors, including Ed and Margaret Genders, the project's major contributors. The elderly couple was prominent in the community, known for their philanthropic efforts and a family dynasty that rose to power after the Great Depression.

As the contractor, Stephanie had already provided the site with a tent, podium, hardhats, shovels and umbrellas. Her crew brought tables, chairs and trash bins, while the hospital offered catering.

The mood was festive as the guests dined on fajitas and lemonade. The president of the hospital opened the ceremony with a huge thank you to the Genders family. As he spoke about their many accomplishments, Stephanie made a decision to do more in their community. She wanted the Stewart name to be as noteworthy as the Genders one day.

After a few short speeches, Texas Builders was invited to the podium. Cameras clicked as Stephanie and Baron stood together, looking dapper beneath the warm, September sunshine. The temperature was a perfect 89 degrees. The crowd applauded as Baron gestured for Stephanie to speak for them. He stood proudly when she walked up to the mic.

"Good afternoon! It's a beautiful day in Overbrook Meadows and a great day in Texas!" She had to pause for more applause. Her bright smile accentuated her beautiful, chocolate features.

"Texas Builders is excited that you've chosen us – *entrusted* us – with such an extraordinary project. As I sat listening to the president and other speakers today, I became more and more proud to take part in this *lifesaving* and *life-changing* cardiac tower.

"This hospital has been a fixture in our community for almost a hundred years," she said. "I was born here, as were many of my friends. The fact that Jackson Memorial continues to expand and *evolve* is a testament to the appreciation this community continues to have in one of our most important landmarks."

Stephanie paused again as the crowd cheered. She looked back and smiled when she saw Baron was clapping too.

"I've heard a lot today about integrity and compassion," she continued. "Those are qualities this hospital is known for, and I'd like you to know Texas Builders will continue in that spirit as we build this tower. Baron Grant is the best foreman in the business," she said, reaching back for him.

He stepped forward, and they stood side by side.

"We look forward to working with you to construct a quality heart center that will last another hundred, two hundred, even three hundred years!" Stephanie shouted.

The crowd rose to their feet and praised the powerful duo.

● ● ● ● ● ●

"Ooh, baby, you were awesome!"

Stephanie leaned over and placed a hand on Baron's chest as he drove to his home. Her smile was ear to ear. He looked over at her and grinned.

"I didn't do nothing. It was all you."

"No, it was *us*, baby," she insisted. "The way you were standing there, looking all *strong* and debonair." She ran her hand from his chest to his stomach. His coat was open. She could feel the hard muscles in his stomach beneath the collar shirt. "I'm so excited," she said. "Aren't you?"

Baron tried to keep his eyes on the road as her hand continued to move southward.

"You know I am," he said. "This is a big job for the company. I think you blew them away, with your speech. And you're wearing the hell out of that suit!"

"Really?" Her hand dropped between his legs. She felt his manhood alongside his thigh. "You like it?"

Baron began to respond to her touch immediately. "Like, like what?" he asked.

"My suit," she said giggling. She began to rub his hardening member until it was hot and rigid.

"Yeah, baby," he said. "That suit is banging. But to be honest, I've been dying to see you take it off."

"That's what I was thinking."

He exited the freeway and stopped at a light on Berry. Stephanie took that moment to turn further in her seat. She scooted over until she was close enough to kiss the corner of his mouth. He turned and met her lips. Her tongue slipped inside his mouth as she continued to fondle him through his pants.

"I like a man who's in charge of things," she muttered as he sucked her bottom lip. "It's so freaking *hot*."

Baron felt the same way about her. He looked up and saw that their light had changed.

"If you don't sit back, we gon' wreck," he warned her.

Stephanie moved back to her seat, but her hand remained glued to his erection. Only a few minutes more, and they would make it to Baron's house.

She checked the clock on his stereo. It was three-thirty. After the groundbreaking ceremony, they had a meeting with the hospital's board of directors and another with the architect. Baron waited until their crew arrived to retrieve their tables and chairs before he and Stephanie left the hospital.

Work on the new site would start on Monday morning, so he and Stephanie were free from work for the rest of the day. Tonight they were hosting a party at Stephanie's house to celebrate the job, but that wasn't until 7 pm. That left three hours for her and Baron to do a little celebrating of their own.

He pulled into his garage and resumed kissing her as the door rattled closed.

"Why you getting me all excited while I'm driving?" he breathed.

He unfastened his seat belt so he could turn towards her. His left hand slipped under her skirt without so much as a *How do you do?* If his plan was to get her back as a form of punishment, he was barking up the wrong tree. Stephanie spread her legs for him and reached past his arm, so she could resume stroking him into a frenzied fit of passion.

His tongue explored her mouth as his fingers rubbed her labia through her panties. It didn't take long before he felt her dampness begin to soak through.

"*Ummm,*" he muttered.

He deftly slipped his fingers beneath her underwear and stroked her slick lips. Stephanie moaned her approval. Her chest heaved as she sank lower in the seat and thrust her body into his hand. She was rewarded when his longest finger disappeared between her folds.

"*Yeah, baby,*" she squealed as a second finger quickly joined the first.

Baron's mouth moved away from hers. He traced steamy licks and sucks from her cheek to her neck. His fingers thrashed in and out of her with a rhythm that matched the grinding of her hips. Stephanie's mouth hung open, her eyes half closed. She loved when he was this raw and uninhibited.

Her heart began to race to the point that she felt lightheaded. Her howls of pleasure filled the car. Her explosion came hard and fast, trapping her in a whirlwind of satisfaction and desire. Her feet pushed off the floorboard, pushing her hips higher. Baron continued to stroke her clitoris, until her cream glistened on his fingers.

Stephanie didn't realize how hard she was gripping his manhood until her orgasm began to subside, and she gradually regained feeling in her extremities.

"*Damn*," he said, kissing her neck, still two fingers deep inside her. "Where'd that come from?"

Stephanie's eyes fluttered open. A thin coat of sweat glistened on her chest. "I don't know, baby."

"You better hurry up and get out of that suit," he suggested. "Before you ruin it."

Stephanie thought that was an excellent idea – not that she cared about sending the suit to the cleaners.

Inside the house, they made it to the main hallway before she turned suddenly. Baron was right behind her, walking stiffly because of his stiffy. Stephanie grinned as she kicked off her pumps on the plush carpet. She pulled her suit jacket off and let it fall to the floor.

"Take it off," she told him, as she dropped to her knees.

Baron watched her, his eyes dark and hungry. "Take what off."

"Everything."

She reached for his waistband and pulled him forward. Her hands moved to unbuckle his belt. By the time Baron got his coat off, she was sliding his slacks and boxers down his legs. His erection popped up to greet her. She gripped him with one hand and squeezed, bringing his pre-cum forward, until she saw it glistening at the tip. She looked up at him with sultry eyes.

"When I visit you on the site..." She leaned forward and licked the offering from the tip of his erection. "Will you take me to your trailer and make me suck your dick?"

She took him into her mouth before he could respond. She knew Baron would never go for that. He was too serious about his work. But Stephanie hoped she could change his mind, with the proper motivation. She applied more suction as her head moved back and forth; coating his dick with saliva. She continued to watch him, knowing Baron loved to watch his dark piece slide in and out of her mouth.

He wanted to respond to her question, but "*Damn,*" was all he could manage.

He held the front of his shirt up with one hand and reached for the back of her head with the other. Stephanie sucked with no hands. She let him guide the action with his hand and hips. With each pump, she took him in as deeply as she could.

As much as Baron cherished the moments she pleased him like this, his one grievance was that he could never last very long, '*Not with your eyes and mouth working together to break me down,*' he had joked.

Stephanie's jaws were nowhere near tired when he pulled out slowly. She continued to stimulate him with her tongue until the last moment.

"*Uh uhn,*" he said, shaking his head.

She grinned. She wasn't opposed to him finishing in her mouth. But whenever he didn't, she knew it was because he wanted to show his appreciation.

"Turn around," he said, hurrying to undo the buttons on his shirt.

Stephanie swiveled on her knees, until she was facing the opposite direction. Her skirt was knee-length. She didn't think – *okay...*

Baron dropped to his knees behind her and pulled her skirt all the way up her lower back. A second later he pulled her panties down, pausing briefly for her to raise each knee, so he could fully remove them.

Stephanie felt her juices on her panties as they moved down her legs, so she knew what Baron was talking about when he said, "Shit, baby. You *dripping.*"

His deep voice brought her clitoris back to life. Her walls gripped him lovingly when he pushed in smoothly from behind. When he was halfway inside, he grabbed her hips and pulled her back into him.

"*Ooh, Baron...*" She lowered her head. Her fingers gripped the thick carpet.

Baron nearly lost it when he looked down and saw the cream coating his dick. He pulled all the way out and marveled at the sight. Stephanie looked back at him. When they made eye contact, he shuddered, and then his gaze returned to her sex.

"Sometimes you just gotta look at it," he muttered.

Stephanie continued to watch as he submerged again. She bit down on her bottom lip. A pulse of ecstasy thundered down her chest, between her legs and continued all the way to her toes.

A few months ago Baron was as eager as she was, when she suggested they get checkups, so they could forgo condoms when they made love and rely on her birth control. It was a huge step in their monogamous relationship. It increased the pleasure they both felt when Baron plunged into her flower. Stephanie loved the feel of his hard, hot skin making direct contact with hers.

He stroked slowly at first. But it didn't take long before his hunger began to override his awe. When he shifted the pound game into second gear, Stephanie's face sank lower into the carpet. She turned her head to the side and cried out with each thrust. The sensations he provided were electrifying.

Maddening.

In the back of her mind, she was still thinking, plotting on how she could convince Baron to accept a blowjob on their new work site. From the sounds of his body smacking her ass with each hard stroke, she was starting to believe it wouldn't take too much convincing at all.

EPILOGUE

Two months later the trees in Overbrook Meadows grudgingly gave up their leaves as the temperature dipped and summertime surrendered to fall.

Korah loved this time of year. The visual aspects of near-barren trees; the oranges and browns mingling with the occasional evergreens had always appealed to her. Even better was the feel-good atmosphere on her worksites. The blistering summer heat was gone, and it wasn't cold enough for her workers to need gloves or stocking caps. Devin agreed that this was the season construction workers lived for.

On Monday, November 2nd, Korah was happy to see everyone in attendance at her weekly meeting. She stood at the front of the room, wearing slacks with a new blouse she purchased months ago but never wore. When she tried it on that morning, she wasn't a fan of the scoop neckline. But Brick said he loved it, and that was all that mattered. He peppered her neck and collarbone with kisses before he took off for work. Korah could still feel his warm breath and sweet lips on her now. She couldn't wipe the smile off her face.

But Brick's everlasting love wasn't the only thing she was excited about that morning. She had several announcements during the meeting. After discussing their current projects (all of them were going splendidly), she held up a framed picture of Beatrice Olsen, their new Human Resources manager.

"Our employee for the month of October is Aunt Bea!" she proclaimed.

Across the room Beatrice looked shocked and then embarrassed that she'd been chosen. The middle-aged woman was not old enough to be an *Aunt Bea*, in Korah's opinion. But Bea had a slew of nieces and nephews who all called her that. She insisted on using the nickname at work. Korah was happy to oblige, especially given Beatrice's reserved nature. She would do whatever it took to make her feel more comfortable and part of the family.

"Don't look so surprised," Korah told her. "Bea started our Human Resources department from scratch," she said to the group. "She and Stephanie created the database, and Bea got all of our employees entered in the system. There's over 300 of us now, so that was no easy task."

Several people expressed surprise over that number.

"Isn't that something," Korah remarked. "We hit the 300 mark a few weeks ago. Bea backed all of their information up with paper files. She's responsible for keeping up with their contact information, vacations, certifications and insurance, and their 401K.

"I know the construction teams don't see much of her," she said to Devin, Baron, Monte and Larry; her top foremen. "But everyone in the office can testify to her diligence and work ethics. Bea is one of the most detail-oriented people I know. That's a much-needed trait in this office.

"Bea," Korah said, looking her way, "we're all very proud of you. You're an asset to this company. I'm delighted to show a small token of our appreciation by naming you employee of the month! Your picture will hang in the lobby for the rest of November."

The crowd cheered for Bea as the woman blushed.

"Thank you, Mrs. Avery," she replied softly.

"This award comes with a gift card," Korah continued, "so your lunch is on me today. Make sure you stop by Malcolm's desk to pick one up. I know we have Red Lobster. You can use that one at Olive Garden too. What other cards do you have?" she asked Malcolm.

"Subway, Chili's and Starbucks," he said. "There may be a couple of others."

"Whatever you like," Korah said to Aunt Bea. "We're grateful to have you on the team."

"Thank you, Mrs. Avery," the woman said again. "This is a great place to work. Y'all treat me really good."

"My last announcement," Korah said, "is a secret I've been keeping from you for months. I signed off on the last of the paperwork on Friday, and I've officially leased a building."

Everyone looked around curiously. Even Stephanie and Devin were in the dark this time.

"As you all know," Korah continued, "now that Stephanie has graduated, I've begun to take a few steps back, *baby steps*, so she can make her transition to CEO of this company."

Stephanie sat a few feet away smiling brightly.

"I still don't have an official date for when I'll step down completely," Korah said, "but we're already giving Stephanie more responsibilities; putting her in charge of things I'd normally handle myself. Her first job as head contractor is going very well. I've received nothing but positive feedback. The folks at the hospital love her."

Stephanie continued to beam as her mother doted on her.

"But back to the surprise," Korah said. "In the future, within the next few months, I'll be even more scarce around the office. I've started a new business that will occupy a lot of my time."

The group responded with more wide-eyed surprise.

"My mind's always working," Korah said, "thinking of ways to improve Texas Builders. On the construction side, there are a few services we're lacking; things we always have to outsource. Next to glass and plumbing, the thing that keeps sticking out when I go over our invoices is *awnings*. We spend an enormous amount of money for awnings and overhead supports. The company I've started is called *Texas Awnings*. Our ultimate goal is to provide all of the awnings needed for Texas Builders' projects, whether they be metal or fabric.

"I'm going to hire welders, so we can build them in our own factory. It'll take a while to get everything rolling. But within six months I want Texas Awnings to provide half of the awnings we need for our projects. Within the next two years, I want that number to be one hundred percent."

The crowd cheered and talked amongst themselves about what this would mean for the company. The new revenue stream was important, but expanding the business and becoming less dependent on others was even more valuable.

"Are you running the new company all by yourself?" Stephanie asked her.

To their surprise, Korah nodded. "All of you have important tasks here at Texas Builders, and I won't be pulling any of you away. I'm starting Texas Awnings from the ground up. This is my new baby. I'm just as nervous as I am excited."

"You'll do fine, Mama!" Stephanie assured her.

"Yeah," Devin said. He shook his head in wonderment. "Just when I thought you were ready to take it easy, you turn around and start a brand new company! Dang. I know me and Stephanie are supposed to work hard to make you proud. But you're the one blowing my mind. I don't even know what to say, Mama. You're amazing!"

Korah glowed as the adulations rained down on her. She took a few moments to answer some of their questions before she concluded the meeting.

"Alright, everybody. We've been here ten minutes longer than usual, and you've all got work to do. I hope you have a wonderfully productive day. Now let's go build something!"

It took a few minutes to get them out of the conference room, because everyone wanted to stop and congratulate Korah personally. Their support alleviated some – but not all – of the anxiety she felt about her new venture.

● ● ● ● ● ●

After such a great morning, Korah wasn't upset when Malcolm entered her office thirty minutes later with bad news.

"Mrs. Stewart, we didn't get those theaters."

The announcement only left her a little deflated. "Oh really?"

"No, ma'am. I thought we were a shoo-in for that contract."

"Me too," Korah said. Individually an AMC theater wasn't a huge deal. But the contract they had bid on was for a dozen of them to be built over the next two years. They would spread from east Texas to western Louisiana.

Korah knew her husband had bid on the contract as well, so she wasn't surprised when Malcolm told her, "I guess Brick House is still your number one competitor."

She grinned. "He beat us again?"

Malcolm nodded. "Yeah, but I've been keeping track. So far this year we've won four contracts both of y'all bid on. This is only his third."

"I guess I'll take some consolation in that," Korah said. "Thank you, Malcolm."

When he left her office, she watched the phone on her desk, waiting for the inevitable. Property owners and investors usually called all of the contractors at the same time, to let them know if they won a bid or not. Korah calculated how long it would take Brick to receive the call, express his gratitude, tell everyone in the office the good news and finally return to his desk to call his wife and gloat.

It took exactly four minutes before Korah got the call. But it was her cellphone ringing, rather than the office line.

She answered with a pleasant, "Good morning."

"Hey, baby," Brick said. She could hear the elation in his voice.

"Congratulations," she told him.

"Oh, you heard already?"

"Yes."

"Sorry you didn't get it," he said. "I knew we only had one company to beat. It could've gone either way."

"Wow. How gracious in victory you are."

"Did you expect any different?"

"You're not too far removed from *I'm better than you, na-na na-na boo-boo.*"

He laughed. Korah didn't think she would ever get enough of his sexy, Texas twang. It was more prominent when he was speaking, but even his grunts, whistles and hums took her to cowboy heaven.

"You left off the best part of that rhyme," he noticed.

"The fact that you're aware of that says a lot about why you really called," she joked.

He chuckled. "I've got news that will make you feel better."

"I don't feel bad right now, darling."

"Sure you do," he said. "Brick House keeps outshining you. That's gotta be taking a toll by now."

"Funny how that memory of yours works best when it suits you," she replied. "This year I've won four out of the seven contracts we both bid on."

"At least one of those was a 7-11," he quipped. "You must be feeling mighty desperate, if you wanna include that."

"It wouldn't take much to pull up the value of those contracts, if you want to find out who's really on top."

"Now, now, dear. You've already experienced a *tremendous* setback today. I don't want you to make things worse by looking at those numbers. You might get so depressed, you won't come home to me tonight."

Korah laughed. "You are such a jackass."

"True. It's a wonder people still like me."

"You got me there," she said. "Despite your many, *many* flaws–"

"Hey, now you're just being hurtful."

She giggled. "You didn't let me finish. I was going to say despite your flaws, I can't get enough of you."

"Likewise," he said.

"Would you like for me to take you out tonight?" she asked, "to celebrate your contract?"

"I would, but I'm not sure when I'll be home."

"How about a bottle of wine?" she offered. "And I can do that thing you like for me to do..."

"Um, yeah," he said gruffly. "I would like that. I'd like it a lot."

Korah found herself blushing, even though she was alone in the office, and even if someone had heard her, they wouldn't know what she was talking about.

She told him, "Hey, I noticed on the blueprints, all of those theaters have an awning over the entrance and exits."

"Oh, you noticed that, did you?"

"Before you get too deep into your subcontracting, I think you should consider Texas Awnings..."

He hummed. "You mean that little, rinky-dink factory with no one working in it? Last I heard there wasn't even a sign on the door."

"You'd be surprised what we can put together in a few months."

"Who is this *we* you're referring to?"

"Me and my new assistant," Korah said.

"You hired someone already?"

"I will this week. It's at the top of my to-do list."

"You know I'd be honored to have your new company install the awnings on every one of those theaters," Brick said, "even if you're unproven and untested."

Korah felt her pulse rate increase, despite the second part of his comment. At the moment, Texas Awnings was nothing more than a barren, dusty factory. But they already had an important contract waiting on them.

"You told your people about it yet?" Brick asked.

"I did today," Korah confirmed. "Everyone's really excited."

"Not me," Brick complained. "I offered you the job of a lifetime, but you'd rather go out and start another company."

Korah knew Brick would've preferred if she joined the ranks his Brick House empire. There were many advantages to accepting that position. The job security was guaranteed, and it would've been nice to work alongside her husband; to continue to propel his company to the forefront of the Texas construction scene.

However, Korah had been in charge for so long, she didn't think she'd be at her best while working for someone else, even if it was her husband.

"But that's what makes you great," Brick said. "I can't think of too many people who retire after thirty years, only to start a new business from scratch. That takes some gumption."

Korah's chest warmed. She was raised in Chicago, where people didn't go around using that word. "You think I got *gumption*?"

"I think you're the most remarkable woman I've ever met," he said honestly. "I know you've got a lot on your plate, so I'll let you get back to work."

"Okay, baby. I love you. Congrats again on the theaters. You deserve it."

"Thanks, baby. I love you too. See you when I get home."

Korah wished the workday was already over, so she could get lost in his hazel eyes and strong embrace. Just the thought of it singed her flesh. "Alright. I can't wait."

KEITH THOMAS WALKER

Thanks for reading my new book! I hope you enjoyed the conclusion of the Brick House series. Don't forget to post a review, if you don't mind. Please continue reading *Hotline Fling*...

HOTLINE FLING

KEITH THOMAS WALKER

KEITHWALKERBOOKS, INC
This is a UMS production

KEITHWALKERBOOKS

Publishing Company
KeithWalkerBooks, Inc.
P.O. Box 331585
Fort Worth, TX 76163

For information write
KeithWalkerBooks, Inc.
P.O. Box 331585
Fort Worth, TX 76163

Manufactured in the United States of America

Second Edition

Visit us at www.keithwalkerbooks.com

This book is for Storm

CHAPTER ONE
NO LEGS

"Good evening, Ma'am. How are you today?"

"*Hellooo*?"

The voice on the other end of the line sounded elderly, hard of hearing and possibly confused. That was generally a good combination, as far as these calls went. But Sonya wasn't feeling it today. She sighed silently before continuing with her script.

"Good evening," she repeated, speaking louder and slower than before. "My name is Sonya Skiles. I'm calling from the Disabled Veterans' Foundation. How are you doing today, Mrs. Colyer?"

"Oh, I'm doing fine," the woman drawled. "What did you say your name was?"

"I'm Sonya. Sonya Skiles. I'm calling from the Disabled Veteran's Foundation."

"Oh, yes," the woman said. "My husband was disabled. We donate every year. But things have been a little hard, now that he's passed on."

"I'm sorry to hear that," Sonya said, trying not to let the donor's sad story tug at her heartstrings. Everyone had a sad story these days. "I'm actually calling because you and your husband have been very generous donors over the years, and your support is always appreciated. This year *even more* soldiers are returning from foreign wars with *many* disabilities, ranging from post traumatic stress disorder to blindness and amputations. There's an even greater–"

"Henry was an amputee," the caller informed her. "He lost both his legs in Vietnam."

"I'm... sorry to hear that."

"They said he would get help when he got back," the woman continued. "They said the *government* would take care of us. They gave him two prosthetic legs that never fit worth a damn, and we got enough to buy this trailer. The social security and disability was good for awhile, but it's never what people think it's gonna be.

"You'd think if you give Uncle Sam both your legs they'd set you up better than this," she grumbled. "But Henry wasn't one to complain. He said as long as we go to church and do what's right, God will take care of us once we pass. I know he's up in heaven now, and he's got both his legs back, too. Yes, he does."

Geez, this was borderline torture. Sonya didn't want or need to hear any of this. She continued with her script, making sure to improvise with the new information the caller had given her.

"The goal of the Disabled Veterans' Foundation is to make sure people like your husband don't have to suffer, while they wait for the government to do the right thing. Our program is in place to fill in the gaps for the funding the government doesn't provide our nation's veterans."

"Henry applied to a few places," the caller recalled. "They were supposed to help out too. I think we got fifty dollars from one of them."

Sonya had no idea how the foundation she represented helped disabled veterans specifically, so she didn't want to speak on it.

"I only get the social security now that Henry's gone," the caller said. "His disability's gone. They gave me enough to bury him, but not much more than that. It was a beautiful funeral, though. The soldiers came and played the bugle for him. Draped a flag over his coffin and folded it up for me. Sent him off real nice. Yes, they did."

Sonya pursed her lips and looked around uncomfortably. Thankfully her workspace had a cubicle wall on either side. No one walking behind her could see her expression.

"How much did you need?" the caller asked.

Sonya was surprised by the question. Judging by the woman's bad-luck story, she was sure this solicitation would end in rejection.

"Um, we have several tiers of donations we'd like to offer you. The first tier would be $100 a month for the next twelve months. That donation would qualify you for—"

"Oh, no. I – no... There's no way I can afford that. We're on a fixed – I mean *I* am. Sorry. Henry just passed a few months ago. I'm still in the habit of saying *we* for everything..."

Sonya didn't think this call could get more depressing. She felt like she was being punked. The supervisors were known to do test-calls ever so often, to make sure the representatives were being professional and giving it their all every time. But those test calls were usually reserved for new hires. Sonya had been with APEX Teleservices for almost two years.

"We also have a package for twenty dollars a month," she offered. "With that donation, you'll get a free veterans' calendar and your choice of a pocket flashlight or a veteran's keychain."

"Would I have to send that in *every* month?" the woman asked, which was another good indication that Sonya had this donation in the bag. All she had to do was reel her in.

"It would be an automatic draft from your checking account," she replied. "I just need you to give me some of the numbers from the bottom of one of your checks. Do you have a checking account?"

"Yes, I do. But twenty dollars a month is a little steep. I hate to do this, but would it be alright if I give just *ten dollars* a month? I'm sorry. I wish I could do more..."

Not only would ten dollars a month be acceptable, but it would satisfy Sonya's quota for the afternoon. She would've been happy with a *one-time* donation of ten dollars. Anytime she was able to get a routing number from someone's checking account, her heart would kick with excitement. Her smile would be ear to ear.

But for some reason, she wasn't feeling this one. It probably had something to do with an image of a legless Henry piddling around his trailer park in a wheelchair because, for whatever reason, the government was too cheap to get the poor bastard a couple of legs that fit him properly.

"Are, are you sure you can afford that?"

The moment the words left her mouth, Sonya's face flushed with heat. Second-guessing a donor was taboo in her line of work. If this was a test-call, her manager would be none too pleased. He would probably come and pull her off the phone personally.

"I, um, well I think I can," the caller said. "I'll just have to cut back on another expense. But the bible says '*Be not weary in well-doing.*' I'm sure a blessing will come our way, if we do all we can to help your charity."

Sonya noticed that Mrs. Colyer was still speaking as if Henry was alive. That oversight was the icing on top of an already depressing tale.

"Why don't you take a look at your finances," she suggested. "Maybe it would be easier for you to make a *one-time donation.* We can take as little as five dollars."

Sonya's stomach twisted uncomfortably. She looked back to make sure none of her supervisors had crept up on her, but the coast was clear. She wiped the sweat that was starting to accumulate on her forehead. It was odd, but she felt like she was robbing a bank, rather than giving sound financial advice to an obviously needy senior citizen.

"Oh, um, well, if you're sure that's enough," the caller said.

"I'm positive," Sonya told her. "Go ahead and check your account and call us back when you decide how much you can donate."

"It's, but I, I don't have your number..."

"That's fine. I'll call you," Sonya offered. "You have a nice day, Mrs. Colyer."

She disconnected before the prospective donor had a chance to respond.

Sonya barely had a chance to blow out a pent up breath before one of her co-workers rolled his chair backwards until he made it past the cubicle wall and was within her field of view. It was Reginald Dukes, aka Mister *Employee of the Month* damned near every month. Reggie was such a consistent top performer, he'd been bypassed for numerous promotions simply because the department was better off with him on the phones. No one brought in more donations. Reggie's voice was deep and silky smooth. He was smart and witty. He was a handsome devil as well, though that didn't play a part in his customer service. But then again, maybe it did. Reggie was so fine, Sonya imagined donors could hear it over the phone.

"That was an interesting call," he commented.

Sonya would've taken offense if not for the smile on his face and the fact that Reggie had been her closest friend at the office the whole time she'd been there. Her eight hour shifts went by a lot quicker with a work buddy who was always eager to cut up with her when they got bored.

Sonya rolled her chair back and looked him in the eyes. His were dark brown and piercing. His eyebrows were thick, in contrast to his clean-shave and low-cut hairstyle. Reggie had an air about him that commanded attention and respect. But Sonya knew he was a teddy bear, especially when it came to her.

"Eavesdropping?" she asked him. "Don't you have your own calls to worry about?"

"Not at this second," he replied. Reggie always wore a tie with his button-downs, even though it wasn't required. A lot of the other guys at the company had trouble keeping their shirts tucked in most of the time. Reggie had fair skin and a smile that oozed confidence.

"Did you just tell that woman *not* to give you her account number?"

Again Sonya was struck by how anti-productive that move was. She hoped she hadn't allowed her moral compass to cost her a job.

"Her husband just died," she told him. "She can't afford to donate like that. And he was a disabled veteran himself. We never did anything to help him. No one did."

"Or maybe you got played," Reggie offered. "Maybe there never was a husband. Or maybe he was sitting there snickering the whole time."

Sonya narrowed her eyes as she considered that. She was a thin woman with peanut butter brown skin. She was usually makeup free at work, and today was no exception. Her hair was straight, pulled back in a ponytail. She never wanted to be flashy at the office, though that didn't stop her from gaining the attention of her horny coworkers. The company was a cesspool for ill-advised hookups. Even some of the married employees had gone too far with their "work" husbands and wives.

"She wasn't playing me," she told Reggie. "I got a pretty good bullshit detector."

"What about your *test-call* detector?" he wondered. "Maybe it was one of the sup's."

"I thought that too," Sonya confided. "But I know all the supervisors' voices. Plus they would've told me it was a test call before I hung up."

Reggie chuckled. His teeth were perfectly straight and white. Sonya loved it whenever his smile was directed her way.

"I don't think they had time to say anything," he commented. "You hung up on them so fast."

"I said I'd call her back."

"But you know you're not gonna. It'll be hard to get your numbers up, if your calls keep going like that."

"What are you gonna do, snitch on me? I thought you liked me." She batted her eyes.

When it came to Sonya, Reggie's nose had been wide open for over a year. He'd find some way to take the blame for her shortcomings, before he would do anything to get her in trouble.

"Why you looking at me like that?" he asked after a pause. "You know I like you. You trying to mess with my head?"

She giggled. "No. I was just kidding."

"You want me to make a few calls for you?"

Sonya's eyes lit up at the thought, but she couldn't let him do that. Reggie would have to switch places with her, because they had to remain logged in to their computers. There were security cameras all over their department. On the off chance someone was watching them at the moment, they would have to come up with a good reason for switching places.

No matter what excuse they offered, the supervisors would know what was going on. Reggie was the best in the department, and Sonya had always been a little better than mediocre. If anyone caught him behind her computer, it would be obvious that he was inflating her numbers. He'd done it twice before, but that was only because Sonya was on the verge of getting fired for her poor performance.

"I'll be alright," she told him with a smile.

"You sure?" His smile deepened.

She nodded. "I'm sure, Reggie."

"'Cause I'll do it," he insisted. "I'll carry you anywhere; past your quota, over a puddle on the sidewalk, over the threshold of our new home... You name it."

Sonya knew he was only partially kidding. She also knew that *he* knew she would never date a coworker. She only had a few hard rules when it came to work, and that was one of them.

"I'll talk to you later, Reggie," she said before tossing him a smile and rolling her chair back to her desk.

The smile caressed his face and warmed his chest. He watched her a moment longer before returning to his own computer.

CHAPTER TWO
SHUT DOWN

After a few more calls (none of which yielded a donation or a legless veteran), Sonya was distracted by a manager entering the department. It wasn't *their* manager, who hadn't been in the office for the past few days. Mr. Price was a manager elsewhere in the building. Sonya thought he might be with the FedEx division. In addition to the Disabled Veteran's Foundation, their company fielded calls for the local water department and the shipping corporation. Sonya tried to get in on the FedEx side when she initially applied for her job, but it wasn't meant to be.

"Everyone, please end your calls now," Mr. Price instructed them as he strolled into the room.

Sonya saw that he was accompanied by Smitty, one of the company's seasoned security guards. It was strange to see Smitty away from his guard station in the lobby of the building, but Sonya didn't immediately sense something was awry.

Many of the customer service reps were speaking into their headsets, so Mr. Price had to repeat himself several times as he rounded the room. "End your call," he told people individually. "Yes, hang up now. Don't worry about the donation. I don't care how close you are..."

Sonya and Reggie exchanged puzzled glances as they stood and watched the short, round man make his way through the department. Rather than follow him, Smitty stood stoically near the entrance. The room had half a dozen work stations with four employees at each one. As Sonya watched the manager, the other two people at her station stood and eyed her and Reggie with confused expressions.

"Did he tell us to get off the phone?" the girl on her left asked. Her name was April.

"Yeah," Sonya said. "I think so."

"What happened?" April wondered. "What's up?"

Sonya shrugged. It was 4:15 on a pleasant Friday afternoon. She was only two hours into her shift. She appreciated the break, but the way Smitty stood with a blank expression gave her bad vibes. Did someone get fired? She'd seen the security guard escort terminated employees out of the building from time to time.

"Maybe they heard about your call," Reggie joked.

"Mr. Price wouldn't shut down the whole department for that," Sonya replied.

"I don't know. It was pretty bad."

"Boy, shut up."

"Please, everyone, put down your headsets and make your way to the front of the room," Mr. Price said as he stepped in that direction. He frowned and spoke sternly to one of their co-workers, who was still trying to secure a donation. "End that call. *Now.*"

Stephanie's eyes bugged as she told the caller, "I'm sorry, Ma'am. I have to, I'll call you back." She yanked her headset off like it was on fire. "I'm sorry. What'd I do?" she asked Mr. Price.

"Everyone, please come to the front of the room," the manager said, ignoring her.

He waited patiently as the employees began to trickle forward. There were around twenty of them there that day. They all questioned each other silently. No one had any idea what was going on. It was clear that some of them didn't like being barked at by someone who was not their boss. But a manager is a manager. Mouthing off to Mr. Price could get them fired, and they all knew it.

It took a couple of minutes, but Mr. Price finally had the whole group gathered before him. Everyone was completely silent while they waited for him to speak. The portly man wiped the sweat from his brow and appeared uncomfortable about the news he was about to deliver. Sonya's stomach twisted uncomfortably. She began to wonder if he really had come to admonish her publicly.

"There's, uh, there's been a shakeup in your department," Mr. Price told them. "Your manager, Mr. Lavigne, no longer works for

APEX Teleservices. Your supervisor, Jason, has been dismissed as well."

The crew wouldn't have been more surprised if he stripped nude and began to belly dance. Everyone's eyes widened simultaneously. They stared at him with their mouths ajar.

"I, um, I don't want to go into too much detail about their *situation*," Mr. Price continued. "But I know you'll hear about this anyway. I think a few reporters were sniffing around here earlier this week..."

Sonya was dumbfounded. Their manager had been with the company for years. He was always top-notch, as far as she was concerned. Their supervisor, Jason St. John, was professional as well. He was a little flirtatious sometimes, usually with the new hires, but he never made one of them feel uncomfortable enough to report him to human resources. Sonya couldn't imagine anything the two of them did that would be of interest to *reporters*.

The room filled with chatter as the employees absorbed the news and made their own assumptions.

"They were accused of embezzling," Mr. Price said, quieting them. "They found a way to steal money from the veterans' fund. I don't know any more than that, so please don't ask me."

He didn't have to provide more information to get the crowd worked up again. There had been a few scandals in the company over the years, but this one sounded like it would be the grandest. Sonya couldn't believe Mr. Lavigne had been involved in such a thing. She had no idea how they would even pull it off. She turned and stared at Reggie, who was equally perplexed. The commotion in the room got so loud, Mr. Price had to wave a hand to quiet them down again.

"Listen," he said. "*Listen.* Calm down, everyone. I'm afraid it gets worse than that..."

It took a few moments, but the team eventually gave him their undivided attention.

"In lieu of Mr. Lavigne's and Mr. St John's alleged thefts, the veteran's foundation has decided to suspend their contract with us." Mr. Price didn't pause long enough to let that sink in. "That means this department will be shut down – *has been* shut down – effective immediately, until further notice. I understand this is unexpected, and I assure you the people in Human Resources are doing their best to find a place for all of you. But as of this moment, there is nowhere for you to go. All of you are being sent home. You're officially laid-off, starting now..."

When he finished speaking, the room erupted again. Among the outbursts, people wanted to know how any of this was their fault, why they had to be punished for their manager's sins and how they were supposed to pay their bills while they were laid-off. Why couldn't they get absorbed by the FedEx team or water department reps?

"Calm down," the security guard warned. He took a step forward to back up the manager. "Mr. Price is just doing his job. I know you're all upset, but we need to deal with this in an orderly manner. We're not going to get out of control."

Smitty was in his mid-fifties. His hair was salt and peppery, but he presented a tall, imposing figure. Everyone at the company knew and respected him.

"But, Smitty, this ain't right," someone shouted.

"It'll be alright," he said, but Sonya knew he had no way of knowing that. "Just be calm and do what the man says, and everything will be fine."

Mr. Price was red-faced by the time he got control of the room again. He looked out upon the crowd and hated that he had to be the one to deliver this news. As expected, people were panicked and pissed. Some were on the verge of tears. They complained that they had families, children to look after.

"If you have PTO, you can contact Human Resources, and they'll use some of it for today and for as long as this transition period lasts."

"How long will it last?" the crowd wanted to know.

"What happens when we run out of vacation days?"

"I'm sorry, but I don't have answers to all of your questions," Mr. Price insisted. "Don't shoot me. I'm just the messenger. On Monday, all of you need to call Human Resources to find out what your status is and to make sure they're putting in your PTO. But at this second, we don't have any answers for you. This is as big a shock to us as it is to you.

"Now, I'm sorry, but all of you need to leave the building. Do not – I repeat – *do not* stop by Human Resources today. They do not have any of the answers you're looking for, and we don't want a riot up there. And lastly, I was told to collect all of your badges before you go. Please don't ask me why, because, as I've stated, I don't know nothing about nothing."

His attempt at humor fell on deaf ears. There was only one reason employees at APEX Teleservices were ever asked to turn in their badges, and that was in the event of their termination. Mr. Price said they were getting *laid off*, but his instructions sounded too much like they'd just been fired.

The emotions he had to deal with at that point were as mutinous as they were depressing. Even Smitty had trouble calming them down. Sonya's heart was in the pit of her stomach, but she didn't burden Mr. Price with her frustrations, like everyone else. She removed her badge from the lanyard around her neck and handed it to Smitty before leaving the room without another word. She hoped this would only be temporary, but she couldn't shake the feeling that she would never return to the department.

CHAPTER THREE
UNHAPPY HOUR

"Hey, Sonya! Wait up!" Reggie had to speed walk to catch up to her.

She stopped to wait for him.

"You okay?" he asked as they began to walk together.

"I just got fired," she quipped. "What do you think?"

"You didn't get fired. No one got fired."

"They took our badges," she pointed out. "They wouldn't do that, if they wanted us back."

"If we were fired, they would've said so."

"No, not necessarily. They didn't want to start a riot."

"They already did that," a new voice said.

Sonya and Reggie looked back, surprised to find another one of their coworkers following them. Tamara had been working at APEX longer than Sonya but not as long as Reggie.

"Are things getting out of control in there?" Sonya wondered.

"Yeah. Jeanine won't leave," Tamara told them. "She won't give her badge to Mr. Price, either. She said she's keeping it until she talks to someone in Human Resources."

"Damn. I should've thought of that," Sonya replied.

"You think we're all coming back?" Tamara wondered.

"It's..." Sonya trailed off as they passed a few people in the hallway. She recognized them as reps who were fortunate enough to work in the FedEx department. Their colleagues quieted down as Sonya and her friends passed them, which made Sonya feel like they were walking the green mile. Did everyone in the building already know what happened to them? She looked back and saw that the rest of her department was slowly trailing behind. The whole group looked lost and stunned.

Sonya held her tongue until they got outside and were greeted by warm, springtime sunrays. A tender breeze kissed her cheeks and swept pink and blue flowers from the dogwood trees across the sidewalk. It was such a gorgeous day. Sonya didn't want to be at work in the first place, but the way they were dismissed tainted the wonderful weather.

Rather than head for their vehicles, most of the crowd congregated in the parking lot. No one had a solution to their dilemma, but there was solidarity in their confusion. As the volume of their discontent steadily increased, Reggie began to look around warily. From his vantage point, the crew looked poised for a revolt.

"We can't, I don't think we should stay here and talk about this. They might make us leave the property, and then we'll be in trouble for sure."

"Man, the hell with them," Byron grumbled. "What they gon' do, fire us again?"

Byron had only been with the company for a few months. Sonya always thought he was a little rough around the edges, but he had a switch he could turn on and off when he made his calls. Last month he brought in more donations than half the group, which surprised everyone.

"No, he's right," Tamara said. "They told us to leave, so we should go. It'll be more trouble, if they have to kick us off the property."

"Y'all wanna get some drinks?" Eva asked. She was in her forties; a single mother with a couple of kids. "Happy hour is about to start at Chili's."

Sonya wasn't normally one to drink that early in the day, but she also wasn't one to get laid off (or possibly fired) in the middle of the day, either. If ever there was a good time to blow off some steam, this was it.

"Yeah, I'll go," she said.

She looked over at Reggie, and he quickly nodded. "I'll go too. The one on Hulen?"

Eva nodded. "Yeah. It's right down the street."

Several other people agreed to join them before they all headed to their separate vehicles.

• • • • • •

Six members of their department showed up and crowded the bar at the restaurant. They laughed at the bartender when he asked who was picking up the tab.

"We all just got laid off," Eva told him. "I don't think any of us wants to buy a round of drinks today!"

They continued to laugh, though her comment was valid. All of their futures at APEX were uncertain. It wouldn't be a bad idea to be careful with their spending.

Five minutes later everyone had a cold beverage and plenty of opinions about their situation. Sonya mostly listened as she sipped a bottle of Miller Lite. Reggie sat next to her with the same drink in hand.

"How the hell they get money from them people in the first place?" Byron wanted to know. "Don't most people write a check directly to the foundation?"

Byron was tall and powerfully built. If Sonya met him anywhere else, she never would've guessed he worked behind a desk.

"I was wondering that too," Phyllis said. "If they write a check to them people, how would anybody else cash it? They don't even send the money to us."

"They couldn't have done it with the checks," Eva surmised. "I bet it had something to do with the credit cards – or when people give us the numbers from their checking account."

"I think you're right," Tamara said. "If the wrong people get their credit card numbers, they can charge up a whole bunch of shit."

"It happened before," Reggie chipped in. "It wasn't a supervisor, but a few years ago some girls started doing that. They only got away with it for a month before they got caught."

"I remember that," Tamara said. "The police came up to the job and arrested them right at their computer. They walked them out the *long* way, in the middle of lunchtime, to make sure everybody saw."

"That's stupid," Sonya said. "They should've known they wouldn't get away with that. Now they're sitting somewhere looking stupid, with a felony on their record."

"Mr. Lavigne's sitting somewhere looking stupid too," Reggie said. "Him and Jason."

"I hope them niggas in jail," Byron spat. "They got us in trouble over some *bullshit*." His sneer was deep and menacing.

Sonya hoped neither her manager nor supervisor would enter the restaurant at that moment. Byron looked like he was ready to whoop up on someone.

"Do y'all think they're gonna let us come back?" Eva wondered. Her eyes looked as doubtful as she sounded.

"They didn't say we were fired," Phyllis reminded them.

"No, but they took our badges," Sonya stated. "Every time they take someone's badge, it means they're fired. I've never seen anyone come back after that."

"They'll take us back," Reggie assured her. "Don't worry."

"Where we gonna go?" Tamara questioned him. "The FedEx side is full, and they're not hiring for the water department, either."

"How you know?" Byron asked her.

"'Cause I tried to get my cousin a job two weeks ago, and they said they weren't hiring," Tamara told him.

"I need my job," Eva whined. "I can't go that long without a paycheck. I'll lose my apartment."

"They said you can use your vacation days," Sonya reminded her.

"I don't have any PTO left. I just got back from maternity leave. They made me use my vacation time for that." She was on the verge of tears.

Reggie told her, "Don't panic. It's only been one day. Mr. Price said they'd make room for us, and I believe him."

Sonya didn't have the same faith in the system, but she liked how Reggie always kept a cool head in the midst of adversity. Not everyone felt the same way.

"Man, shut up," Byron told him. "You just saying that because you *know* they'll take your ass back. You like, the number one suck up in the building."

"I'm not a suck up," Reggie replied. He spoke calmly, but Sonya saw his eyes narrow slightly. One of the larger veins in his neck began to swell against his skin.

"Yeah you are," Byron retorted. He outweighed Reggie by over fifty pounds, so there was no need for him to back down.

"You do anything them people tell you to: *'Get us more donations,'*" he mocked. "*'Yes, sir. Yes, sir, boss. I'll get that money for you.'*" He laughed. "Nigga, they got you running around like Stepin Fetchit."

Sonya didn't find that amusing. Out of all the people in her office, she liked Reggie the most. She didn't appreciate Byron bullying him. She didn't think Reggie would respond, given his calm demeanor and preppy dress, but he surprised her.

"Oh yeah? Why don't we *step* outside, and you can *fetch* my foot out your ass."

"*Ooh!*"

Sonya didn't know which one of the ladies said, "*Ooh,*" because her eyes were locked on Reggie. She'd never seen him angry before. She couldn't believe he stood up to Byron, who was not only bigger but was clearly from the other side of the tracks.

Everyone watched Byron as he took a slow swig of his drink and placed the glass on the table. He chuckled. "Boy, you know you don't want none."

The tension at the bar thickened as they waited to see if Reggie would respond again.

"I see you're still sitting down," Reggie told him.

A sneer curved Byron's lips. "Why you talking shit? You ain't about that life. You know your ass ain't like this at work."

"We're not at work," Reggie pointed out. "You wanna take it outside or what?"

Sonya couldn't believe what she was hearing. Her work buddy had a death wish!

"Hey," she said. "Y'all need to cool it."

"Yeah, why are you doing this?" Tamara interjected. "We're all mad about our job. But we don't have to take it out on each other."

"For real," Eva said. She pushed Byron on the shoulder. "You need to chill."

"Alright," he said. "My bad."

He didn't direct the apology at Reggie, so he felt no need to respond.

● ● ● ● ● ●

An hour and a half later everyone had had a few rounds, and the mood at the bar was somewhat back to normal – as normal as it could be considering none of them had a job to go to tomorrow. But tomorrow was Saturday, so that meant they all had the weekend off.

One by one the group from APEX began to call it a night as the sun receded in the western skies. When they were down to just three people, Eva told the bartender she was ready to settle her tab.

"How long are you guys staying?" she asked Reggie and Sonya as she slid her credit card across the bar.

"I think I'm done too," Sonya replied. "I know I've had enough to drink." She wasn't tipsy, but her body felt warm and loose. One more drink and she might have to consider taking a cab home.

"Me too," Reggie said. "But I was thinking about getting something to eat before I leave. Watching these waitresses deliver food has got my stomach growling. Are you hungry?" he asked Sonya.

She shrugged. If they had remained at work, this would be around her lunchtime. And she knew a full meal would help sober her up. "I can eat."

"You wanna get a booth?" he asked, looking around the restaurant.

Sonya nodded. "Okay."

Reggie slipped off his stool in search of a hostess.

Eva told Sonya, "Y'all have fun."

There was something about the way she smiled that made Sonya cock her head slightly.

"We're just getting something to eat. It's not like we're on a date or nothing."

"I know," Eva said, but her smile became even sneakier. "You two have fun," she said again. She retrieved her card and signed the receipt for the bartender before she rose to her feet. "See y'all next week, I hope," she told her coworkers.

"Alright, girl. I hope so too," Sonya said.

CHAPTER FOUR
ONCE BITTEN

"Are you okay?" Sonya asked.

She and Reggie sat in a cozy booth near the back of the restaurant. She ordered baby back ribs, while he opted for an Angus burger. The food was great. Sonya didn't realize how ravenous she was until she took the first bite and nearly swallowed one of the bones.

"Yeah, I'm fine," Reggie told her. "Why do you ask?"

"You seem a little different," she said, "ever since you and Byron got into it."

"Oh." He shrugged. "I'm not worried about that. It was just a little thing."

"I can't believe you talked to him like that. Were you really going to fight him?"

"If I had to. What choice would I have?"

"You could've let him punk you..."

"Not in front of you and the other ladies. You think I'm a coward?"

"No. I never said that. I just never took you for a fighter."

"I'm not," he confirmed. "I think I've had four fights my whole life. I'm sure Byron would've demolished me."

She laughed at that. "But you were willing to fight him anyway – just so you could save face?"

Reggie grinned at her. "When you put it like that, I guess it sounds pretty stupid."

"That was a good rebuttal though: *Step outside and fetch my foot out your ass.*"

He chuckled. "You liked that?"

"Yes! How'd you come up with it so fast?"

"I don't know. I guess I'm a quick thinker."

"That's how you get those donations at work," she surmised. "You always know the right thing to say."

"Not only that, but I have to be convincing," he divulged. "If people don't believe what I say, then it doesn't work. That's why Byron backed down. He believed I was confident about whooping his ass – or at least holding my own."

She picked up another rib and grinned at him. "But you weren't?"

"To impress you, I think I would've won that fight," he said honestly.

She looked away, still smiling.

"You don't like it when I flirt with you, do you?" he noticed.

"I just don't wanna get your hopes up."

"Damn. You make it sound like I have no chance at all."

Her face flushed with heat. Sonya had fair skin, so Reggie saw the crimson in her cheeks.

"Are you still trying to get with me?" she asked.

He hadn't put forth an earnest effort in over a year and a half, back when she first started working for APEX. She had shut him down, as she did all of the men at the office who hit on her.

"I never stopped wanting to go out with you," Reggie confided.

He looked her in the eyes. His were dark and serious. Hers still had a trace of amusement. She wasn't sure what to make of his boldness. Byron was right; this wasn't the same Reggie she knew from work. She guessed it had something to do with the alcohol coursing through his system. But he didn't look tipsy. She was the first to look away.

"*And* I see you're still rejecting me," he observed. He shook his head. "Some things never change."

"It's not you," she said. "I think you're a great guy. But I told you: I don't date guys I work with."

"And why is that again?" he asked.

"I told you that too."

"When?"

"When you first asked me out, back when I was in training."

"That was over a year ago. Why don't you refresh my memory?"

"You wanna hear about one of my ex-boyfriends?"

"Might as well," Reggie said, leaning back in his seat. "You got me in a platonic bubble already."

She shook her head, giggling. "*Platonic bubble*? You make it sound so terrible."

"No, it's not all bad," he replied. "It's cool because I get to hang out with you."

"You're my best friend at work. I love that we work together."

"But it sucks because sometimes I wanna grab your ass," he divulged.

Her eyes widened. Her mouth fell open as well. "*Reggie!*" He was full of surprises tonight. First he was willing to go toe-to-toe with Byron, and now this bold confession. She laughed. "What's gotten into you?"

"I dunno. Must be the alcohol."

Sonya didn't buy that. He only had a few drinks at the bar, and he'd eaten a whole burger since then. He was by no means blitzed.

"Tell me your story," he said.

Sonya still hadn't gotten over his ass-grabbing ambitions, but if he wanted to change the subject, she was okay with it.

"I dated Morris five years ago," she said, "when I worked at Red Lobster."

"*Morris?*" Reggie frowned. "I can already tell he's an asshole."

"Okay, *Reginald*," she teased.

"What? You don't like my name?"

"No, I do. I was just kidding."

"*Reginald William Dukes* is presidential," he informed her. "*Morris* was a cat from the *9 Lives* commercials."

"*Hmmm.* Touchy," she noticed.

"Nah, I'm just kidding. I don't like him because apparently he ruined my chances of going out with you. Go ahead and tell me what the bastard did."

Reggie's cocky demeanor heated her chest, her whole body. She didn't think she could've held him at bay if he behaved this way at work over the past year. She eyed him curiously before continuing.

"Well, Morris started hitting on me right after I got hired. And he was cute, so I went out with him. We got to dating pretty heavy, over the next couple of months. I started hearing rumors about him flirting with others girls at work, but he denied it, saying it was innocent, and they were taking it the wrong way. I was falling in love, so I believed him."

She paused, thinking Reggie would call her stupid, like her girlfriends did when she told them about Morris. But he kept his lips sealed.

"As you probably guessed, the girls at work weren't lying on him," Sonya said. "Morris was definitely a dog. I got confronted by another waitress he was sleeping with. I wasn't down for any of that hoodrat shit, so I let her run her mouth. She was the one who got fired for that."

Reggie nodded slightly.

"Morris swore she was his *ex*-girlfriend, and she was jealous because he moved on," Sonya said. "And I believed him again."

Just thinking about her decision-making made her feel so dim-witted her face reddened. She shook her head.

"I was a fool."

"Nothing wrong with being a fool in love."

Sonya didn't know if he meant that, but it made her feel a little better. She looked into his eyes. "Thanks."

He grinned and waited for her to finish.

"So anyway," she said, "Me and Morris stayed together, and it didn't take another month before I got confronted again. This time one of his baby-mamas came up to the job–"

"*One of them?*" Reggie's eyes widened.

"Yes, *one of them*. He had three kids. Look, don't judge me. You've been doing a great job up till now."

"I'm sorry. Go ahead." He managed to do away with his frown, but his smile returned.

Sonya rolled her eyes. Some stories were not worth reliving. "I didn't fight her either. But she was starting mess in the lobby, and the manager had had enough of us by then. He fired me and Morris. It wasn't the best job in the world, or anything like that. But to lose it over a man made me feel like a loser. That's why I would never date anyone I work with."

"But that was only one incident," Reggie pointed out. "And that kind of stuff can still happen, even if you're dating someone away from work."

"Maybe. But at least I can maintain some integrity if it doesn't happen in front of my co-workers. Plus APEX is full of whores. And even if the guy I'm with doesn't cheat, I'll still have to worry about seeing him every day if it doesn't work out. I don't want that. If I break up with somebody, I don't want to have to ride the elevator with them every day."

"I understand," Reggie said. "It's a lot to think about."

"It's a lot of drama that can easily be avoided."

"Okay, but, you know, it's different now. For us."

Her eyes narrowed. "How so?"

"Well, I don't wanna bring up bad news, but we just got laid off. They said they'd take us back, but we don't know that for sure. So technically we're not working together anymore."

She laughed. "So I should embrace unemployment, because it gives me an opportunity to go out with you?"

"Maybe. Everything happens for a reason."

"I need my job, Reggie. I'm in school. I don't have any help with my bills."

"I know. And I'm sure everything will be alright. But I still wanna go out with you. So for now, while our work status is up in the air, will you go out with me?"

Again she was intrigued by his boldness. Was this the real Reggie? She liked the guy she'd been working with for the past year and a half. But this *new* Reggie... She *really* liked him. The loophole he presented her with was rather lame, but she could roll with it, if she wanted to.

"Okay," she decided.

He looked surprised. "For real?"

She giggled. "Yes, for real. I've known you for a long time, and I like you. And I trust you. I know you're nothing like most of those losers at APEX."

"No, I'm not," he agreed. He smiled. "So this can be, like, our first date."

She smiled too. "If so, it's going very well."

He leaned forward with his elbows on the table. "Even after I said I wanted to grab your ass sometimes?"

She felt butterflies in her stomach. She nodded. "Yes, even after that."

• • • • • •

It was after 8 pm when they left the restaurant. Sonya had eaten well and drank well. She couldn't remember the last time she stayed at a restaurant for so long. It was also interesting to note that after getting laid off from her only job, she was having a great day somehow. She knew Reggie was the cause of that, so she was not opposed when he took hold of her hand as they crossed the parking lot. His touch was soft. A pleasant pulse of electricity traveled from his body to hers.

When they reached her car, Sonya was surprised when he embraced her. But she wasn't opposed to that either. His hands were unexpectedly strong and comforting. He slightly caressed her back during their hug. The feel of his chest pressed against hers heated Sonya's body to the point that she felt like she might melt.

After sitting next to Reggie at the same workstation for over a year, she couldn't deny that she wondered what it would be like to have his arms wrapped around her. She had no idea it would feel this good.

She initiated the kiss. She felt Reggie's body stiffen for a moment before he returned the gesture. He pecked her bottom lip and then sucked it slowly. Sonya did the same. Her tongue seemed to slip into his mouth on its own accord. If Reggie had reservations, it didn't show. He sucked her tongue, and his hands gradually moved down her back until they claimed the ass he'd been coveting for over a year. Sonya felt her juices flowing as he squeezed her cheeks and pulled her hips closer to his. Her heart thundered.

She had so many thoughts running through her mind, it was hard to know which one to follow. She gathered her courage and threw caution to the wind before she spoke. If he rejected her, she would've lost nothing. But if he didn't...

She backed away and asked him, "Do you want to follow me home?"

His lips parted, but he didn't speak – not right away.

"It's not like I just met you," she said, her voice barely above a hush. She sighed quietly. "All I know is today has been an awful day, but you make me feel good. I just wanna..."

He took so long to respond, she began to regret offering the invitation. But Reggie grinned slightly and said, "I want that more than anything else in the world."

She blew out a pent up breath and smiled. "Okay. Go get your car. I'll wait on you."

CHAPTER FIVE
NETFLIX & CHILL

Sonya lived in a one bedroom apartment in Woodhaven, on the east side of town. The area was once a bright spot in the city; picturesque with rolling hills and densely packed trees from a variety of species. But overpopulation was its downfall, as was the case with many beautiful locales across the state. Woodhaven was now host to dozens of sprawling apartment complexes, most of them catering to low income families. The neighborhood could appear downright dangerous at times, especially on a Friday night, but Reggie was pleased to find Sonya's apartment clean and neat, with mostly new furniture.

He took a seat on the sofa, and she tossed the remote control into his lap as she continued towards the bedroom.

She told him, "I'll be back in a second. I have to freshen up."

"Okay," he replied.

"You can make yourself something to drink, if you want," she called before she disappeared into one of the rooms on the far end of the hallway.

Reggie didn't plan to drink more that night, but after a few minutes he heard the muffled sound of running water. When it didn't stop, he knew that Sonya had slipped into the shower. That brought everything home for him, even more than the invite to her apartment, and he began to feel antsy.

This really was happening. He wasn't opposed to being there. He had hoped for it countless times over the past year. But he never expected things to progress so quickly between them. He was poised to go from first base to a homerun with the woman of his dreams, all in a matter of hours, rather than the months he thought it might take. That was enough to make his legs feel rubbery as he stood and approached Sonya's bar.

He chuckled to himself and tried to shake off the nerves as he poured himself two fingers of Hennessey. Before he returned to his seat, he walked around the room, admiring his friend's style and décor. He appreciated that she chose to go with simplicity, rather than cram the small space with more than was necessary. Sonya didn't have a dining table, which made the living room more spacious. There were a couple of books on her coffee table. Reggie took one to the sofa with him and flipped through it while he waited for the woman of the house to return.

She emerged from the bedroom ten minutes later wearing a tee-shirt with pajama bottoms. Her hair was still pulled up and away from her face. Despite the basic attire, Reggie thought she looked beautiful, even more so than the outfits she wore to work. This was the first time he'd ever seen her barefoot. He felt like he'd been allowed a peek into her private life. He finished his drink and placed the empty glass on the table.

"Sorry I took so long," she said as she sat next to him. "You didn't wanna watch TV?" she noticed.

"Actually I've been caught up in this book," he said and returned it to the table.

"You think psychology is interesting?"

He nodded. "It's been a long time since I read a text book."

"Maybe you should do my homework for me, if you like it so much," she joked.

"You don't like psychology?"

She shrugged. "It's alright, I guess. It's one of the classes I need for my major, so I gotta take it, regardless of whether I like it or not."

"You're majoring in business?" Reggie knew that from conversations they'd had at work.

She nodded. "Two more years, and I'll be done."

"And then what?"

"And then I can finally get away from customer service jobs."

She grinned. Reggie loved her lips, the way her mouth curved when she was amused. He wanted to kiss her again, but it was Sonya who had initiated their first kiss at the restaurant. Despite all of the green lights she'd given him, he remained a little unsure of himself.

"What about you?" she asked him. "Are you ever going back to school?"

"I don't know. Sometimes I feel like I need to, but I've been doing okay without it."

"What are your long-term goals?" she wondered. "I know you don't want to work at APEX forever..."

"I'm really good at my job," he pointed out. "I may still be in an entry-level position, but I get nice raises every year."

"What about promotions?" she asked. "It looks like they wanna keep you right where they have you."

"I like being on the phone," he told her. "But I don't think I'll be stuck in a cubicle indefinitely. I'm one of those people who believe you can take a job flipping burgers and work your way up to owning the building one day. I think hard work and integrity can get you just as far as a college degree will."

Sonya was surprised by his response. She never thought Reggie flat out lacked ambition, but she didn't know that he expected his work ethics to pay off so grandly. He was a couple of years younger than her, which put him in his late twenties. He would probably never own APEX Teleservices, but at the rate he was going, she could see him sitting in a boardroom with the president and shareholders one day.

Of course that was all contingent on whether either of them returned from their layoff.

"Do you think they'll take us back?" she asked. "Well, I know they'll take *you* back. You're *Mr. Company Man.* But what about me?"

His features quickly filled with concern. "Why wouldn't they take you back? You never call-in. You're hardly ever late."

"Yeah, but what about my performance? Remember, I was on probation last year, because I couldn't get my numbers up."

"Yeah, but you got past that. There are some people in our department who *shouldn't* come back. But you're not one of them."

"You're only saying that because you have a crush on me," she said with a smile.

She sat with her legs tucked beneath her. Her knee was in steady contact with his thigh, which warmed him more than the alcohol he'd consumed.

"I do," he admitted.

Her smile deepened. "Are you blushing?"

His skin was so fair, there was no point in denying it. "Do you even wanna go back to APEX?" he asked, rather than respond to her question. "I know you don't like making those calls."

"I just need to remain gainfully employed until I graduate," she said honestly. "I live by myself, and I don't have anyone helping me."

"Even if they don't get the veterans' contract back, they'll find a place for you," he predicted. "Everyone likes you."

"I don't know about that, but I know *you* like me." Her grin was flirtatious. She leaned forward and kissed him softly. "Don't you?" she asked when she backed away.

Reggie wanted to tell her that he was in love with her, but he didn't know how she would react. Was it possible to fall in love with someone you worked with but only dated once? He felt like it was.

"I like you a lot," he said. "I'm glad you invited me. If us getting laid-off led to this, then I'm glad we got laid off. I can't tell you how happy I am right now."

His unshakable sincerity made her heart flutter. The way he stared at her, with those piercing eyes, made it clear that he meant every word. She looked around and noticed his empty liquor glass.

"What were you drinking?"

"Hennessey?"

"Straight?"

"I needed a stiff one, but I like it better with Coke."

"Want me to make you another one?" she asked as she rose to her feet.

Reggie noticed her current outfit didn't hug her figure at all, but the pajama pants couldn't hide the sexy swell of her ass. He grinned, thinking of how he grabbed it in the restaurant parking lot. If he lived to be 100, he knew that memory would always be one of his fondest.

Sonya lifted his glass and asked, "What's so funny?"

He shook his head slowly. His smile remained devious.

"You wanna watch Netflix?" she asked as she walked to the bar.

He couldn't help but chuckle at that.

She turned back and smiled. "What?"

"Netflix and chill?"

She giggled. "You make it sound all *nasty*."

With her back to him, all Reggie could do was watch her booty and think about touching it again.

"It doesn't have to be nasty," he replied, although he hoped he was wrong about that.

● ● ● ● ● ●

They couldn't immediately agree on a show to watch, because Sonya hadn't been keeping up with his favorites, and Reggie wasn't interested in hers. Neither of them wanted to watch a movie they had already seen before. They settled on *Orange is the New Black*, which was at the top of both their next-up lists.

"I can't believe you haven't watched this," Reggie commented.

"I can't believe *you* haven't," Sonya replied. "Maybe it was destiny."

"You mean we both avoided this show for reasons unbeknownst to ourselves, so we could watch it together on this special night?"

"Damn," Sonya said. "I think you just gave me chills."

"Come closer," he said. "I can help keep you warm."

"Who *are* you?" Sonya wondered aloud as she leaned towards him and settled into his embrace. "*Work* Reggie is not this bold."

"Work Reggie is not full of Hennessey."

"Yeah, but it's more than that. I think you know it is."

Reggie did feel different today, and he agreed the alcohol only played a part in it. He was on cloud nine because Sonya finally broke down the walls of the platonic dungeon he'd been trapped in. His soul was so free, he felt like he could fly, which was a little scary, considering they'd only been on one date. He didn't look forward to how hard he'd crash back to earth if she changed her mind about him.

They were both fully enthralled in the show midway through the first episode. By the second one, they were drunk and giddy. Reggie blushed the first time they watched a sex scene together. But after a while, the girl-on-girl action started to turn him on.

Sonya must have felt the same way, because she looked up at him in the midst of one such scene and said, "You like that, don't you?"

"Meh," he said, trying to play it cool. "It's alright. It's just TV. And they're not really showing *anythiiii – Oh Lordy...*"

His exclamation was because Sonya reached into his lap unexpectedly. She found things very stiff down there.

"What were you saying?"

Reggie couldn't find his tongue, with her touching him like that. Sonya upped the ante by rubbing in addition to touching.

"Damn, Reggie. Is this all you?"

She hoped he didn't think she was too forward, but she already showed her hand when she invited him over. He didn't respond to the question, so she reached with her other hand and unbuttoned his pants. Given his reserved nature, she thought he'd stop her, but he just watched. By the time she got him unzipped, he was fully erect. His boner pushed at his boxers at what she assumed was an uncomfortable angle. She pulled his shorts down to free the beast. When she saw what he was packing, her clitoris began to throb with excitement.

"*Damn, Reggie.*" Her voice was breathy now, a few octaves lower than normal. She wrapped her fist around his meat but was unable to connect her thumb and forefinger. He had a nice amount of length to accompany the girth.

"Well look what you've been hiding," she whispered.

His piece looked so good, she wanted to devour it. She wanted it so badly, her mouth watered in anticipation. But she couldn't go down on him tonight – not on their first time. It was bad enough she'd invited him to her home after their first date.

She watched his stomach rise and fall as he took a deep, slow breath. His manhood pulsated in her hand. She gave it a squeeze, and it jumped again. Sonya felt slick between her legs as she looked up at him. His steely gaze made her walls clench and her chest tighten. Had she really been sitting next to this beautiful creature for a year and a half and not once thought to give him a shot? She cursed herself for being such a fool. But then again, it looked like Reggie was well worth the wait.

She began to stroke him as she stared at the fat head poking out of her fist.

But he told her, "No, don't."

Sonya knew she couldn't comply with that. She looked up at him and asked, "Why?" Her eyes were dark and lust-filled. His were low and slightly glazed.

"I can't handle that," he revealed. "It's been a while for me. And I've wanted you for so long. You gonna make me..."

"You gonna cum?" She continued to stroke him as she spoke. She returned her attention to his erection, hoping he would explode in her hand. She thought it would be awesome to watch.

"I am," he replied. "I'm sorry. You, you make me feel like a virgin."

His revelation caused another flow of juices to dampen her panties. How was it that he hadn't had sex in awhile? Who were the stupid women in his life who were passing up on this smart, handsome and well-hung brother? Sonya smiled when she realized she was one of those stupid women up until 5 pm today.

She let go of him and asked, "You got a condom?" She stood and pushed her pajama bottoms down in one quick motion. She wasn't wearing panties.

Reggie's eyes bulged when he saw her standing bottomless before him. His nostrils flared, and his manhood somehow grew another half inch. He shook his head vaguely, in response to her question.

"I'll be back," Sonya said, as she headed for her bedroom.

Reggie felt they were way past pretenses at that point, so he turned fully on the sofa so he could watch her as she walked away. The sight of her bare ass made his whole body shudder. He wasn't aware that his mouth hung open, and he panted slightly.

He was still facing the hallway when she reappeared a moment later with a condom in hand. Reggie felt guilty for ogling her neatly shaved kitty. But when his eyes traveled up to hers, he saw that she was smiling.

She approached the couch and asked, "Why didn't you take your pants off?"

"I'm, I'm sorry. I thought..." He was about to inquire about going to the bedroom. But Sonya stood impatiently before him, and he couldn't get his mind or his eyes off the glory between her legs. She was standing no more than two feet away. She was so close. He inhaled deeply, but her scent wasn't strong enough for him to catch an aroma. He wanted to bury his face in her love and lap her juices until he was satiated and her skin was red with passion.

He kicked his shoes off roughly and yanked his khakis down, all while his eyes remained glued to her kitty. He felt self-conscious when he looked up and saw that she was watching him.

She grinned. "Why are you looking at me like that, Reggie?"

"I – I don't know."

"Do you like my body?"

She raised her shirt up to her bra line as she spoke. She even did a half-turn, so he could check out her ass again. Reggie had never experienced anything like this. She was not only confident with her sexuality, but she *owned* it. He knew he was awake, but what he was witnessing defied the logical world he was accustomed to. Vixens like this never visited him outside of wet dreams.

But if he wasn't dreaming, then he had to be the luckiest man alive. He tried to hide his shock and act as if this type of thing happened to him all the time.

"You're super fine," he said. "I love your body."

"Here." She handed him the condom as she pulled her shirt up and over her head.

Reggie thought he'd be able to subdue his reaction, but Sonya didn't have on a bra. The sight of her bare breasts held him spellbound once again. They weren't huge. He thought they were the perfect size. Her areolas were two shades darker than the rest of her skin. Her nipples were small and erect. He longed to suck them. He wanted to lick and taste all of her. He hadn't had an oral fixation like this since he was a toddler, but it was back in full force. Sonya's whole body was a pacifier.

He was so excited, even the slight friction of rolling the condom down his shaft nearly set him off. He knew he wouldn't last long, and he hated it. Thankfully he was sure he could go a second or even a third round tonight. He felt like he'd popped a Viagra.

Once he was protected, Sonya stepped between his legs and pushed his shoulders back against the sofa cushions. His piece continued to point skywards. She straddled him, with both hands on his shoulders. Reggie felt the heat radiating from her box as she hovered over him. She was so slick, she didn't have to reach down to guide him in. She lowered her hips until he penetrated her. She gasped and her body shuddered as she continued downwards, causing him to spread her walls until they could accommodate him.

She looked into his eyes, her chest rising and falling. She sank lower, until their pubic hair touched and she had every inch of him. Reggie relished her sweet heat, the way her body soothed and squeezed him. He knew she was perfect, even before she flexed her hips and began to slide up and down his pole. She closed her eyes and sucked air between her teeth as she rode him.

"*Ooh. Damn, Reggie.* You feel so good."

He wasn't able to speak, but he loved that she could. He had never been with a vocal lover before – not one who could formulate coherent sentences, rather than simply scream or moan.

The only problem was Sonya continued to push him closer to his climax. It wasn't just her sexy talk, it was the whole package; the curves of her nude physique, the drunken look in her eyes, the feel of her body caressing and coaxing him as her hips moved up and down.

He thought he'd lose it when she took him in all the way and remained there. She grinded her hips to a rhythm only their souls could hear. Her grip on his shoulders strengthened. Her bottom lip slipped halfway into her mouth, and she bit down on it. Reggie could smell her essence now. The primal scent invaded his nasal passage and set his mind on fire. He was glad she was on top. He wouldn't have been able to handle this if he was in control of the action. He would've been howling at the moon.

"*Do you like it?*" she breathed.

He had been staring at her breasts. He looked up and saw that she was watching him again. He nodded, but Sonya desired more from him.

"Say it," she insisted. "*Tell me how you feel.*"

Reggie knew he couldn't match her on a sexual level, so he spoke with honesty, from his heart. "This feels like a dream," he told her. "*It's like heaven.*"

He thought his response was corny, but the smile that lit Sonya's face said otherwise. Her eyes slipped closed, and her hips began to move up and down again. This time her pace increased until the incredible sensation caused Reggie's toes to curl and dig into the carpet. Her expression was pure bliss. His was the same.

He breathed a silent *thank you* when he felt her legs tremble, and she told him, "*I'ma cum.*"

But before he could rejoice in the fact that he outlasted her, his own eruption rolled through his body so forcefully his mouth and eyes flashed open. He felt a tingling sensation in each of his extremities.

"*Oh shit.*"

"*No, baby. Wait,*" she urged.

"*I'm trying. I – shit. I can't.*"

"It's okay," she told him.

Her body moved so majestically, he would've sworn she was part serpent. She was so wet and delightfully tight.

"You like it, baby?" she asked. "*I'm making you cum?*"

Any hopes of restraint were certainly lost then. Her body and her words were a double threat. Reggie gave up on trying to hold back and became fully immersed in the moment, in her. His hips pushed up off the couch, and he plunged in deeper.

She screamed; a real one, with her head thrown back, her eyes squeezed closed. Reggie surprised her by rising and lifting her off the couch completely. For a brief moment Sonya was suspended in air. He turned and deposited her on her back. They never unlatched. Her eyes fluttered open, and she saw him hovering over her. His skin and eyes were dark with hunger. He began to pump harder as his manhood swelled and spilled his seed.

Sonya's clit pulsated, and her essence flowed as well. She spread her legs wider for him. The clapping sound of their hips filled the small apartment. The sound was mostly drowned out by her moans of pleasure. She feared her neighbors would hear them, but she didn't care. She didn't care if all of them knew her lover's name.

"*Reggie! Oh, Reggie! Yes!*"

Her orgasm flowed down her body like lava, sweet and sticky. Reggie continued to stroke her, hitting rock bottom, even after he was spent. That pleased her immensely. She reached and held onto him, gripping his flanks. He lowered himself as the speed of his hips gradually slowed. He continued to please her. Even when they were both panting and she could barely feel her legs, he kept grinding, pumping his hips with slow, deliberate strokes.

Her eyes fluttered. When she tried to open them, she could only see a soothing, pink and gray abyss. She wasn't sure if she was staring at the back of her eyelids, or if Reggie's sex was so good she had gone blind. Either way, a smile parted her lips as they continued to ride the wave of ecstasy.

CHAPTER SIX
THE MORNING AFTER

Reggie was an early riser. He was up and out of the bed by eight am, which was not the norm for Sonya on a Saturday. He emerged from the shower a few minutes later with one of her towels wrapped around his waist. He looked so delectable, with his fresh, bronze skin radiating the sparse sunlight, Sonya almost didn't mind him waking her up so early. Almost.

"Morning," he said. He approached the bed and sat next to her. He leaned and kissed her softly on the cheek.

Sonya grinned and burrowed in her sheets. "Morning."

"I'm hungry," he announced. "Wanna go get something to eat?"

"Uh-uhn," she moaned as her eyes slipped closed again. "It's too early."

"Okay," he chuckled. "Is it alright if I cook? You got something in the fridge?"

"The usual," she mumbled. "Eggs, bacon. Some biscuits."

She opened her eyes when he didn't head to the kitchen right away. Reggie had a startlingly fit physique. She never considered him the athletic type, but his chest was broad and defined. The muscles in his arms were toned just right. She smiled, thinking of how he put his endurance to the test last night. "Can you cook?" she asked him.

"I think I can handle bacon and eggs. Are you going to eat? If not, I can take off and grab something on the way home."

"No, I wanna eat. I'm getting up now."

"Cool," he said as he rose from the bed. "I'm going to..." He looked around the room. "... find my underwear."

She giggled. "Have you checked the living room?"

"No, I haven't." He offered a conspiratorial grin before he left the room.

Sonya continued to watch him until he was out of sight. She tried to restrain herself during their lovemaking, but one small scratch stood out on his back. All things considered, he was fortunate to get away so unscathed.

Fifteen minutes later she was still gathering the strength needed to crawl out of bed. The sounds and smells coming from her kitchen were certainly enticing. She couldn't remember the last time a man cooked for her. But it was her cellphone that finally got her moving. She recognized the ringtone as one she used exclusively for her sister.

She rose from bed without gathering a sheet to hide her nudity and hurried to the dresser on the other side of the room. She plucked her cellphone from her purse in time to catch the call before it went to voicemail.

"Hey. What's up?"

"What's up with *you*?" her sister exclaimed. Sonya could tell she was excited about something. "Why you didn't tell me about this *scandal* at your job?"

Sonya was not happy to be reminded of that. It was a terrible part of what had otherwise been an awesome day. The time spent with Reggie was like an erotic fairytale. Carla had just dragged her back to reality.

"What do you know about it?"

"It's on the news!" her sister informed her. "They're talking about y'all right now. Y'all be stealing from veterans? Ain't that the department you work in? I knew that begging for donations shit was trouble."

Sonya's heart sank as she searched for the television remote.

"Did you say you had biscuits–" Reggie stopped in his tracks when he came face to face with Sonya's full moon. He'd seen her bare-naked ass quite a few times last night. But it was daytime now, and they weren't having sex. He felt like he'd intruded. His sense of guilt was so strong, he turned away and looked down the hallway. "Oh, I'm sorry."

Sonya looked back and told him, "No, it's alright."

"Who is *that*?" Carla blared in her ear. "You got somebody over there? *Girl, who you sleeping with*?"

Sonya was not surprised or even annoyed by her big sister's nosiness. She'd been putting up with it since she was in diapers.

"I'll call you back," she told her.

"*Wait!* Sonya, who is that?"

"I said I'll call you back." She hung up on her, knowing Carla would have enough respect for her privacy to leave her alone until she returned her call.

"I'm sorry. I didn't know you were on the phone," Reggie called from the hallway. "I'll, uh, I'll keep looking." He continued to back away.

"It's okay," Sonya said. "My sister said they're talking about APEX on the news. Don't you wanna see it?" she asked as she turned to the television with the remote in hand. She realized she didn't ask her sister what channel was airing the story. She figured it was one of the local networks.

"I'm sorry," Reggie said again as he returned to the bedroom. "I didn't know you weren't dressed."

"Boy, what are you talking about?" She took a seat on the bed. "You tripping 'cause I'm naked?"

He risked a few glances and saw that she was not going to cover up.

"What do you have against naked people?" she asked as she flipped channels on the remote.

Reggie shook his head and allowed his eyes to roll over her figure without gawking. He was constantly reminded that Sonya was not like any girl he'd ever dated. He liked that she was such a free spirit when it came to her sexuality. But he feared that he might have trouble keeping up with her.

"Look. Here it is!" she exclaimed.

Reggie saw that Channel Six's star reporter Chad Collins was indeed covering the corruption story at their place of business. Stunned, he sat next to her, with his eyes glued to the screen. He was fully dressed, while Sonya remained as naked as a jay bird.

"So far police have made two arrests in this case," the reporter was saying. "David Lavigne, a manager at APEX Teleservices, and a supervisor, Jason St. John, were apprehended by officers yesterday afternoon."

As the reporter spoke, his image on the screen was replaced with what appeared to be mug shots of Sonya's former bosses. A chill rolled down her frame as she stared at them. Both men looked like they were past the point of being shocked over their arrest. They wore the embarrassed expressions of someone who knew full well that what they had done was very wrong.

"Stealing from disabled veterans?" Chad Collin's cute sidekick asked when the view returned to the reporters in the newsroom. "That's about as low as you could get."

"It is," Chad commented. "Representatives from the Disabled Veterans' Foundation said they were shocked and disappointed by the findings. They have since suspended their funding drive at APEX. They gave no word on whether they would continue working with the company in the future. Meanwhile a spokesperson for APEX had this to say..."

The view changed again, this time to a woman Sonya had never seen before. She was smartly dressed, seated in an office. She appeared poised and confident.

"We are certainly disappointed to find that two of our employees were involved in this theft. We are working with the police to discover how they managed to pull it off and exactly how much they were able to take from the foundation before this issue came to light. Both of those men have been terminated, and we will continue to assist with their prosecution."

"We will have more on this story as it develops," the reporter said before they cut to a commercial break.

● ● ● ● ● ●

Sonya wasn't hungry after she showered and dressed for the day. But Reggie had gone through the trouble of cooking for her. She felt it would be impolite if she didn't eat it. Plus he waited until she took a seat at the table before he served himself. He remained upbeat about their predicament. Sonya wished she could share his optimism.

"I still can't get over how they took our badges," she told him. "If it wasn't for that, I would feel better about what happened."

"I'm sure they know some of us aren't coming back," Reggie replied. "It would be easier to call and tell them they're fired, instead of making them come back to work to turn in their badges."

"You're probably right," Sonya agreed. "How long do you think it will take before they figure things out?"

"I'm hoping only a few days. I don't want to be out of work for too long."

"What if they don't take me back?" she wondered.

"They will," he assured her. "Both of us. They have slackers in every department. You're better than a lot of them."

"It doesn't matter if I'm better. They're not going to fire people to make room for us. They might make us wait until the veterans decide if they'll continue our contract. And who knows how long that will take..."

"It'll be alright. Have a little faith."

Reggie didn't indicate where her well of faith should come from. Sonya didn't like the idea of her future being up in the air.

"Anyway, what are you doing today?" she asked him.

Reggie felt like she was telling him to get lost. Or maybe she didn't mean it that way. "Oh, um, I was gonna stop by my dad's house. He needs help with a '67 Corvette he's restoring."

He hoped she'd ask for more details about that. Working on old hotrods was a hobby most people found interesting. But Sonya was preoccupied as she stared down at her plate.

"Are you okay?" he asked. "I know you're upset about the job, but–"

"I'm fine," she said. "It's just one of those things, right?"

"Yeah. I suppose. But, uh, what about us? Are you, you're not having second thoughts... Are you?"

She looked up at him and frowned slightly. "No. I'm – what gave you that idea?"

Reggie felt like he'd been getting a chilly reception from the moment she woke up, but he didn't mention it. He hoped this wasn't a one night stand. He'd yearned to be with her for so long. Now that they'd gone all the way, he hoped for a meaningful relationship. There was no way he was going back to that platonic bubble she had him in. But saying all of that would scare her away for sure.

"It's, nothing," he said. "I know you're just scared about our job. I'm worried too."

"Except you don't have anything to worry about."

Reggie left the house five minutes later with a "Thanks for the breakfast," but no kiss goodbye. Sonya didn't offer one, and he didn't feel like he'd be welcomed if he attempted it. She said she wasn't having second thoughts, but as far as he could tell, their future remained uncertain.

CHAPTER SEVEN
CARLA

By noon Sonya found herself bouncing a baby on her knee while another child clamored around the living room, pushing a lawnmower toy that made quite a racket. A third child practiced playing a recorder in an adjacent room. Luckily this was her sister Carla's house, and none of these rug rats were her responsibility. Sonya loved her nieces and nephew dearly, but the best part about them was they weren't hers. She could cut her visit short the moment they started to get on her nerves.

Carla sat on the sofa next to her hoping to get the 411 on a couple of hot topics. Sonya didn't mind being interrogated. She had a lot going on, and it wouldn't hurt to hear someone else's opinion.

"Tell me about this Reggie," Carla said, smiling from ear to ear.

The mother of three had fair-skin, like her sister, but they didn't have many similarities past that. Carla was shorter, and she never lost the weight she started to put on after her first child. And she'd been dyeing her hair different shades of red since high school, because she thought it made her look cute and jazzy. Sonya had told her on more than one occasion that she actually looked better (and more mature) with her natural hair color. So far this suggestion went unheeded.

"I've been working with Reggie for almost two years," she replied.

"You never liked him before?" Carla wondered. "It took this long for you to decide to bring him home?"

Sonya wondered if her big sister lived vicariously through her, seeing as how Carla was married now and settled-down. Flings and one-night-stands were no longer a part of her repertoire.

"It's not that I didn't like him," she said. "But you know my rule against dating men at work."

"Yeah, you been saying that ever since that lady came up to Red Lobster and tried to whoop your ass."

"*Whoop my ass*? Oh, excuse me, precious," Sonya said to the baby in her lap. "Those are bad words."

"Girl, please," Carla said, waving her off. "She done heard way worse than that. And she can't even talk yet. You think she understands what we're saying?"

"No," Sonya said. Carla's latest bundle of joy couldn't even hold her head up by herself. "But you know *that one* picks up on *everything*," she said, referencing her sister's middle child.

"No, I don't," the boy said as he continued to play with his lawn mower.

"Case and point," Sonya commented.

"Boy, take your eavesdropping tail to your room!" Carla yelled at him. "You know you need to stay out of grown folks' business!"

The boy laughed as he pushed his toy out of sight. Sonya wouldn't doubt if he'd continue to listen to them from the hallway.

"You didn't like him when you first met him?" Carla asked again when they were relatively alone in the room.

"I always liked him," Sonya told her. She noticed the baby was starting to doze, so she positioned her so that she could take a nap in her arms. "I just wasn't interested in dating him. And you need to get the story straight about Red Lobster. If anything, that girl was going to get her butt whooped; running up on me like that at work. The only reason I let her get away with it was because I didn't want to lose my job."

"Didn't they fire you anyway?" Carla recalled.

"They did. If I had known they were gonna do all that, I probably would've yanked some weave out that bitches head. Bet she wouldn't have been doing all that talking then."

Carla laughed. "No, it's a good thing you didn't. Getting beat up in front of all your coworkers is not a good look."

Sonya cut her eyes at that comment, but her sister was probably right. As children Sonya was quick to run and get reinforcements when she got into an altercation. Carla loved to rumble, whereas Sonya dreaded rolling around on the dirty ground.

"Anyway, get back to Reggie," Carla pressed.

"Reggie has been liking me since day one. He's a good dude."

"What does that mean? He's ugly?"

"Hell no. When have you known me to go out with some Shrek-looking thing?"

"What he look like?"

"Tall. He's light-skinned. No beard or moustache. He keeps his hair cut low. Always clean cut and professional. He's smart. He's really smart. He's the best worker in my department – well he *was*, before we got shut down. I like Reggie. He's funny. He always has me cracking up at work."

"How was he in bed?"

Thinking about their time together gave Sonya a sweet rush of heat.

Carla noticed her dreamy expression. "Damn. That good?"

Sonya grinned wickedly. "He's packing, and he knows what to do with it. Had me second guessing myself last night. If I knew he had it going on like that, I would've jumped on him a long time ago."

"*Umph.*" Carla grinned. "You keep saying how smart he is. It sounds like he's a nerd. That's probably why you thought he wasn't working with nothing."

Sonya considered that. "I guess he is a little nerdy, but I don't mind."

"You never went out with a nerd before," Carla pointed out.

"No, I don't think I have."

"What line did this nerd feed you to make you think he was worth a shot?"

"Stop calling him a nerd. He just told me we'd gotten laid off, so technically we weren't working together anymore." She chuckled, thinking of the smile on his face when he said that.

Carla found it amusing too.

"But that wasn't all," Sonya said. "After they sent us home, we went to Chili's; me and Reggie and some more people from work. We got drunk and got to talking about stuff. And then everybody left, and it was just me and him. While we were at the restaurant, Reggie had me looking at him differently. And then when we got ready to leave, he grabbed my booty, and that was it."

"Hmmm." Carla's smile grew wider.

"That's when I knew he wasn't a punk," Sonya recalled. "That, and he was about to fight this tough guy from our job. It was a lot of stuff that made me want to take him home."

"So the cavemen had it right all along," Carla said with a laugh. Before Sonya could question that, she said, "Women like a man who'll whoop some ass and then drag them to their cave!"

Sonya wanted to dispute that, but on a base level, she knew her sister was on to something. "And now it looks like everything I was worried about has already started," Sonya complained.

"What do you mean?"

"Like this morning, I felt a little weird around him."

"Damn," Carla muttered. "What the hell did you do last night, that would make you feel weird about it in the morning."

"Nothing too crazy," Sonya replied. "I mean, you know I'm not shy when it comes to sex."

"Don't I ever," Carla said, thinking about the time she'd stayed with her when they were both single. Even with a guest in the house, Sonya and her boyfriend at the time made so much noise one night, Carla went from covering her ears to wondering how much longer the two could keep it up.

"We're not even back to work yet, and I don't think things will be the same," Sonya confided. "He's so reserved. This morning he saw me naked and looked away. His face turned red."

Her sister hummed.

"I know this sounds crazy, but I'm kinda glad we don't have to see each other at work on Monday."

"But if you lose your job, what will you do?" Carla wondered. "Unemployment will only pay some of what you were getting."

"I know. It would be hard to keep up with the bills."

"You know you can come live with us."

"I don't wanna live over here." The thought of it made Sonya's nose wrinkle up. "You got way too much going on. You're like the little old lady who lived in a shoe."

"Whatever. I got three kids."

"And a snoring-ass husband."

"He do be snoring," Carla conceded with a shake of her head. "What about Debra?" she asked, referring to their other sister.

"Nope. Nope. Nope. You know she's struggling. Nothing in the refrigerator. She owes me money right now. Two people struggling in the same house end up fighting all the time."

"I guess," Carla said. "You know you can always go live with Daddy, just until you finish school. You wouldn't have to work, if you don't want to."

Sonya rolled her eyes at that suggestion. "Yeah right."

"You know Daddy will take you in. No matter how old you are."

"If it was just him, I might actually consider it. But there's no way I'd live with *Cruella DeVille*."

Carla laughed at that. Sonya never ran out of insults, when it came to their father's new wife.

"You know, she's not that bad," Carla said. "I wish y'all would get over whatever is going on with you two. You see me and Debra don't have a problem with her."

"She rubs me the wrong way," Sonya said vaguely. "And I know she's doing it on purpose."

"Only because of the way you treat her," Carla countered. "Y'all feeding off each other's negativity."

Sonya knew her sister had a point, and she appreciated her honesty. But she didn't think the problems she had with the new lady in her dad's life would go away if she simply played nice with her. They'd been feuding for four years. By now the animosity was deeply rooted.

"I hope you get your job back," Carla stated. "And I hope things work out with you and Reggie. Sounds like he would be good for you."

"I hope so too," Sonya said. "I really like him. We might even be okay working at the same job. But if we *don't* work out, I don't wanna have to see his ass every day at work – not after last night."

"Mmm hmm. That's what you get for being freaky," Carla chastised her.

Sonya didn't think she was freaky, and she had no plans to change her bedroom activities. Her sister made her sound like a certified nympho.

"I was gonna ask if you wanted to go to the movies with us," Carla said. "But I know yo broke ass can't afford it."

"I been laid off for one day, and now you calling me broke?"

"Oh, my bad. You wanna go then?"

"Hell no. I don't got no money to be wasting at the damned movies!"

They both laughed.

CHAPTER EIGHT
CRUELLA

On Sunday morning Sonya made a trip to the north side of town to visit her father. She purposely picked that day and time because she knew her dad's wife would be at church, and he would be home alone.

It took Calvin a while to make it to the door, because his house was fairly large, and he didn't move around as well as he used to. But Sonya would gladly take a slow, disabled dad over a not-there dad any day of the week. After thirty years of heavy smoking, Calvin was diagnosed with lung cancer. During his treatment, he endured multiple invasive procedures; the worst being a partial lobectomy of his right lung.

Thankfully his treatment was successful. Calvin was fortunate to be cancer free, going on five years now. Sonya hoped he'd make a full recovery, considering he still had one perfect lung and most of the other. But the doctors warned that was not going to happen. In addition to getting winded easily, Calvin was now experiencing heart problems. His doctors were confident he would live another decade or maybe two. But sometimes when Sonya saw his ashen face covered with beads of sweat, her heart bled for him. She feared he wouldn't make it that long.

But today she had no worries. Calvin's cheeks were full of color, and the trip to the front door didn't fully exhaust him. He invited his youngest child inside and gave her a big hug in the foyer. He would've looked like his old self, if not for the oxygen tank that was forever tethered to him and the tubes that ran from the tank to his nostrils.

"Morning," he told her. His smile was wide and toothy. Sonya saw a lot of herself in his features.

"Morning, Daddy." She felt twenty years younger whenever she was around him.

"You staying for lunch?"

She checked her watch and saw that it was ten a.m. His wife would be home from church at twelve-thirty. "Probably not."

"Can you stay long enough to watch some Feud with me? I got four or five of them recorded."

Calvin's voice was deep and raspy. His hair was mostly gray, though he was only 55. He always enjoyed *The Family Feud*. His love for the show was reignited when Steve Harvey became the host. One of his favorite pastimes was watching a few episodes with his baby girl. Sonya enjoyed their time together, but sometimes she wished Mr. Harvey wasn't so darned funny. There had been times when Calvin would bowl over with laughter and begin to cough so hard she thought he'd hack up the rest of his lung.

"Yeah," she said. "Let's go see who Steve is making fun of today…"

• • • • • •

The host was in rare form in the shows they watched that morning. He was so entertaining, Sonya didn't realize how long she'd been with her dad until she heard the garage door rolling open.

"Whoop. Gotta go," she said as she shot to her feet.

"Wait. Stay and have lunch with us," her father suggested.

"You know I can't." Sonya snatched up her purse and walked to his easy chair. She knelt to kiss him on the cheek.

"I wish you girls would get along," Calvin complained. "I don't know why the two special women in my life are always at each other's necks."

"The *two* special women?" Sonya said with a grin. "Did you forget you have two more daughters? I know I'm your favorite, but you're not supposed to tell me."

"I didn't say you were my *favorite*," he backtracked. "I said you were *special*. A lot of people are special. Hell, the Unabomber is special."

"Whatever old man. The cat's out of the bag. I love you, Daddy."

"Love you too, Squirrel."

He'd been using that term of endearment since she was six, supposedly because of Sonya's fondness for climbing trees.

She gave him another hug and hoped to reach the front door before Cruella made it inside, but luck wasn't on her side that afternoon. Calvin's wife entered through the kitchen and made a B-line straight to the den. She was so swift, Sonya imagined she raced to the room the moment she saw her step-daughter's car in the driveway.

"Leaving so soon?" Joan said as she appeared in the doorway. She looked Sonya up and down, slowly. Her smile was big and phony. If Sonya could read her mind, which she was pretty sure she could, she knew Joan was thinking, *Yeah, caught you, bitch.* "Why do you always run off as soon as I get home?"

"I'm not running off," Sonya said. She tried not to let on how her skin was crawling all of a sudden. "I have plans to meet someone," she lied. "As a matter of fact, I'm running late."

"What a shame," Joan said. "I stopped by Boston Market on the way home. We'd really like it if you joined us for lunch."

"Yeah, baby. Have lunch with us," Calvin said.

"Sorry, Daddy. I really have to go."

Joan didn't immediately move out of the doorway when Sonya turned back to her. She stood smiling in her church clothes, a hand on her hip. Sonya had always thought Joan was pretty. She was tall and thin with rich, dark skin and big brown eyes. They first met at Jackson Memorial Hospital, where Joan worked as a nurse on the oncology floor. Calvin was her patient many times over the course of a year as he fought the cancer that would later claim a portion of his lung.

Initially Sonya loved that Joan was so doting towards her father. She considered her level of care a little over the top at times but never complained. Her daddy was sick, and his nurse treated him like a king. Who could ask for more? She was not surprised when Joan continued to call after her father was discharged. But she was taken aback when Calvin announced the two of them were dating.

"Isn't that against their code of ethics or something?" Sonya had asked him.

"I don't think so," Calvin had replied. "Even if it is, I'm not her patient anymore. What we do away from the hospital is our own business. Why? Don't you like her?"

"I do," Sonya told him. "She always takes good care of you. If you like it, I love it."

"Well, I like it very much," Calvin had said with a grin.

"Then go for it," Sonya replied. "I hope everything works out."

But over time Sonya became less and less enthused about her father's new love interest. Whenever the family would get together, she felt like Joan was judging her. She was always asking about Sonya's aspirations and career goals. Sometimes she'd appear disappointed with her step-daughter's lackluster responses.

The final straw came a few months before their wedding. Calvin and Joan moved into a new home and threw a housewarming party. It was the first time most of their friends and family had a chance to meet each other. The beaming couple found themselves alone in the kitchen for a moment – except they weren't completely alone. Sonya was headed that way, but she stopped dead in her tracks when she heard Joan mention her name.

"But what's her plan?" she was asking. "Is she going to keep jumping from job to job, sleeping around as she pleases? Why didn't you make her go to college right after high school?"

"You can't *make* anyone go to college," Calvin had countered. "Sonya said she wanted to get a taste of the real world, and it was her decision to make."

"It doesn't sound like you expect much from her," Joan stated. "At least Carla got married and is starting a family. And Debra's in school. But Sonya has no responsibilities."

"Baby girl is fine," Calvin insisted. "She's young. She's got the whole world in front of her."

"She's almost thirty. That's not so young."

"Drop it. It's not your place to speak on that."

"I'm sorry. I didn't mean anything..."

"It's okay," Calvin told her. "Let's just get back to the party."

Sonya had been so stunned to hear Joan speaking negatively about her, she remained frozen in the hallway for a few seconds after her dad and his new *bitch* returned to their guests. She loved that Calvin stuck up for her, and she hated Cruella from that moment on. Who gave that woman the right to judge her? And how the hell did she know Sonya was sleeping around? She wasn't even *sleeping around*, for that matter. She had boyfriends and she had sex with some of them. Since when was that a crime?

Later, it was Carla who helped Sonya understand that the reason the barbs hurt so much was because everything Joan had said was technically true. Sonya wasn't doing anything with her life at the time. And in the five years Joan had known her, she'd gone through quite a few boyfriends. But none of that mattered. Sonya was done with her dad's stuck up, bougie girlfriend. She wouldn't have even gone to the wedding, if it hadn't meant so much to her father.

Since then, Sonya refused to credit Joan for giving her the incentive to better herself. She was now two years into a business degree. She was independent and responsible. Calvin was exceedingly proud of her, and it felt good to please him. Deep down, Sonya was also grateful that her dad had a real-live nurse as a wife. His condition was sure to deteriorate in the next ten years, and Joan knew more about his medical needs than anyone else.

"Excuse me," Sonya said as she tried to exit the den.

"Sorry," Joan said. "I didn't mean to keep you." As she stepped aside, she told her, "I'm sorry to hear about what happened with your company. I hope none of that mess affects your job."

Sonya bristled visibly. Her eyes narrowed, and she sneered at Joan as she waited for her father to reply.

"Squirrel! What's going on with your job?"

Bitch, Sonya thought.

"Oh, baby, it's all over the news," Joan announced as she stepped to him. "They were stealing donations from *disabled veterans*. They arrested a couple of people. The veteran's group said they're cutting all ties to APEX. I hear a lot of people got laid off."

"Why didn't you tell me you were having trouble at work?" Calvin asked. "What's going on at that company? Did you lose your job?"

Sonya's face burned as she turned slowly to face him. Somehow she managed to paint on a smile for him. Joan stood next to his chair now. She smiled brightly as well.

"No, Daddy. It was just a couple of people involved in that. Everyone else is okay."

Joan knitted her eyebrows. "But I thought that's what you did; make calls for the disabled veterans. Isn't that your department?"

Sonya didn't have to wonder why Cruella was doing this. After she overheard the insult at the housewarming party, Sonya had been unable to hide her disdain for Joan. Without knowing why Calvin's youngest child was suddenly being such a bitch to her, Joan responded with venom of her own. The feud had been simmering for four years now.

"I did take donations for the veterans," Sonya confirmed dryly. "But it's a big place. We take calls for a lot of companies. They're moving us to another unit; either the water department or FedEx."

"Oh, well that's good," Calvin said. "So you'll be okay?"

Sonya didn't like lying to him, but his messy-ass wife left her no choice.

"Yes, Daddy. I'm fine. They only fired the people who were actually stealing."

"I'm glad you're okay," Calvin said. He sighed. "I'll feel better when you graduate, so you can quit that damned job."

"Me, too," Sonya said. "Just two more years."

"And I'm glad you decided to go back to school," Joan chipped in. "I'm so proud of you."

She was such a good actress, Sonya almost believed her.

"Thank you, Joan. See you later, Daddy," she said and quickly left the house.

● ● ● ● ● ●

When she made it to the freeway, Sonya got a call from Reggie. She was surprised when seeing his number on the Caller ID increased her anxiety, rather than make her smile, like a new lover should. She didn't fault him for anything she was feeling or anything that had transpired. But he was inexorably tied to a source of stress in her life. She felt guilty for letting the call roll over to voicemail, but she breathed a sigh of relief when her phone stopped ringing.

CHAPTER NINE
IMPATIENT

On Monday Sonya was happy to return to classes at Texas Lutheran University. She wasn't always gung ho when it came to her studies, but going back to school was a welcome change to moping around all weekend, worrying about her job.

The morning classes were a breeze. She didn't have any tests or taxing assignments due anytime soon. When her last class ended at noon, she headed to the student union building to do a little studying.

It felt weird to have time to chill, rather than head home and get ready for work. Her sister advised her to enjoy the layoff. Carla thought she could use the time off as a little vacation. Sonya wished she could see it that way, but she couldn't shake the apprehension that had been eating away at her since Friday.

She took a seat at an empty table and scrolled through her phone, catching up on things she missed while she was in class. She had a new voicemail from one of her coworkers. Sonya returned the call, hoping Marie had good news.

"Hey, what's up?"

"Hi," her friend said. "What you been up to?"

"Nothing much. I'm at school now. Just waiting to hear from APEX. Have you heard anything?"

"Yeah. They called me today. They want me to come back on Wednesday."

Sonya was stunned. Her heart began to squeeze uncomfortably. The crowd of students moving around her became a blur.

"When did they call you?" she asked.

"A couple of hours ago," Marie said. "Around ten. They didn't call you yet?"

Sonya would've thought the girl was trying to be funny, but Marie was an *okay* friend. They never had any problems before.

"No. I didn't hear from anyone."

"Oh." After an awkward pause, Marie said, "Well, I'm sure they'll call you some time today."

"What did they say when they called you? Who was it that called?"

"It was some lady from Human Resources," Marie reported. "Mrs. Cook. I don't know her. She just said there have been some changes at the company, she was sorry for what happened on Friday, and they were ready to start taking back some of the people who got laid off. Wednesday is the first day they want us to come in."

"What department?" Sonya wondered. "Did they say where we'd be working?" She caught herself. "*We*" may not have been the best choice of words. Just because they asked Marie to return, didn't mean she would be so fortunate. She didn't have any missed calls from APEX.

"She didn't say," her friend replied. "I'm just so happy to get my job back. I've been worried all weekend. I thought I was going to have to start filling out applications again. It took me a month to find that job. I didn't want to go through that again."

Sonya was growing annoyed with her friend's glorious sense of relief, but she knew it wasn't her fault. When (or if) Mrs. Cook got around to calling her, she would feel the same way.

"Did they call other people from our department?" she asked.

"Yeah, but only two that I know of. I got a call from Jorge, and he said–"

"Who's Jorge?"

"He works in that other department, with the water company. He said he saw Reggie at work."

Sonya's eyes widened. Now she felt sick to her stomach, in addition to frustrated. "Reggie was at work *today*?"

"Yeah," Marie said.

"At, doing what?" Sonya stammered. "What department did they put him in?"

"I don't know. Jorge said he was in a meeting."

"A meeting with who?"

"I don't know. Do you have Jorge's number? Maybe you could call him…"

"No, that's alright," Sonya replied. Why did she need to call Jorge, when she could go directly to the source?

"I knew they were going to take Reggie back," Marie said. "He was the best one there."

"Yeah," Sonya said vaguely. Her mind was racing. She had to figure some things out, and Marie didn't have any more useful information. "Hey, let me give you a call back."

"Okay. But don't worry, girl. If they called me, I'm sure they'll call you too. You're a good worker. You never call-in, like some of the others."

Yes, that was true. But showing up every day didn't mean a lot in their department if you couldn't bring in donations. Sonya thought back to one of her last calls. She told a widow to keep her money and even hung up on her when the potential donor insisted. If any of the higher-ups knew about that, there was no way they'd take her back.

"Alright, thanks," she told Marie. "I'll talk to you later."

Sonya sat quietly and weighed her options after she disconnected. She didn't want to upset anyone, but when Mr. Price took their badges, he said they could call Human Resources on Monday to make arrangements for their PTO. That sounded like a green light to Sonya. She dialed APEX's main number and asked the operator to transfer her.

"Human Resources," a friendly voice announced.

"Hi. My name is Sonya Skiles. I work, well, I worked for the disabled veterans' department. I was told to call today to make sure you were using my PTO while we're laid off."

"One moment," the woman said. Half a minute later, "What was your name again?"

"Sonya Skiles."

"Okay… Yes, Sonya, you have 121 hours of vacation time. Would you like to use 40 hours to cover this week?"

"*Forty hours?*" Her body grew numb. "We're going to be out all week? I thought you were taking people back already."

"I don't know how long you'll be out of work," the woman said. "But you do have enough PTO to cover this week."

"I don't want to use all of my PTO," Sonya complained. "What if I get sick or want to take a vacation or something? I want to come back to work."

"Yes, Sonya. I understand."

Sonya doubted that. This woman got to clock-in for work this morning, same as always. "Aren't y'all taking people back already?" she asked again.

"I'm not sure. I think they will try to get some people from your department back this week."

"Who gets to decide who comes back?" Sonya pressed. "I know they've already taken at least two people back."

"I'm sorry. I'm not at liberty to discuss that."

"Well, who do I need to talk to then?" Sonya realized she was raising her voice. She caught herself. "I'm not trying to be rude. I just want to know what's going on."

"I understand," the woman repeated. "Employees from your department have been calling all morning, and we've been telling them the same thing: We don't have any answers right now. All of you are upset and worried about your jobs. We're doing everything we can to make room for you, but you have to give us time. It's only been one day since you were laid off. We need you to be a little more patient."

Sonya sighed. She didn't think she would've had a problem with the wait if not for the fact that they had already asked Marie to return. And Reggie was there for a meeting this morning. But it was clear that the woman she was speaking to didn't have – or wouldn't give her – the answers she needed. Arguing with her could make things worse.

"I'm sorry," she said. "You're right. I'll wait to hear from you."

"Thank you, Sonya. We're working things out as quickly as possible. We apologize for any inconvenience this has caused you."

• • • • • •

She waited until six o'clock before she called Reggie. She figured if he was in a meeting that morning, he may have worked a full day shift. He answered after a few rings.

"Wow. You actually called me back."

257

Sonya was confused by the comment. She didn't miss any calls from him that day. "What do you mean?"

"I called you Sunday afternoon," he stated. "I didn't leave a message, but I thought it would show up on your Caller ID."

Sonya remembered that he had called when she left her father's house that day.

"Sorry," she said. "I meant to call you back."

"Oh yeah? Why didn't you?"

She didn't have an explanation. "It was a busy day," she offered.

"I hope you're okay with me saying that's not a great excuse."

He was right, but Sonya didn't expect him to call her on it. She was surprised by his confrontational tone. Then again, Reggie had been awfully ballsy as of late.

"I know," she said. "I'm sorry."

"So I guess it was just a one night stand."

She frowned. "No. What do, I never said that."

"You've been acting shady since we woke up the next morning," he informed her. "I saw it then, but I didn't want to believe it. I didn't want it to be like that."

"Neither did I. I don't know why you're saying that – just because I didn't call you back one time?"

"I think if you make love to someone on *Friday* and don't hear from them until *Monday*, that says something. But, we didn't make love, did we?"

Sonya knew she deserved this aggression, but she didn't like it from Reggie. She didn't even call him to talk about that. With everything going on in her life, relationship drama was on the back burner. They weren't even in a relationship.

She rubbed a spot of tension on her forehead and told him, "Reggie, I'm sorry I didn't call you back. But it has nothing to do with you being a one night stand. I'm just under a lot of pressure right now. You know that. I didn't think it would be a problem if you didn't hear from me this weekend, but now I see that I was wrong."

A few long seconds passed before he said, "Alright. I'm sorry for getting an attitude."

"No, it's my fault," she told him.

He didn't respond to that, so she figured he agreed.

"Um, can I ask you something?" she said.

"Yeah. What's up?"

"Someone said they saw you at APEX this morning. Did they take you back already?"

There was another break in the conversation. This one lasted longer than the first.

"You didn't call to talk about us," he deduced. "You called because you're worried about your job."

Damn, Sonya thought. She knew she'd handled this completely wrong. "Reggie, it's not like that."

"What's it like then, Sonya? Tell me what I'm missing."

So far everything she said ended with a foot in her mouth, so she opted for complete honesty. "I like you a lot, Reggie. And I didn't want us to be a one night stand. But I need my job more than I need a relationship right now. That's not to say I don't wanna be in a relationship with you – but I haven't been worried about what's going on with us all weekend. I've been worried about my job. I'm sorry if that sounds wrong..."

"No, I understand," he said. "The only thing on my mind since Friday is *you*. I get it. We're on two completely different pages."

"I didn't say I don't want to be with you."

"Nah, it's cool. I said I get it."

"Reggie, stop that. You're being–"

"Hey, listen, I gotta go."

Her eyes widened. "What? Why are you getting off the phone?"

"Oh, my bad. I didn't let you use me for information about your job yet, did I? I'm sorry. What did you want to know?"

Sonya felt lower than dirt. Her heart began to ache as her eyes filled with tears. She didn't think she was the bitch he was making her out to be. But she couldn't deny that she had done him wrong.

"Reggie, I'm sorry."

"Yeah. You keep saying that."

"You don't have to tell me about the job, if you don't want to. I'll be fine if we could just, you know, keep talking. I want us to work this out." A tear spilled from her eye as she spoke. It had been a long time since she cried over a man.

"You know, I wish I could believe you," he said. "Let me, I'll call you back."

Sonya's eyes slipped closed, and another tear rolled down her cheek. "Alright," she breathed.

"Okay. Bye."

She went to sleep early that night.

When she awakened the next morning, feeling just as miserable as she did the night before, she checked her phone to see if she'd missed Reggie's call.

No such luck.

CHAPTER TEN
THE FINAL CHAPTER
BOSSY

Sonya finally got a call from APEX on Tuesday.

"Hello?"

"Hi. Sonya?"

"Yes, speaking."

"This is Betty from Human Resources."

Her heart sank. This is when they'd tell her they couldn't find any room for her at the company. Her mouth went dry as she said, "I hope you have some good news."

"I do," Betty replied.

Sonya could tell the woman was smiling. She could hear it in her voice.

"You've been reassigned," Betty told her. "We would like for you to come back to work tomorrow afternoon, from 2 to 10, the same time as your regular shift."

"Really?" Sonya's storm cloud was immediately vanquished. The huge weight lifted from her shoulders and made her feel like she could breathe again, for the first time in days. She never thought she'd care so much about what she considered a dead-end job. Her smile was ear to ear when she asked, "Did they move me to a different department?"

"Yes, but they're still shuffling people around, so I'm not sure which one. They'll let you know when you get here tomorrow. You'll need to report to room 112."

"Okay," Sonya said. She didn't think she'd been this happy when she first got the job. "I'll be there. Thank you."

"You're welcome," the woman replied. "We'll see you tomorrow."

● ● ● ● ● ●

Sonya remained in good spirits the next day at school. She wondered which department they would assign her to and how many of her work buddies were asked to return. As far as departments, she was cool with wherever they put her, as long as they didn't patch things up with the veterans' foundation and send her back to them.

She found herself daydreaming about Reggie during her morning classes. Were they dating? Did he still think their time together was a one night stand? She hadn't spoken to him since their argument. She knew it would be awkward when they saw each other later at work. She didn't need to remind herself that this was exactly why she didn't get involved with men at the office.

When she got to work that afternoon, she was ushered to a training room that was filled with familiar faces. Everyone was happy and excited to be back. There appeared to be more than half of her original department there. The rest were new faces, who Sonya later learned were new hires. They were greeted by Leticia Forney, who had been a supervisor at APEX for over a decade.

"Good evening everyone!" She stood at the front of the room and looked over the new crew. "For some of you this is welcome back, and for others this is your first day at APEX. I'm happy to have all of you here. I apologize for the little shakeup last week, but we've got everything straightened out, and this is going to be an awesome day!"

Sonya never worked with Leticia before. She found her upbeat and energetic. Her enthusiasm transferred to everyone in the room.

"The new hires are aware of this," Leticia continued, "but for those of you who are coming from the veterans' department, I'm pleased to announce that we have a new contract. Your department will now take customer service calls from Sears appliance customers in the Dallas/Overbrook Meadows area."

All of the old employees were surprised to hear that.

"All of the calls will be *incoming*," Leticia continued. "You will access the customer's account, verify their warranty and schedule service appointments. This will be completely different types of calls, for those coming from the veterans' department. I can already tell by the look on your faces that you'll enjoy this a heck of a lot more!"

A number of people in the crowd voiced their approval, Sonya included.

"Now, we don't want there to be any rumors circulating through the office," Leticia stated, her smile turned down a few notches. "So we're going to get all of the dirty business out of the way right now..."

Everyone quieted down for this.

"First of all APEX Teleservices will no longer seek contracts for donation collections. The trouble with the veterans' foundation is a black eye for the company, and it taught us a valuable lesson."

The crowd received the news solemnly.

"The second thing I'm sure you've all noticed," Leticia said, "is not everyone from the veterans' department is here today. The layoffs gave us an opportunity to re-evaluate all of the affected employees. After much consideration, some were not asked to return."

Sonya and her friends looked around, taking note of those who weren't in attendance. She could only come up with five missing faces off hand. She knew the number would grow when she and her work buddies got together to gossip later. Two notable absentees were the men from their happy hour outing last Friday.

Byron was a little ghetto, or *rough around the edges*, as the higher ups would describe him, so she wasn't surprised that he got canned. But where was Reggie? After spending half the day girding herself for their encounter, Sonya was both relieved and disappointed that he wasn't in the training room. She was pretty sure he didn't get fired, since they called him to a meeting on Monday. Or maybe it wasn't a meeting. Maybe they had summoned him so they could give him a chance to plead for his job.

But how unlikely was that? Reggie was the best of the best. And if he got axed, he would've told her about it when they spoke yesterday, wouldn't he? They didn't talk for very long, but he had time to squeeze in that little bit of information.

Whatever the case, Sonya had to wait a few hours before she could start asking questions. Leticia was ready to get down to business.

"Okay, everyone," she said. "Whether you're a new hire or transferring from another department, the work we're doing for Sears will require all of you to complete a training course. Training will last two days, and you lucky people get to train with me. We'll have snacks and beverages brought in, so things don't get too tedious.

"And we've wasted enough time talking about it, so let's get started. If you'll turn and face the computers in front of you, you'll notice a packet of information and your new log-in screen..."

● ● ● ● ● ●

As happy as she was about being back to work, Sonya found the first couple of hours of training boring and repetitive, which reminded her that this was still a crummy job that she would probably grow to hate in six months. But it was a means to an end. She probably wouldn't like any of her jobs until she graduated and got started on a real *career*, though she wasn't exactly sure what that would be, either.

When it was time for their first break, she was eager to hook up with her friends and get their opinion on the new position and the ten or so folks who were missing. But Leticia stopped her before she could exit the room and said, "Reginald would like to speak with you."

Sonya stopped short, thinking she hadn't heard her right. Her eyebrows were bunched together as she said, "*Reginald*? Reggie Dukes?"

"Oh, yes, you two worked together in the veterans' department, didn't you? His office is around the corner. Do you need me to show you where it is?"

Sonya couldn't hide her surprise. Not only was he *Reginald* now, but Reggie had an office? She nodded stiffly and followed the woman down the hallway.

When they made it to the office, Leticia stepped aside and allowed Sonya to enter alone. Sure enough Reggie sat behind a desk in a sparsely decorated room that was presumably all his. He noticed the look of confusion Sonya wore and smiled impishly. He looked over her shoulder and told Leticia, "Thank you. How's training going?"

"Everything's going great," she said, in her typically upbeat fashion. "I'll get with you before I take off."

"Okay," Reggie said, and Leticia walked away.

He wore a powder blue shirt that fit him well. Every button was fastened, except the one at the collar. He was clean cut and dashingly dapper. His eyes were dark with a hint of humor as he watched Sonya. She had so many emotions rushing through her mind, she couldn't do anything but stare at him.

"Have a seat," he said, smiling again.

She did, and she offered a small grin. "You're going by *Reginald* now?"

He chuckled at that. "No. Reggie's fine. I've been meaning to tell her."

"No," Sonya said. "I like Reginald. It's..." She trailed off, looking around the small office. Everything was in perfect order, like the man behind the desk. "You got a promotion?"

He nodded. "Supervisor."

Sonya's eyes widened. "*No way.*" She didn't think he was undeserving, but they'd passed him up multiple times. She thought they would rather keep him on the phones.

"They said I was highly recommended." He didn't sound smug about that.

Sonya loved his confidence. It made a fire glow in her chest. "No doubt. You deserve it."

"I..." He took a slow breath. "I don't know. It's a lot of responsibility."

"You got this," Sonya said. "You know you're the best."

His eyes softened. "Thanks."

The way he watched her made goose bumps sprout on her arms and neck. "What department?" she asked.

"Oh, um." He looked away for a moment before his eyes returned to her. "Yours. I guess I'm your boss. Sorta."

Sonya felt a chill in the air. "Oh."

"I hope you don't think that's a bad thing."

"No, it..." She sighed. She shrugged. "I don't know what to think. Why didn't you tell me?"

"I did, I mean, when we talked on Monday, I was going to tell you. But, you know, that conversation didn't go so well."

"I know. I'm sorry."

"Nah, it's not your fault. I understand you were worried about your job, and I was coming at you with something totally different. That was my bad. But, as you can see, even though we had a little disagreement, I still made sure you got your job back. You know, 'cause I'm cool like that."

Sonya found his smile adorable. "Well, I appreciate it. Did you get to decide who came back?"

He shook his head. "Not every single person. But they listened to my suggestions." He frowned. "Byron was a no-go. That asshole wasn't getting back in here."

Sonya covered her mouth as she laughed at that.

"Don't worry about what happened between us," he said. His smile fell away, and he lowered his voice. "I would never say anything or do anything to put your job at risk."

Sonya shook her head. "You don't have to tell me that, Reggie. I know you wouldn't. I trust you."

"Okay," he said and nodded. He returned to his usual demeanor and said, "So, what do you think about Sears so far?"

"Wait. What about us, Reggie?" Sonya couldn't believe she had the courage to ask him that, in his office, after he'd just made it clear that he was ready to let bygones be bygones.

"It's... Sonya, it's okay. You don't have to—"

"You were not a one-night-stand, Reggie." She caught herself, mostly because of his startled expression. She looked back to make sure no one was walking past his doorway.

He grinned. "You're not just saying that because I'm a supervisor now?"

"Don't you say that. Don't even joke like that."

"Okay, I was just kiddi—"

"Maybe if you were a *manager* I'd try to get with you, but..." She trailed off giggling. When she quieted, she said, "For real, though, Reggie. I know this is probably way more complicated than before, but I want to try. I mean, if you do."

"Tell me what happened," he said. "Why were things so different on Saturday morning?" His smile was gone now. Hers was too.

She looked back again and asked him, "Can I close the door?"

He nodded.

She closed it and returned to her seat. "This is, it's hard for me to talk about this..."

"I can tell." His eyes filled with concern. "Is everything alright?"

"Yeah, I'm fine. The reason I don't like to talk about this is because it makes me feel like I have a problem. But I don't think I do. I guess it's up to you to decide."

Reggie was intrigued. He leaned forward with his forearms on the desktop.

Sonya took a deep breath and let the honesty flow from her. "I told you I don't like to date men I work with because it's too much drama."

He nodded.

"But that's only part of it," she revealed. "The bigger problem is the way I am, in bed."

His eyes grew larger, but he didn't interrupt her.

"It's one thing for a guy to come back to work and say we had sex," Sonya continued. "But I know it would be more than that. If he's really mad at me, he can come back to work and tell them *everything* I do in the bedroom. And, as you know, I do a little bit more than the usual..."

She watched Reggie's skin redden right before her eyes.

"I don't think I'm a ho," Sonya said defensively. "I don't sleep around, and I don't sleep with strangers. I don't cheat. But I do get wild sometimes – in the privacy of my home. I don't feel like I should have to follow people's *rules* when I'm naked. If I feel like talking dirty, I will. I do a lot of stuff most girls would wait months or even a year before they tried. Some guys can't handle that. The immature ones, sometimes they say bad things about me."

Reggie understood what she was saying. He'd experienced her bold sexuality first hand. And while it was unexpected at first, *scandalous* even, he never thought less of her because of the way she made love to him.

"I think you're a good balance for me," Sonya said. "You and me are exact opposites, in a lot of ways. But I think that's a good thing. I want to be with you. Do you still want to be with me?"

She didn't like how tense and miserable she felt as she waited for him to respond. Is this what it was like for the men who put their hearts on the line for her in the past? How many times had she broken those hearts without giving a second thought to the tears they shed? She'd just given Reggie the power to do the same, but she didn't think he would hurt her.

"I want that so bad, Sonya. I've wanted it for – how long have I known you?"

She giggled. Her goose bumps were washed over by a soothing rain. Her heart had been torn all weekend, but he made it whole again. She sighed pleasantly.

Dating a supervisor. How tastily forbidden. Whether they could pull it off or not was anyone's guess. But for Reggie, it was worth it.

His next comment made keeping it a secret seem even less likely.

"I know we shouldn't, but do you mind if I kiss you?"

Sonya shook her head as she looked back at the door. It wasn't locked. Anyone could barge in without warning.

"I'm just kidding," he said.

His smile was so delectable! Sonya wanted to devour him.

"What time do you get off?" she asked.

One of his eyebrows rose. "Um, around the same time as you. Why? What you got in mind?"

"Nothing," she said, with a bat of her eyes. "I have to go to school in the morning, so I can't stay up too late. But if you wanted to come over, we could watch Netflix or something..."

His eyes brightened. "I would love that so much, to Netflix and chill with you."

"Cool. I'll make hot wings."

"I'll bring a bottle of wine."

"Call before you come," Sonya said as she rose to her feet. "Talk to you later, *boss*."

She wore slacks that day with a loose fitting blouse. The slacks weren't tight, but the fabric got a little snug around her hips and ass. Reggie continued to smile as he watched her exit his office. Before she was out of sight, a stiffness in his khakis confirmed he had a bonafide boner.

He didn't like their chances of keeping their office romance a secret any more than Sonya did. But it would be a hell of a lot of fun trying!

EPILOGUE

It wasn't easy to keep their relationship a secret. After a couple of months the affair began to weigh heavily on both of them. Reggie turned out to be a great supervisor. He was hands on, and he knew the new system better than anyone in the department. Sonya didn't like to watch his interactions with some of her coworkers. The ladies thought he was a dreamboat, and a bare ring finger meant he was an eligible bachelor. Sonya was confident none of the skanks flirting with him would ever get his attention, but that understanding didn't suppress her jealousy.

And then there were the times she needed his one-on-one assistance. Her temperature would rise when he'd reach over her shoulder to press a button on her keyboard or point something out on the computer screen. They would steal glances at each other across the room and try not to smile too much. Sonya avoided his office at all costs. But that wasn't enough.

Some of her coworkers began to make shady, little remarks about Reggie liking her. One commented after Sonya returned from a four-day weekend.

"You can take as many days off as you want to, huh? You got Reggie wrapped around your little finger."

Sonya just stared at the woman, wondering what she and Reggie had done to give her that impression. They certainly never touched at work. They tried to keep their conversations strictly professional.

"I'm just kidding," her coworker had said with a chuckle. "But I do think he likes you. You're crazy, if you don't see it."

After three months of this, Sonya had had enough. She surprised her boyfriend with a request: "Can you help me get transferred to a different department?"

They were in bed at the time, completely nude and satisfied. Reggie didn't have enough strength to register surprise. He yawned and asked her, "Why?"

She rolled over and placed a hand on his warm chest. "Because I don't want you to get in trouble if they find out about us. I can always get another job, but you're doing good there. I think you can go all the way to the top."

"Not without going to college," he replied lazily.

"And you need to go to college. If I can do it, I know you can. You're way smarter than me."

"I don't think so," he said, blowing her off. "But how will you getting a transfer help any?"

"Everybody knows Seth and Amy are dating," she said, referring to a manager and a customer service rep at the company. "It's okay for them, because they're not in the same department, right?"

"Yeah. I guess so," Reggie said. "But I like working with you."

"How? It's nothing like before. We used to kick it, crack jokes all night. We can't even have lunch together now. We're there at the same time, but you're like a ghost. I might as well be in a different department. At least then we can meet up for lunch."

Reggie gave it some thought and said, "Alright. But I'll miss not having you there, in my face all night."

"You couldn't possibly want to see me that much."

"You're wrong," he said, closing his eyes. "I can see you, right now. And it's beautiful."

His romantic nature never failed to send tingles down her spine.

"I love you." She was surprised that she said it first. But she didn't regret it. Reggie was everything she wanted in a man. She wished she hadn't waited so long to figure that out.

His eyes fluttered open as his head rolled towards her. When they were face to face, he said, "I love you too, Sonya."

She kissed him softly. "So you'll go back to school?"

"What? Where did that come from?"

"Baby, you need an education," she said, kissing him again.

Her lips set his heart on fire. She had to know that. "Okay," he murmured. "Anything you say. I'll go chop some firewood too, if you want."

She giggled. There wasn't even a fireplace in her apartment. "You can get it tomorrow," she commented as her eyes slipped closed.

Minutes later they were both fast asleep.

● ● ● ● ● ●

True to his word Reggie got Sonya transferred to the FedEx department. She didn't like it better over there, but the move did relieve a lot of the pressure from her and Reggie's relationship. They waited another month before they went out to lunch for the first time. There were plenty of eyes on them when they returned to the building together, but there were no rules against employees dating. After another two months people started saying they looked good together. Sonya wholeheartedly agreed.

● ● ● ● ● ●

A year and a half later, Sonya graduated from Texas Lutheran with a bachelor's degree in business administration. It was a beautiful ceremony in the university's auditorium. All of her nearby relatives were there, including *Cruella*, who hadn't been such a bitch lately. Sonya was glad that Joan's love burned so strong for her father. She learned to forgive her for the negative things she said behind her back.

Reggie appeared to be the proudest face in the crowd as Sonya stepped across the stage and accepted her diploma. Thanks to her, he already had a year of college under his belt. There was a manager position waiting for him at APEX the moment he graduated, which confirmed what Sonya had been saying for years: He was the ultimate company man.

● ● ● ● ● ●

Two weeks after graduation, Sonya's crew in the FedEx department threw her a going away party. She had recently been hired by Dinder & Mifflin, one of the largest advertising firms in the south. They were based in Dallas, which made for a 45 minute commute. But she and Reggie were on the lookout for a new home. They had maintained separate apartments the whole time they were dating, but their wedding date was right around the corner. Sonya was finally ready to settle down, for good.

She beamed when one of her coworkers announced her fiancé had stopped by the party. Reggie toted a shiny gift bag with a red ribbon affixed to it. He stepped to her, grinning sheepishly, while Sonya and her girlfriends' hearts melted. Her man was the finest thing in the building. Always clean cut and smelling good.

"We sure are gonna miss you," Reggie said. "Congratulations on your new job."

Sonya laughed. Even this late in the game, he was the utmost professional at work. The crowd cheered when she pulled him closer and planted a hot kiss on his lips. Her heart was completely full as they embraced before their peers.

"I love you," she said, close to his ear.

"I love you too, babe. I'm so happy for you!"

● ● ● ● ● ●

Later that night, after second shift had cleared out of the building, and the janitors began to show up for their nightly cleaning, Reggie sat behind his desk putting the finishing touches on a spreadsheet he had to present to his team tomorrow. The work was tedious, but he loved it. They were grooming him for a manager position, and he was ready to prove himself.

When a shadow darkened his doorway, he assumed it was Priscilla, the housekeeper he sometimes ran into when he worked late. He looked up from his computer, surprised to see his bride-to-be enter his office. She kicked the door closed and then turned to fasten the deadbolt. Reggie's eyes were narrowed when she turned back to him. She rarely closed his office door and had never locked it. He found her smile contriving as she sashayed to his desk and took a seat on the corner.

"I didn't know you were still here," he said, his eyes running up her bare legs.

That day she wore a pencil skirt with pumps and a sleeveless blouse. Her hair was pulled up and away from her face. Everything about her was prim and proper, except her eyes and her smile. Reggie knew she was happy about this being her last day at APEX, but there was something more. He felt like she was harboring a secret of some kind.

"I thought you'd be the first one to clock out tonight," he commented. Sonya's shift ended at ten, which was over forty minutes ago.

"I've been off the clock," she confirmed. "I was saying goodbye to some people. I stayed and talked to Marie for a while."

"I know she's gonna miss you."

"I'm gonna miss her, too," Sonya replied. She turned slightly on the desk, until her legs dangled on his side. Reggie watched as she began to slowly unbutton her blouse.

"Um, what are you doing?"

"You said we could never make love in your office," she recalled. "You said we would both get fired, if someone found out."

"Uh, yeah, I did say that." It had been over a year since they had the conversation.

"But now that I'm not working here anymore," she said as she continued to undo her buttons, "I think you should reward me for being so patient. I've been a good girl, haven't I?"

She unfastened the last button and pulled her shirt open, exposing a red, lace bra. Reggie had never seen the undergarment before. She knew he had a fetish for lingerie. He inhaled sharply as his eyes darted around the room, confirming what he already knew to be the case: His office didn't have any windows, and there was but one entrance. The janitors had a key to the door, but they would knock first, wouldn't they – especially if they heard noises coming from inside the room?

Or would they place their ear against the door for a while and then walk away smiling? Sonya was never known to be the quiet type. And he wasn't the risk-taking type. She knew that full well, yet there she was, sitting on his desk, almost topless. The overhead lights seemed especially bright. He could see everything, including the small bulge of her nipples beneath the thin fabric of the bra.

As Reggie took in everything he was seeing and attempted to rationalize what was clearly irrational behavior, Sonya uncrossed her legs and attempted to spread them. Her pencil skirt was a hindrance. She stood briefly and raised the garment to her ass before sitting down again. This time she could spread her legs. A few beads of sweat dotted Reggie's forehead as his eyes were drawn to her oasis. He expected to see red panties that matched her bra.

Nope.

His beautiful vixen wore no panties at all.

Reggie had seen her neatly trimmed kitty many times before – but he'd never seen it at work. Certainly not on his desktop. There was so much wrong with the whole scenario, he couldn't decide what to complain about first.

"You, you don't have any panties on," he muttered.

"I know." She planted her hands on the desk and leaned back slightly. "Isn't that something?"

"What, what happened to them?"

Out of all the questions he could've asked, she didn't expect that. "I have them right here in my purse," she replied. "Why, Reggie? Do you want them?"

"It was, I was wondering if you came to work with no panties."

"Why?" she asked with a chuckle. "Are you jealous? My face is up here, by the way."

He grinned as he looked up at her. "You spread your legs on my desk and then complain that I'm not giving you eye contact? You got some nerve."

Sonya continued to grin. She bit down on her bottom lip.

"But to answer your questions," he said, "yes, I'm jealous. And yes, I want your panties."

She laughed and retrieved them from her purse. "Here."

She tossed them at his face. He let them bounce off his nose and fall into his lap. Sonya watched as he slipped them into his front pocket.

"What are you gonna do with those?"

"They're mine now," he commented. "Not your business."

"Oh. Okay."

"And... I don't think we should do this here," he told her.

"I know. I knew you'd say that."

"But you're trying to seduce me anyway?"

"It's my last day," she complained. "And it's my fantasy."

"You have a lot of fantasies," he noticed.

She leaned back until she fully reclined on his desk. Reggie found her a lot less intimidating, now that they lost eye contact.

His gaze returned to her pleasure center just as her hand did the same. She stroked herself with her longest finger.

"I'm going to cum on your desk," she announced as she stared up at the ceiling. "You can watch me, or you can help me, or you can leave, if you want to. Either way, it's going down. On your desk."

She continued to caress herself as she spoke. A second finger joined the first. They both slipped between her labia and spread them, exposing her pink, wet center. Reggie's heart thudded so loudly, he was sure it was audible outside of his office. He thought he heard a vacuum cleaner approaching. He imagined his housekeeper standing outside his office. She would reach for the door, find it locked, and then shuffle through her keys. Reggie knew he would hear the keys jingling, which would give him enough time to cease whatever activities he and his fiancé might be engaged in.

He shook his head, surprised that he was considering it. But it wasn't like he had much of a choice. The scent of Sonya's forbidden fruit was in his nostrils. His manhood began to respond the moment she tossed her panties at him. His lips parted as he watched her fingers slide up and down her slick opening. He was pretty sure he could force her to stop this foolishness, if he put his foot down. But Sonya's spontaneous nature was one of the things he loved about her. He would much rather enjoy her than attempt to tame her.

"Baby, you know you're too loud. This isn't a good idea."

She lifted her head and peered between her legs. Reggie licked his lips, and she knew she had him. "I'll be quiet," she whispered. "I promise."

"I don't believe you."

"If I'm too loud, feel free to stuff something in my mouth."

His heart skipped a beat. "Some, something like what?"

"Whatever you want, baby."

He leaned closer. When he spoke again, she felt his breath on her clitoris. The sensation sent a pleasant pulse of energy through her chest.

"Just because you don't work here anymore," he said, "doesn't mean I shouldn't worry about my job."

She arched her back and hummed quietly. "Don't worry," she said as her eyes slipped closed. "You worry too much. Live for the moment."

Reggie wondered how many times she'd told him that since they'd been dating. Initially he was against the idea. Living for the moment was the exact opposite of his permanence and reliability personality type. But while Sonya's lifestyle seemed carefree, he knew that she cared about a number of things. He was happy to say he was one of them.

He threw caution to the wind and buried his face between her thighs. Sonya gasped but didn't cry out as he expected her to. She moved her hand out of the way, to make room for his lips and tongue. Reggie's cunnilingus skills were only amateur level when they first met, but she'd taught him a few tricks since then. She marveled at his gains as he licked her up and down. He sucked her clit before penetrating her with his hot tongue. He returned to her clit and gnawed on it with his lips until her chest heaved and her ass slid to and fro on the desk.

He grabbed hold of her hips and held her still.

"Don't run now," he told her.

"Ooh, baby. Shit."

"You said you'd be quiet," he warned between sucks.

"You said you'd shove something in my mouth," she panted.

"It's coming," he growled.

Sonya closed her eyes and got lost in the ecstasy as he continued to pleasure her with his mouth. She walked into his office with a plan tonight, but she wasn't sure if she could pull it off. She loved that Reggie was willing to explore all facets of her sexuality. He was–

"Oh. Oh shit!"

Sonya was so high on lust, she didn't realize Reggie had stood and jerked his pants down to his knees. He invaded her smoothly and fully as he stood next to his desk. She was rewarded with the most erotic friction as her walls spread to accommodate him. She opened her eyes and saw him standing over her. He gripped a thigh in each hand. He stared down at her with a powerful gaze that made her body go numb.

"Shhh," he warned. "You said you'd be quiet."

"I, I am," she whispered. "I'm sorry."

"What is it gonna take for you to be good?" he asked as he stared down at her.

He loved the look of unparalleled bliss on her face. He loved to watch himself slide in and out of her. He was so glad that he and Sonya went to get blood tests, so they could eliminate condoms from their lovemaking. Safe and monogamous never felt so good.

"Marry me," she breathed. "Give me some babies, and I'll be good."

Her words touched him to the very core. She would never know how much his soul soared at the thought of her having his children.

His pumps were slow and stiff as he told her, "I don't want you to change, baby."

"Good."

She grinned, and he stroked her quietly. Between her hushed breaths, she thought she heard the sound of keys jingling beyond the door. Or maybe it was bells ringing in her head. She opened her eyes to see if Reggie had heard anything and saw him glancing at the door as well. If he expected someone to open it, she couldn't tell. His hips kept pumping, and his pants continued to slide towards his ankles. He hit her spot with each long stroke. Sonya decided she didn't care about the door either.

She couldn't keep from moaning when he plunged deeper and harder.

"Baby, you gotta be quiet," he warned again.

"*Uhn. Make me.*"

His eyes widened at her insolence. The thought of his erection in her mouth made her lips tingle. Reggie prayed their relationship would always be this impulsive as he slipped out of her wet warmth and duck-walked around his desk.

"I will make you."

Sonya watched with low, eager eyes as he drew nearer. Despite all that had transpired, she managed to appear startled when he guided himself into her mouth, forcing her to taste herself.

Her man could be so bossy sometimes.

KEITH THOMAS WALKER

ABOUT THE AUTHOR

Keith Thomas Walker, known as the Master of Romantic Suspense and Urban Fiction, is the author of nearly two dozen novels, including *Life After, The Realest Ever,* the *Brick House* series and the *Finley High* series. Keith's books transcend all genres. He has published romance, urban fiction, mystery/thriller, teen/young adult, Christian, poetry and erotica. Originally from Fort Worth, he is a graduate of Texas Wesleyan University. Keith has won or been nominated for numerous awards in the categories of "Best Male Author," "Best Romance," "Best Urban Fiction," and "Author of the Year," from several book clubs and organizations. Visit him at www.keithwalkerbooks.com.